MURDER KEY

by

H. Terrell Griffin

www.hterrellgriffin.com

First Printing: November 2006
Printed in the United States

Published by: Tangerine Press LLC
                28 East Washington Street
                Orlando, Florida 32801

ISBN: 987-0-9774047-1-1

Cover design by Sandy Ingledue/Adman Graphics
Author photograph by Richard Wright

Dedication

For Jean, my love,

and for

Vernell and Margaret

who gave us life

ACKNOWLEDGMENTS

Thanks to Peggy Henger for her gracious help in turning words into prose, and to her special friend, Dave Kendall for his patience during the process.

Deputy Chief Martin Sharkey of the Longboat Key Police Department provided invaluable insight into the workings of the Blue Light Task Force, and the cooperation among the various law enforcement agencies chasing bad guys. In the telling of this story, I was not always faithful to Martin's descriptions, but they would not be here if not for his help. Any mistakes are entirely mine. Martin is too good a cop to screw it up.

Debbie Stowell and Eric Lamboley were, as ever, generous with their time and advice. They are an industry unto themselves when it comes to helping authors, both rookies and masters. We need more booksellers like them.

My buddies, John Allred of Houston and Miles Leavitt of Longboat Key, are truly two people without whose friendship this book would have been very different. They know why.

Vanessa Brice, my erstwhile paralegal, now a first year law student at Florida A & M University's College of Law, somehow juggles all her duties as wife, mother, student and right hand to a struggling writer. I'm very proud of you.

And finally, to Jean Griffin, whom I have loved desperately and joyously for most of my life, thank you for putting up with me. Your wit, your intelligence, your beauty, and your passions have sustained me, and made me a better person. Your encouragement as I have struggled with my new passion, writing, made this book possible. Your sharp pen, and even sharper mind, made it better.

The other Matt Royal Mystery by H. Terrell Griffin

LONGBOAT BLUES

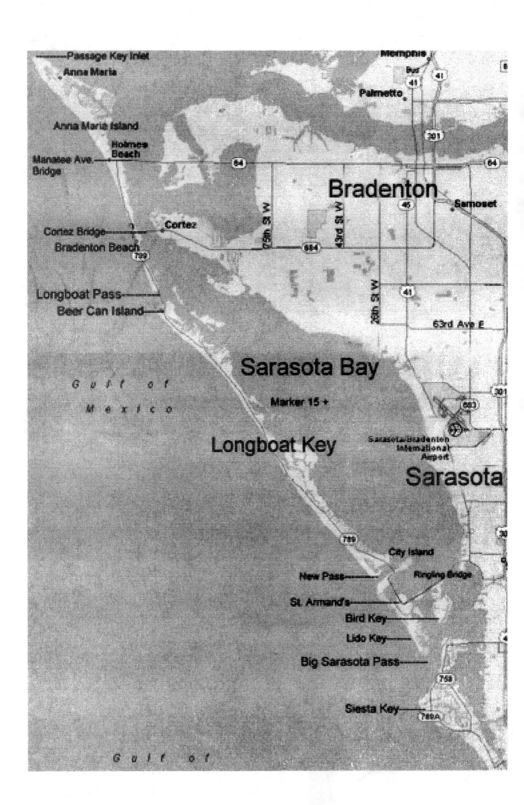

ONE

At dawn, the naked man squatted in the surf, building sand castles. A boat, no longer than fifteen feet, lay on its side near him, its occupants sprawled lifeless and unnoticed on the sand. Attached to the boat's transom was a small outboard engine with a rusted propeller. The lower unit was pitted by electrolysis, and bare metal showed through the black paint, sure signs of neglect. The placid green water of the Gulf of Mexico provided an incongruous back-drop to tragedy and farce.

An accident, I thought. *There shouldn't be dead men on our beach on a bright fall morning.* Pulling my cell phone from the pocket of my shorts, I approached the bodies. There were three small dark men wearing jeans and T-shirts. They were barefoot, lying askew on the beach, like so much seaweed discarded by the tide. Two of the men had gunshot wounds to the head. I thought I saw chest movement in the third, and I leaned down close, listening for breath sounds. He was alive. I dialed 911 and told the operator that we needed ambulances and police on the beach behind the Isla Grande Condominiums on Gulf of Mexico Drive.

I sat on the sand next to the nearly dead man and held his hand. If he was about to die, he would at least have the touch of a human being in his last moments. I'm not a religious man, but I said a little prayer. I sat. And I waited. There was nothing more that I could

1

do for him until the paramedics arrived.

The naked man had not changed his position. He sat on his haunches and piled more sand on his castles. His eyes were vacant, staring straight ahead.

"Joe," I said to the naked man, "did you see the boat?"

"What boat?" He turned to look at me.

"The one behind you."

"Oh, yeah. With the greasers."

"Did you check them out?"

"Nah, the police will do it."

"Well, they're on their way."

"Shit, am I going to be arrested again?"

"I'll take care of it." He went back to his castle building.

I heard the siren of an approaching ambulance, growing louder as it rushed toward us. It stopped, leaving the morning silence unbroken. In a few moments, two paramedics scampered down to the beach, their medical bags sitting on a wheeled stretcher that bounced over the packed sand.

I held the man's hand as I watched the medics trot toward us. I told him help was coming. Did he hear me? Who knows. I hope so. I wanted him to know that somebody gave a shit about him and his dead buddies.

The medics bent over the patient, using a blood pressure cuff and stethoscopes. One of them spoke into his radio, relaying the man's vitals. The hospital, I assumed.

I told them what I knew and walked the few steps to where Joe was intent on his building project. "Let's get you up to Grace," I said.

"She'll be pissed at me," he said, petulance written on his face.

We walked across the beach to the condo complex where Joe and his wife Grace lived. As we neared the steps leading over the dunes, an ancient lady met us coming down.

"Morning, Joe," said the woman, looking him in the eyes.

Joe nodded.

Turning to me, she said, "Hey, Matt. Grace will have his hide for this."

"I know," I said. "There are some dead guys on the beach, and the police are on their way. I've got to get back. Will you take him home?"

"Sure," she said. "What's this about dead guys?"

"I'll tell you later," I said. "Just take Joe home."

As I turned toward the surf, I could hear the police sirens in the distance. Glancing over my shoulder, I saw the elderly woman gently leading Joe back across the dunes.

* * * * *

Tiny's was jumping, the Friday evening crowd in full swing. Susie and Debbie were behind the bar, and a shaggy looking man sat in a corner playing his guitar and singing the oldies. My buddy Logan Hamilton was perched on a stool, sipping an amber drink. A brown bag was next to his glass, an unopened liter bottle of Scotch peeking out of the top. Logan had been to the package store next door, stocking up for the weekend.

Dotty Johansen, a widow in her seventies, the doyenne of the North End, held court at her usual table. She was surrounded by her friends, all retired ladies who had lost their husbands to the grim reaper. Smoke filled the place with a volume that even the best air handlers couldn't dent.

It was Friday evening on Longboat Key, and the crowd was breathing a sigh of relief at having survived another week in the workaday world. There was the usual mix of wealthy retirees, middle-aged professionals and construction workers, all come to Tiny's to sit and talk and drink. It was late October on this barrier island just south of Tampa Bay, halfway down Florida's west coast. Our summer had ended the week before, when the humidity dropped to a bearable level and the temperature hovered in the mid-to-low-seventies. Except for a few cold days in January and February, this would be our weather until the middle of May, when summer again blew its hot breath down our necks.

Tiny's was not really "Tiny's." Some new people had come to the island a few years before, bought the place from a guy named Tiny, and renamed it. The locals didn't like the new name, and most couldn't remember it, so Tiny's remained Tiny's. It's a little bar, tucked away in the corner of a building in a small shopping plaza on the north end of the key. When the voters of Florida passed an amendment to the state constitution a few years back requiring all places that served food to be smoke-free, Tiny's, because it was the only bar on the island that didn't serve food, became the oasis of necessity for thirsty smokers. There are more of those people than you might expect, and Tiny's gained a popularity far above its humble status in the world of bars. The new owners, who had already become part of the island fabric, were content with the place as it was, and so were the patrons.

"Hey, Matt," Dotty Johansen called to me as I walked in, "I heard you found those dead Mexicans this morning."

Dotty knew everything, and perhaps the greatest mystery on the key was how she knew so much, so quickly.

"Actually, Joe Turnicoff found them," I said.

Dotty laughed. "I heard he was out naked again," she said. "He's crazy."

I nodded. "Yeah, but he still has some good days," I said.

Dotty made a face. "Not enough," she said. "Grace is going to have to put him in a nursing home. He scares the tourists, and Bill Lester's going to run out of patience with him."

Bill Lester was the Longboat Key Chief of Police, a well-liked

4

cop who had worked his way through the ranks of the small force until he was in charge. Joe had once been a powerful businessman in Chicago, but Alzheimer's was taking a terrible toll on him. His wife Grace tried to keep him at home, but once in a while Joe would get up early in the morning, before her, and sit on the beach naked. During the winter season, tourists would call the police about the crazy man on the beach, and a cruiser would come. The patrol officer would drape a towel around Joe and take him home. Most mornings though, Grace found Joe before he could cause any trouble.

Dotty swallowed a little of her vodka. "I heard one of them was still alive," she said.

I said, "He is, but he's still unconscious. The docs don't know if the guy will pull through or be a vegetable."

Logan turned on his bar stool. "Do they know what happened?" he said to me.

I said, "Bill says it looks like the one still alive shot the other two, then fell and hit his head. His fingerprints are on the pistol, and blood and hair were on the gunwale."

Logan said, "That was a big onshore wind last night. It must've pushed the boat up on the beach."

I took the seat next to Logan and sipped from the Miller Lite Debbie had set on the bar. "Looks that way," I said.

A heavily accented voice said, "Are you Matt Royal?"

I turned to my left. A man I had never seen before was standing behind Logan. The accent was Spanish. His face was pitted with acne scars, and his black hair was combed back from a widow's peak, no part. He had a thick mustache and a trim goatee. A big man, a couple of inches taller than my six feet. He was wearing one of those gray sweatshirts with a hood. There were slits in the front, giving access to the pocket in which his hands were concealed. The sweatshirt had "Property of University of Florida

5

Athletic Department" written across its front in bold orange letters. I remember thinking that those preppie kids in Gainesville would never wear such a ratty-looking thing.

"That would be me," I said, sticking out my hand to shake, a reflex action among us lawyers. His right hand came out of the pocket holding a snub-nosed revolver. He was raising it toward my chest, his eyes starting to squint in anticipation of the report that would follow the bullet entering my body. My world slowed down, like in those cheesy movies where the lovers are running toward each other in slow motion. I was starting to react, to reach toward the gun, to grab the hand that held it and twist downward, as the Army had taught me so long ago. But I knew I'd waited too long. The shock of death stalking amid the gaiety of Tiny's slowed my reaction time just long enough to seal my fate. My killer was grinning. He was enjoying this.

A hand holding a full bottle of Scotch by its neck, shot into my line of vision. The bottle came down onto the arm of my killer. I was expecting to hear the sound of a gunshot, but instead I heard the bones of the shooter's forearm breaking. Two people screamed, Logan in anger as he followed through with the chop that saved my life, and the Hispanic guy in agony, as he dropped his revolver.

There was silence. Nobody moved for a second, except the shooter, who turned and headed for the door. He was gone before anyone could react. As I rushed toward the entrance to stop him, I heard a motorcycle revving its engine. Several agitated people were right behind me, all of us pushing out the door at the same time. All we saw of the shooter was his back as he climbed aboard the bike, placing his good arm around the driver's waist and holding the broken one between his chest and his rescuer's back. The bike shot out of the parking lot and headed for the Longboat Pass Bridge, less than a mile to the north. He'd be across Anna Maria Island and onto the mainland before the police could get organized to chase him.

I returned to my seat at the bar. Logan was still nursing his Scotch. He hadn't moved during the rush to the door.

"You saved my life, buddy," I said, patting him on the back.

"Your turn to buy," he said.

And he ordered us two more drinks.

TWO

Susie had picked up the phone as soon as the shooter dropped his gun. As we were settling down, she announced that she had called 911, and the cops were on their way.

"Don't touch that gun, people," she said. "The CSI's will want to see it. This is a crime scene."

I didn't have the heart to tell her that the Longboat Key Police Department didn't have Crime Scene Investigators. We could hear the sirens in the distance, and they quickly grew louder, drowning out the din of voices as Tiny's customers told each other what they'd seen. My adrenalin rush was subsiding, and I was beginning to shiver all over. I couldn't seem to stop. I was drinking my beer in small quick swallows, trying to stop my hands from shaking and hoping I wouldn't throw up, when the first patrol officer arrived.

Susie pointed to the gun on the floor near my bar stool, and the cop told everyone to calm down. He added that more police were on the way, and they would have to take statements from each one of the customers.

The patrolman told Susie to shut down the bar. "No more drinking," he said, "until we get to the bottom of this."

He was new to the force, and none of us knew him. It was obvious that he didn't know this crowd either, not if he thought

8

he could stop them from drinking just because they had witnessed an attempted murder.

The young officer took a small notebook from his shirt pocket. "Who can tell me what happened?" he said.

A cacophony of voices rose from the crowd. Everyone was talking at once. The cop was nervous, didn't seem to know what to do. He was looking around the room, his eyes darting from one speaker to the next. They probably didn't teach this kind of thing at the police academy.

"Everybody calm down," said Dotty Johansen, talking over the buzz of excited voices. She stood, took a big swig of her vodka, and said, "Young man, why don't you ask Matt Royal? He's the one the guy was trying to kill."

"Which one is Matt Royal?" he asked.

I raised my trembling hand.

He turned to me, "Why was he trying to kill you, Mr. Royal?"

"I don't know," I said. "I never saw him before in my life. I don't think I have any blood enemies, and as far as I know, I haven't pissed anybody off lately."

The cop stood there, dumbfounded. He didn't know what the next question should be. I was feeling sorry for him, and about to make some inane comment, when Chief Bill Lester walked in the door.

The rookie snapped to attention. The chief was about five- feet-eight, with a head full of black hair and a small well-trimmed mustache. He was wearing a golf shirt over a pair of chinos, his small belly beginning to push at the shirt, a sign of too much desk and not enough exercise. He came over to me and put his arm across my shoulder.

"You all right, Counselor?" he asked.

"Yeah, thanks to Logan."

"What happened?"

I told him the whole thing, leaving nothing out. I couldn't imagine why anyone would want to shoot me, and I'd have thought it a case of mistaken identity if the guy hadn't asked me if I were Matt Royal.

Turning to Logan, Bill asked, "Where'd you learn that kung fu crap?"

"Ah, that's just bar fighting 101, Bill. A full bottle of hootch can do a lot of damage. You think I could get another Scotch? Matt's buying."

"Sure," Bill said. Several Manatee County Sheriff's deputies had come into Tiny's while we talked. They helped the Longboat police as needed. Lester had probably called them in to help take statements while the crowd was reasonably sober. He would've known before he reached Tiny's that there'd be a crowd on a Friday night. The chief was a regular himself and knew most of the people in the bar.

Bill asked the crowd to calm down, and then told them he would appreciate it if each of them would give a statement to the deputies. There was a murmur of agreement, and the deputies began to move about the bar, talking to the witnesses.

Bill turned to me. "You feel like talking now?"

"Yeah," I said. "Let's get this down before I start to forget things."

We moved to a table in the corner where it was reasonably quiet. "What can you tell me about this, Matt?"

I gave him the facts, as best as I could remember them.

"What were your impressions?" Bill asked.

"Impressions? I was scared to death."

"I can imagine. But there must have been some thoughts going through your head."

"I was hoping I wouldn't crap my pants when the bullet hit me."

"Okay, but think. Try to let your mind just flow around the

10

memory. Is there anything else you saw, or thought you saw, or sensed?"

"The shooter was wearing latex gloves. I don't think that registered until now. But he was wearing surgical gloves."

"Anything else?"

"I don't think so," I said.

"What about the motorcycle, the rider, the tag number, anything?"

"The driver had on dark clothes and a black helmet. One of those that covered his head completely. It had a tinted visor, and I couldn't see his face through it. There was mud on the license plate. It was a Florida plate, but I couldn't read the numbers."

"Anything else strike you about the driver?" the chief asked.

I thought for a minute, concentrating on the few second glimpse I'd had of the driver. "He was small," I said. "Maybe he was a teenager. His jacket seemed too large."

"Could it have been a woman?"

I hadn't thought about that. I nodded. "I suppose it could've been," I said.

"What kind of bike?"

"I don't know. It wasn't a Harley. What do they call those others? Crotch rockets?"

"Yeah. Harley drivers are a lot more sensible than those kids on the rockets. Could you tell the make?"

"No. Sorry."

"No problem, Matt. You've done better than most."

"I think I need to get home, Bill. I'm beat, and I can't seem to stop shaking."

"Do you want me to get Doc Britt to look in on you?"

"No, I'll be okay. I just need to settle down some."

"Okay. I'll put an officer at your condo tonight. We'll talk more about this in the morning."

"Thanks, Bill. I'll see you tomorrow."

The chief and I agreed to meet at the Blue Dolphin for breakfast the next morning, and Logan insisted on driving me home. I'd retrieve my car the next day.

THREE

Logan walked to the door of my condo with me. "Want me to come in?" he asked.

"No, thanks. I'm fine. I'm still a little shaky, but I'll get over it.'

"Okay. Call me if you need anything."

I couldn't sit still. I roamed my condo, drinking a beer, trying to talk myself out of this odd state I'd been in since the shooter pointed his pistol at me. I looked out the window and saw the Longboat Key patrol car in the parking lot. I could just make out the figure of a cop behind the steering wheel. I knew another officer was outside my door. They'd be there all night, because the chief told them to, and because they were my friends. We islanders take care of each other.

I was not happy with myself. I had crafted a self-image that ran to the macho, and I was feeling a lot like a wuss tonight. I'm not sure what a wuss is, but I think it's the opposite of macho.

I had been to war, killed some people, got shot up, survived and lived a pretty good life. A few months before, I thought my life was over when three men tried to kill me on Egmont Key. I killed two of them, took some injuries to my own priceless hide, and never looked back. I was glad they were dead, and not me. It seemed like a good trade off, and I didn't suffer the remorse that I've always heard good cops feel when they have to shoot some scumbag.

But now I was scared. I didn't like that feeling. Where had my old macho self gone? Perhaps it was just the result of that instant when I knew with absolute certainty that I was about to die. In every other time I'd faced death, I'd been moving, in action, trying to save my skin. At Tiny's, I was frozen in place, unable to move. I'd waited for death for what seemed like a long time, although it was only a moment. It scared the hell out of me. That was an emotion I hadn't felt in years.

I knew I was going to have to get over this. Whoever tried to kill me was not likely to give up. I had no idea who wanted me dead, or why. But I figured if I was to survive, I'd have to find out who and why and put a stop to it.

I owned a thirty-eight caliber snub-nosed revolver, the same kind of handgun that had almost killed me a few hours earlier. I hadn't fired it in years. I took it out of the safe in my closet and spent an hour cleaning it. I clamped the holster to my belt and practiced drawing and dry firing the gun. I felt a little bit like Tom Mix, the old movie cowboy, but I was getting the hang of it. Old habits return quickly, and I'd once kept a weapon close at all times.

Several years before, the Florida legislature had passed a law that allowed any citizen who took a one-day course and passed a perfunctory test on the use and safety of firearms, to be issued a concealed weapons permit. I had one. I thought it was time I took advantage of it.

The phone rang. I answered.

"Mr. Royal? This is Ken Brown at the *Herald Tribune*." I hung up. It rang again. I ignored it.

I knew some of the islanders would be worried when they heard about Tiny's, and they'd be calling. I'd let the answering machine pick up, and I'd call my friends back later. The press could go to hell.

I lay down on the bed with my revolver on the bedside table. The front door was dead-bolted and the sliding glass doors to my balcony overlooking Sarasota Bay were secured with steel rods in the slide-ways. I felt relatively safe as I drifted off to sleep.

The dreams came that night, murky with dread and remorse. I hadn't had them in a long time, but I knew the men knocking on my psychic door during that long night. I woke with the dawn, glad the specters were gone, but knowing they'd be back, and that I could do nothing about it, except drink myself into a stupor. I didn't want to start that again.

FOUR

The Blue Dolphin Café sits in the middle of the Centre Shops, a small strip mall with a tree lined parking lot near the north end of Longboat Key. Bill Lester was waiting in a booth when I came in. I was wearing a light windbreaker over a golf shirt, cargo shorts and boat shoes. Bill was in uniform, the two stars on his collar glinting in the flourescent light.

He said, "I hope you've got a permit for that thing."

I looked down at my belt line. "Is it that obvious?"

"Only to a trained observer, such as myself. Permit?"

"Yeah, I got one. Want to see it?"

"Your word's good enough for me, Matt. Do you really think you need a gun?"

"After last night, I'll feel better just having it."

"Well, try not to shoot any innocent bystanders."

"Bill, I appreciate the cops at my place last night. I'm really spooked by this. Have you found out anything?"

"No, and you know it's being handled by the Manatee Sheriff's Office. You're not one of their favorite people."

Longboat Key is a small island, about ten miles long and a quarter-mile wide. The Town of Longboat Key encompasses the whole island, but it's divided by the county line that runs across

16

the key at its middle. Manatee County is to the north, and Sarasota County lies to the south. When the very rare major crime is committed on Longboat Key, the Sheriff's Office of the county in which the crime occurred handles the investigation. The Longboat Key Police Department is in charge however, and the deputies report to Bill Lester.

"I'm not sure why I'm in such bad favor at the Manatee Sheriff's Office," I said. "I did what I had to do to save an innocent man, and Banion was a bad guy."

I'm a lawyer by training, but I retired early and moved to Longboat Key. Some months before, I'd come out of retirement and tried a case defending Logan Hamilton from a charge of murdering his girlfriend. In the process I'd destroyed the reputation of a drunken Manatee County detective named Michael Banion, and Logan had been acquitted. Banion was a mean drunk who should have been put out to pasture years before.

Bill said, "I think everybody was happy to see Banion retire, but the sheriff thinks he should have been the one to make that happen. Some of the deputies think you were overly aggressive in taking the guy on."

"Do you agree with them?"

"Hell, no. And most cops I know think you did all of us a service. But there are those in Manatee County who spent their careers with Banion, and they feel that you brought about his death."

Two months after his retirement, Banion had put his service revolver in his mouth and pulled the trigger. The psychological scars on his buddies, and on me, were still fresh.

"So, you don't think Manatee is going to go out of its way to find the shooter?" I asked.

"They're good cops, and they'll do their jobs, but I don't think anybody's going to be putting in overtime on this one."

"Where do we go from here?"

"Can you think of anyone who'd want you dead?"

"Maybe some of Banion's friends?"

"I thought of that, but I don't think he really had any friends. The deputies are just mad at you because he was a cop, not because they gave a shit about him. And they're good cops. None of them would commit murder to avenge a dirtbag like Banion."

"What do you think I should do?"

"Be careful. I can keep my men at your place for a few days, but I'm sure you don't want them following you around."

"I appreciate the effort, Bill, but those guys have other things to do. If the shooter wants me, he'll just wait until you pull the guard off and come for me then. We might as well give him his chance sooner rather than later. Maybe Manatee will come up with something. Is there anything new on the dead Mexicans?"

"No. The survivor is still in a coma. Sarasota County is investigating, but they think the forensics point to the survivor as the killer. Maybe they'll know more when he wakes up. If he does."

"Has anybody figured out where the boat came from?"

"Not yet. It didn't have any registration numbers, but they're trying to track it through the serial number on the transom."

"Will you let me know if they figure it out?"

"Sure."

We talked about fishing as we ate our breakfast. After Bill left, I lingered over a last cup of coffee, reading the Sarasota *Herald Tribune*. A front-page article reported the previous evening's fracas at Tiny's, identifying me as the intended victim, and stating that "Mr. Royal was unavailable for comment."

I'd be getting calls all day from concerned friends, and I didn't feel up to discussing the damn thing. I didn't know who was trying to kill me or why. Maybe it was some kind of horrible mistake, and the threat would go away. I heard a nagging voice in the back of my mind telling me not to get my hopes up, that somebody was really trying to do me in. There was obviously somebody out there who didn't think I was as good a guy as I thought I was.

I paid my tab and left the restaurant. I drove to a public firing range on the mainland and put in a little practice time. I needed it.

FIVE

I had once been a trial lawyer in Orlando. I'd always loved the law, the give and take of the high-stakes poker game that a trial usually turned out to be. I missed that part of the practice, but there was too much of it I didn't miss. The law had lost its high calling and turned into a business where the name of the game wasn't justice, but billable hours. I mourned the law's loss of its nobility, and I quit. I moved aboard a boat moored at a marina on Longboat Key, and spent much of my time getting drunk. A good man pulled me out of that losing proposition and talked me back into the practice to handle his case. We won, and I ended up with enough money to retire completely, buy a condo on the bay, and spend the rest of my days without the need to work for a living. I didn't have enough to live lavishly, but I was comfortable, and that suited me.

The key had become my home, and I had been accepted into the community of friends who lived there year-round. It was a good life of fishing, boating, and drinking with people who had come to the key from all over the world. Our circle included wealthy retired industrialists, working professionals, government employees and blue-collar workers who clung to their lives in the Village, the oldest settlement on the key. People cared about each other, rallied around in times of need, and never let the widows and widowers get too lonely.

The rhythms of life beat more slowly on our small island, cosseted as we are by our isolation from the world at large, protected by bridges and bay and white sand beaches.

In the gathering dawn, the sun rises from behind the mainland and gives our slice of paradise its reason for being. At the end of the day, when the sea birds head for their rookeries and the beach stragglers watch in amazement, old Sol sinks slowly into the Gulf, clothing its surface in brilliant colors and, on rare occasions, a quick flash of green that bedazzles his worshipers.

It's during the interval between those times, the alpha and omega of our day in the sun, that the islanders live and love and play and congratulate themselves for abiding in paradise. And when the sun goes down, we move from the beaches and the bay and into the bars. We drink and talk and tell the stories of our former lives in cold places, faraway.

And when death comes to one, the others gather round the survivors, like elephants in the wild, to comfort the grieving and jolly them back to life.

With each dawn, the cycle begins anew. Our key is a small place on the edge of a great ocean, and perhaps it is the awareness of our own insignificance that brings us a kind of frenzied serenity.

I was content. Life was good on Longboat Key.

I was ruminating on this as I drove from the firing range in eastern Manatee County and across the Cortez Bridge to Anna Maria Island. I turned south where the Cortez Road ends at the Gulf. I drove over the Longboat Pass Bridge onto Longboat Key and a couple of miles farther turned into my condo complex.

I called Logan, and he told me he was going to Tiny's to watch some college football on the giant screen TV, and then would probably go to the Hilton for a drink to wind up the evening. I told him I thought I'd stay in with a good book.

I was sitting on my balcony, halfway through Bob Morris' latest novel. The phone rang occasionally, and I let the machine answer. I wasn't in the mood to talk to anybody. The sun was low in the western sky, its rays reflecting off the cumulus that hung high over the bay, giving me a vision of pastel colors lightly daubed on fleecy clouds. The bay was still, the temperature in the low seventies. The roar of a go-fast boat assailed my ears as it headed south, its wake disturbing the wading birds on the edge of the channel. My cell phone rang. Few people had that number, so I answered.

"Matt, it's Billy. I hate to bother you, but we've got a pretty big crowd, and Logan isn't holding up too well, if you know what I mean."

My old friend Billy was the bartender at the Hilton, and I knew exactly what he meant.

"I'll be down in a few minutes," I said.

"Thanks, buddy." He hung up.

I slipped on my boat shoes and headed south.

* * * * *

The Hilton has an outside bar with a clear view of the beach about 200 feet away. Billy was mixing drinks as he'd done for twenty years behind the same bar. He was somewhat of a tourist attraction himself, as people from all over the world would return year after year to visit with Billy and have a few with the locals. He and Logan had been friends since they'd first gotten out of the Army as the war in Vietnam wound down.

The sun was beginning its daily dip into the Gulf. Everyone at the bar, except Logan, was turned on his stool watching it. It was an event that never failed to move even the most cynical locals. I always watched for the flash of green that is said to show on the horizon just as the sun sinks finally beneath the surface of the Gulf. I had seen it once in Key West, but never here.

The bar was full, and Logan sat at his usual place, squeezed between Mike Nink and an obese woman in a bathing suit done in a garish floral pattern. Her butt was the size of Indiana, and it appeared to be devouring the bar stool upon which it was perched. She had obviously been there awhile.

The woman was leaning in close to Logan. "I'm jazzed, jazzed. Aren't you?" she said.

"What in the hell are you talking about?" asked Logan, as he leaned away from the boozy breath of the tourist from hell.

"Jazzed. You know. I just left Milwaukee this morning and it was snowing, and now I'm sitting at a bar on the beach wearing a bathing suit. I call it the Longboat Jazz. You know, excitement, happiness, warmth. Don't you feel it?"

"Jeez," murmured Logan. He had that look on his face that I knew well. He'd had one scotch past what should have been his limit, and he was about to unload on the fat lady.

"Logan," I said. "Drink up and let's go see Sam at Patti-george's for a nightcap."

"Okay. 'Bout time you got here. Jazzed. Christ, where the hell do these people come from?"

He took a big swallow of his drink, got unsteadily off his stool, and started for the parking lot. Billy mouthed me a thank you from behind the bar. The fat woman gave Logan the finger.

Pattigeorge's was only about a mile down Gulf of Mexico Drive, but I didn't think Logan would make it. The key was getting crowded with the snowbirds coming in for the winter, and our main street was packed with cars. It wouldn't take much for a driver with too much scotch in him to cause an accident.

My Explorer was parked in the lot bordering the beach. Logan was waiting on the passenger's side for me to open my door and unlock his. Suddenly, the rear door window on my side exploded. Almost simultaneously I heard the crack of a high powered rifle.

Logan and I both hit the ground, our military training taking over. I was lying on my stomach, trying to melt into the pavement. I could see under the car, Logan on the other side, hugging his piece of asphalt. He began to rise slowly, and I yelled, "What are you doing? Get down."

"I'm trying to see where the shot came from," he said, sounding completely sober.

He was on his feet, his head poking over the hood. "The shooter's gone," said Logan, as I heard the roar of marine engines on the Gulf.

I stood and watched a dark blue go-fast boat of about thirty feet coming on plane as it headed for deep water. Dusk was on us, and what light was left was quickly disappearing.

"The shooter was in that boat," Logan said.

"The guy from Tiny's?" I asked.

"I don't think so. I didn't get a good look at him, but he wasn't wearing a cast, and that guy definitely had a broken arm last night."

"Who the hell are they?"

"I'd sure like to find out."

We heard sirens headed our way. A cruiser and an unmarked screeched into the parking lot, their blue lights throwing a strange pattern in the darkening night. The sirens stopped abruptly as the cars came to a stop. Someone in the bar had apparently called 911.

"You guys all right?" asked Bill Lester as he strode toward us, gun drawn, but hanging down along his right thigh.

"Yeah," I said, "whoever it was is gone."

Logan began to tell him about the shot and the blue boat. When he finished, Lester looked at me, and said, "Matt, do you know a lawyer named Dwight Conley?"

"Never heard of him. Why?"

"Conley was an immigration lawyer in Sarasota. He was jogging on the beach on the southern tip of Longboat early this morning, and somebody shot him through the head with a high-powered rifle. A witness down the beach heard the rifle shot and saw a dark blue or black go-fast headed straight out into the Gulf."

"You think it was the same guy?" asked Logan.

"Seems reasonable," said Bill.

"But," I said, "the shooter must be a hell of a shot if he could hit somebody in the head from that distance. The way the bottom slopes up out of New Pass, his boat must have been fifty yards from the beach."

"He was a lot closer to me and he missed. Could he have just been trying to scare me for some reason?"

"I wouldn't bet on that, Matt. He might have caught a little swell that threw his aim off. But I don't think he was just trying to scare you."

"How would the shooter have known I was here?" I told Lester how I had come to be at the Hilton that evening.

"Aren't you usually here on Saturday evenings?" said the chief.

"Yeah. That's true."

"Then there's your answer. It's just like Conley. He always jogged on the beach at daybreak. It's just a matter of learning your schedules. If somebody wants you badly enough, they can watch you for a couple of weeks, or maybe just ask around. We're all creatures of habit, and sometimes those habits can kill us. What the hell have you gotten yourself into, Matt?"

"I don't have a clue, Bill. Not a clue. But it seems like more

25

than a coincidence that two different people tried to kill me right after I found those bodies on the beach. If they're connected, nobody had time to figure our my daily patterns. What do we do from here?"

"Since we're in Sarasota County, the sheriff will take over the investigation. That's the good news. They're also investigating the Conley shooting .They found the slug that killed Conley."

"How?" I asked. "Surely that thing didn't lodge in his head."

"No. The witness had one of those metal detectors. He goes out every morning looking for stuff in the sand. He found the slug, or what we think was the slug. We probably can't use it for evidence, but we can compare it to the one that almost got you. I'm willing to bet the slug they'll find in your car will be a match. It was 7.62 millimeter round."

Logan cleared his throat. "That's an M-14 or something like it, right?" he said.

"Yep. That's the bad news," said Lester.

* * * * *

An hour later, Logan and I were sitting quietly at the bar at Pattigeorge's. I wasn't too sure we needed any more merriment that night, but Logan said we deserved a drink after another near-death experience.

Sammy, who knew everybody on the island, was behind the bar. We'd been there for about thirty minutes when a tall blonde woman came in and took a seat. She was about five-feet-eight, with shoulder-length hair. Her face was a bit angular for my taste, but her pale blue eyes made up for that. She was a beautiful lady, probably in her early thirties, and I was not surprised that Sam knew exactly what she drank. He started the martini as she walked through the front door, shook it, put it on the bar and introduced us to Marie Phillips as she sat down next to Logan.

We were the only three at the bar, and we talked for an hour or so in the desultory manner of people at ease in a familiar place. Marie was new to the island, and lived in one of the big condos at the south end of the key that was reserved for the very wealthy.

She told us she was in the "corporate world," but made no effort to explain further. It was against the code of the key to delve too deeply into someone else's life, so we left it at that.

She said she was a Florida native, and she spoke with the accent of the central part of the state; not quite southern in her inflection, but enough so that it fooled the Northerners. Marie didn't tell us where she had grown up, but I assumed it was in the Orlando area.

She had another martini, said her good-byes and walked out into the night. Sam told us Marie had been in several times over the past few months, but she never talked much about herself. She was pleasant enough, but a little secretive. That was okay. Many of the islanders had fled to Southwest Florida to get away from a past they didn't like to remember, and the people of the key respected their silence.

Sam told us that Marie had come in for dinner a couple of times with an older man, and he suspected that she might have a sugar daddy. Or, maybe she'd inherited a bundle, and the old gent was her father or a kindly uncle. It wasn't likely that a corporate job for one so young would generate the income necessary to sustain a life on the south end.

Sam had also seen her with a younger man, late thirties or early forties maybe, at the Haye Loft bar late one evening. They were sitting at a table in the corner, and if Marie noticed Sam, she didn't acknowledge it. Sam didn't know the man she was with.

"A mystery woman," said Logan. "The best kind."

Sam laughed. "Don't get your hopes up, Logan. I think she's

a five star gal and you're about a two star kind of guy."

Logan laughed. "Go to hell, Sam," he said.

The conversation moved on to other things, and Marie was forgotten.

SIX

Logan drove me home and dropped me at the elevator entrance to my condo complex. Earlier, I'd been advised by a Sarasota County detective that the Explorer was a crime scene and it would have to be processed at the forensics lab. The Sheriff's department would have it towed there, and I should be able to pick it up in a couple of days.

The cell phone rang as I entered my condo. "Matt, are you all right? I just got back from Lauderdale and read this morning's paper."

It was Anne Dubose. The sound of her voice always made me feel like a better person than I am. She was my girlfriend, sort of.

We'd met in the summer and had a hot affair that lasted for a couple of months. She had been a lawyer in Ft. Lauderdale, but recently moved to Sarasota and gone to work with a small firm. Our relationship had cooled substantially, but we saw each other every week or so, and we were good friends. We even shared a bed once in awhile, but I figured that wouldn't last long.

That bothered me, because I had developed some deep feeling about Anne. I knew that she was bound to meet someone who would become a permanent fixture in her life, and I would be left, like detritus, on the roadside of What Might Have Been

Boulevard. Ouch. That phrase sounded bad to my own ears. Maybe Willlie Nelson could us it.

"I'm fine, Anne. Logan got the bad guy before he got me."

"That's a relief. I don't have anything to wear to a funeral."

"Right. How was Lauderdale?"

"Same old. I took a couple of depositions yesterday and spent the night with friends. Nothing has changed, and I'm glad to be living here."

"Do you know a lawyer in Sarasota named Dwight Conley?"

"I don't think so. Why?"

"He was shot and killed on Longboat this morning, down near New Pass. Apparently, the same guys took a potshot at me about an hour ago."

"Somebody shot at you?" Her voice held a hint of fear.

"Yeah. Missed, though."

"I'm coming out there."

"You don't have to," I said, without any conviction whatsoever.

"I know, silly. I want to. I'll bring a pizza."

* * * * *

Anne arrived an hour later, bringing a large pizza with everything but anchovies. We sat on the balcony, eating pizza and drinking beer. She was wearing shorts and a midriff blouse which exposed her delightful belly button as she leaned back in her chair. Barely past thirty, she was tall with short dark hair, hazel eyes and a body that men would have killed for in other ages. Her bare feet were propped on the balcony railing, her toenails painted a bright red. I told her the details of both shootings and repeated what the police had told me.

"You don't have any idea who might be trying to kill you?"

she said.

"None. I can't come up with a reason, either. I'd tend to think it was somebody from my past with a grudge, but what's the connection to Conley? I never heard of the guy before this evening."

"Maybe the gunmen were hired by different people with different reasons to kill you and Conley? Then there'd be no connection, other than the hired gun."

"I think that's way too much of a coincidence. It may not even be the same shooters, but the parallels are too great. I guess we'll know for sure when the police get the ballistics done."

"Is my toothbrush still here?" Anne asked.

"Of course."

"Good. Then I can stay?"

"Of course."

And she did.

SEVEN

I awoke Sunday morning to the smell of coffee. Anne had beat me out of bed, and I could hear her rattling around in my kitchen. I took a quick shower, shaved and dressed, and joined her.

Anne was wearing one of my T-shirts, and I noticed when she reached for a plate on a high shelf that she wore nothing else. Bacon was draining on the side board, and eggs were frying on the stove. I couldn't think of a better treat on a Sunday morning than coffee, eggs, bacon and Anne's bare butt. I kissed her cheek and wished her a good morning. The cheek on her face, that is.

She smiled, and said, "Sleep well?"

"Like a worn out old man. Your fault."

"Maybe we ought to stop that if it tires you too much."

"Don't even think it, woman."

I retrieved the Sarasota paper from my door step, and read while Anne finished cooking breakfast. The large headline was about the Conley murder, with a side story about the shooting at the Hilton. Again, the reporter wrote that I had not been available for comment. I'm sure his voice was on my answering machine.

Anne and I hadn't seen each other in a week, and we caught up over breakfast. She was working on a civil case involving a fraudulent bank transfer, and she was enjoying it.

32

"Still glad you moved here?" I asked.

"Even more so after spending a couple of days in South Florida. This is home."

"Want to take the boat out?" I said, as we finished our coffee.

"It's going to be a gorgeous day. Why not?"

Anne drove to The Market at Whitney Beach Shopping Center to stock up on deli sandwiches and beer, while I cleaned up the breakfast dishes.

My twenty-seven foot Grady-White, with its twin 150 horse-power Yamahas, rocked gently in its slip in front of my condo. She was a center console fishing boat, white with black trim. With all that had been happening I hadn't been aboard in a couple of months, and that was unforgivable. As always, the engines cranked on the first try, and we maneuvered out of the harbor and into the Intracoastal Waterway, headed for Longboat Pass and the Gulf of Mexico.

We cruised north, moving at thirty knots and staying about two miles offshore. The sea was calm and the boat handled like the thoroughbred she was. We came into the beach at Egmont Key, near the north end where the remains of an ancient gun emplacement provided a concrete backdrop to the white sand and turquoise water.

At the end of the Nineteenth Century, the U.S. Army had turned Egmont into a fortress protecting Tampa Bay. Gun emplacements were situated at strategic points on the small island, and barracks, bunkers and, curiously, a red brick road had been built in the interior.

When the Army gave up its garrison there, Egmont became a state park and wildlife sanctuary. People were not allowed onto the southern third of the island, and it was populated by every kind of seabird that lives along the west coast of Florida.

The beaches of Egmont are still pristine, although the normal ebb and flow of the tides has eaten large portions of the shore. On a Sunday afternoon, there were families from all over the Tampa Bay area using the island and enjoying themselves, their boats anchored in the shallows.

We lay on the sand on towels, swam when the spirit moved us, ate our lunch, drank our beer and napped. Anne's lithe body was barely clothed in a bright yellow bikini, and I found myself hoping she would stay another night. The revolver was in the picnic basket, and if Anne noticed it, she didn't comment.

As the sun began to sink toward the horizon, we headed south for home. As we neared Longboat Pass, a pair of dolphins appeared in the bow wave, surfing along, enjoying life. The sun hovered just above the horizon, its orange and red glow burnishing the water. After a few minutes the dolphins peeled off and left us with a feeling of wonder at nature's small displays of elegance.

I secured the boat and washed it down as Anne took our belongings upstairs to the condo. When we were finished, she thanked me for a wonderful day, and left for Sarasota and an early morning hearing on Monday.

EIGHT

I decided not to jog the beach on Monday morning. If the shooters were counting on me keeping a schedule, the easiest way to throw them off was to vary my routines. I planned to jog later that day.

I was sitting in my living room drinking coffee and reading the morning paper when I heard a knock on the door. It was only a little after seven, early for social callers. I peered through the spy hole and saw John Algren.

He was about six feet tall, with a wiry build that belied the power that could surge out of his body when needed. He was very tan, and had a U shaped fringe of black hair setting off his bald pate. A small area of skin was peeling from a sunburn on the crown of his head. He'd been playing golf without his hat again. He was the smartest man I'd ever known.

I opened the door to a bear hug from my best friend since junior high school. "Jock, my God it's good to see you," I said, coming up for air. "What brings you to paradise?"

"I thought you might need somebody to watch your back."

"How did you know?"

"Anne called me last night. I caught an early plane into Tampa, and here I am."

John, who had acquired the nickname of "Jock" in high school, was a frequent visitor to the key. He had gotten to know most of the islanders, and a couple of months before, on his last visit, Dotty Johansen threw an elaborate party on the beach behind the Hilton, where she formally decreed "that henceforth and forevermore, Jock Algren was an honorary Longboater."

"I'm glad you're here, old buddy. How about some coffee?"

"That'd work."

Jock had left high school on the same day I did. While I headed for the Army, he went to engineering school on scholarship. He played on the basketball team, and was a member of the school's ROTC unit. Near the end of his senior year, he'd taken a bad fall on the basketball court, and the college newspaper reported that Jock had ruptured the ligaments in his knee. The injury and the surgery to repair it would end his basketball career and any thoughts he had of being commissioned in the Army.

Jock was heavily recruited by the major oil companies, and when he graduated he went to work for one of them in its international department. Jock was still with the company.

A couple of people at the very top of his company, a few people in the government, and I knew that Jock had never hurt his knee, never had surgery, and was certainly not medically unfit for military duty. He had been recruited by the most secretive intelligence agency our country has.

My friend spent a couple of years in training, and then became a deep-cover operative, doing things for the government that no one ever wanted known. Jock had maintained his cover with the oil company, and now was in fact an employee, living in Houston. However, the government would call on him when needed, to do things that needed to be done.

When the call came, and it always did, the chairman of Jock's company would send out a memo that Mr. Algren would be off somewhere in the world on a special mission for the chairman, and Jock would be back in the field hunting and killing people who would do harm to the United States.

Years before, his boss in the government had given Jock permission to tell me what he did for the country. Jock had no living family, and he had convinced the boss that somebody had to know the real story in case anything happened to him. He still complained about phantom knee pain, and he couldn't play golf worth a damn.

I brought the coffee back to the living room and sat in my recliner. Jock was on the sofa, his stocking feet propped on a low table. "Tell me what happened, Podner," he said.

I gave him the whole story. "I don't know who they are or why they're trying to kill me. It doesn't make any kind of sense."

"How's Logan?"

"Logan's Logan. He's staying in town this week to give me whatever help he can. You know Logan; generous to a fault."

Logan had a job in the financial services industry that kept him traveling most of every week. He was sticking around this week for me, but now that Jock was here, I'd tell him to go on and do his work, and I'd see him on the weekend. I picked up the phone to call him.

Logan agreed to meet at Lynches Pub on St. Armand's Circle for lunch. He and Jock had become good friends during Jock's visits to the key.

"You got a gun?" Jock asked me as we got back to our coffee.

"Yep." I got it out of the drawer in the coffee table. "A thirty-eight caliber revolver."

"That's good for close work. Anything else?"

"No. If they come after me with that M-14 again, the only thing I could defend myself with would be a rifle. I can't be carrying one of those around with me. If they get close, the thirty-eight will do the trick."

"You're right. I guess we'd better try to figure out who these bastards are."

My cell phone rang. It was Marcie McFarland, Anne's law partner in Sarasota.

"I heard you've taken up target shooting for a hobby, except you're the target."

"Not by choice, Marcie. Not by a long shot."

"Is that a pun?"

"Maybe. I hadn't thought about it."

"Anne mentioned that you asked about Dwight Conley. I knew him, and I thought I could fill you in a little."

"That'd be a big help. What can you tell me?"

"He was a nice guy. My sister, Dawn, used to date him, but not seriously. Dwight came to Sarasota about ten years ago, about the same time I did, and opened an immigration practice. He'd built it up into a pretty thriving operation. Dwight was well respected in the Bar Association, and by the U.S. Immigration Judge up in Bradenton. He did a lot of work for the Mexican migrant workers that seem to congregate in Manatee County. Dwight lived on Bird Key, and nobody I've talked to can figure out why anyone would want to kill him."

"I think the same guys who tried to kill me Saturday night killed Conley that morning. I didn't know the guy, and I can't see any connection between us. If you hear anything else, let me know. Oh, and tell Anne that Jock got here."

We said goodbye and hung up. I related the conversation to Jock. "Still not ringing any bells," I said.

Just before nine, my cell phone rang again. It was Bill Lester telling me that ballistics had matched the slug in my car to the one that killed Conley. A canvass of the local hospitals had failed to turn up any evidence of a Hispanic man with a broken arm.

Murder Key

"He could've had it looked at by any number of doctors, and we'll probably never figure it out," Bill said.

He also told me that I could pick up the Explorer at the crime lab. I called a company that repairs car windows and arranged for them to pick up the car and fix the window and plug the bullet hole in the unholstery. I'd pick it up late that afternoon from the repair shop.

* * * * *

At noon, we drove south in Jock's rental car and crossed the New Pass Bridge onto Lido Key. I marveled at the beauty of the inlet, its surface painted in pastel shades of blue and green. Several boats were anchored on the sand bar just seaward of the bridge, filled with people fishing and taking the sun.

We found a parking place near Lynches and walked back a block to the small restaurant. Logan was waiting at a table just inside the door.

"Good to see you, again," he said to Jock as they shook hands.

"Same here, Logan."

We ordered lunch while Jock and Logan caught up with each other. Just as our meal was brought to the table, a large man, probably six-feet-three and weighing 220 pounds entered the restaurant. He had a lot of blonde hair set off by a deep tan. His sun-wrinkled face put him in his mid-forties.

"Matt," he said, as he spotted us. "I've left a couple of messages on your answering machine."

"Sorry, Buddy. I haven't checked it since Friday. Say hello to Jock Algren. Jock, this is Buddy Gilchrest."

"Nice to meet you, Jock. You doing okay, Logan?"

"Can't complain."

"Matt, I heard you found those Mexicans on the beach on

39

Friday," said Buddy. "The one who's still alive is the brother of one of my crew chiefs."

Buddy ran a lawn maintenance business that had sewn up much of the condo business on Longboat and Lido Keys. Most of his workers were Mexican immigrants, some even legal.

"How's he doing?" I asked.

"Still in a coma, but the cops are going to charge him with murder as soon as he wakes up. I don't think he did it. I was wondering if you knew anything."

"I don't. What makes you think he didn't do it? The evidence seems pretty solid."

"Well, first of all, I doubt Pepe knows how to use a gun. Secondly, he's here legally, and I don't think he'd want to do anything to jeopardize his status. He's supporting a pretty big family in Mexico."

"I wish I could help, Buddy, but you probably know more about this than I do."

"I also heard that you almost got killed a couple of times this weekend. Do you think there might be some connection with the guys you found on the beach?"

"I don't see how. All I did was find them and call it in."

"The cops think this has to do with drugs. I know Pepe wouldn't be using. He had too much to lose."

"Could he be in the importing business?" Jock asked.

"I doubt it. Call me if you hear anything, Matt. Take it easy Logan." He went to the bar to order lunch.

We finished our meal, and Logan left for the airport. Jock and I had another beer, paid our bill, and walked out of the restaurant. Just as we got to the sidewalk my cell phone rang. It was Bill Lester.

"Where are you, Matt?" His voice was agitated, louder than normal.

"Just leaving Lynches. What's up?"

"Get back inside and stay away from the windows. I'm on my way." He hung up.

"Back inside," I said to Jock. He didn't question me, just headed for the door. "That was the police chief. He'll be here in a few minutes. I don't know what the problem is, but he said to get inside and stay away from the windows."

I patted my thirty-eight in its holster and asked Jock if he were armed.

"Yes," he said. "I brought it in checked luggage."

We sat. In about ten minutes Bill Lester strode through the door. I introduced him to Jock. "What's wrong?" I asked.

"Your Explorer's been shot up again. The guy from the auto-glass shop went to the crime lab to pick it up, and as he was coming out of the parking lot, somebody shot through the wind-shield with an assault rifle."

"Shit," I said. "Anybody hurt?"

"Yeah. The shooter got the driver right between the eyes. A hell of a shot."

I said, "This had nothing to do with my habits."

Jock shifted in his chair. "I wonder if somebody put a locator beacon on Matt's car," he said. "That'd make it simple to find him whenever they wanted."

"I'll have the crime lab check for one," said the chief. "In the meantime, Matt, you'd better lay low. I'll let you know what I find out. Any more of this and we'll have to change the name of the island to Murder Key." He left.

"I think we need to get out of town," Jock said.

"That's a hell of a note," I said.

"Well, at least until we can get some idea of who's trying to kill you."

I thought about it for a moment. I had to do something more

41

than sit around waiting to be shot. "Let's go to Orlando," I said. "I've got an old friend in the U.S. Attorney's office who might be able to find out what's going on with this mess."

"What are you thinking?" asked Jock.

"We've got two dead Mexicans and one in a coma. The guy who tried to kill me Friday at Tiny's was most likely Mexican. Conley was an immigration lawyer. I think I may have somehow stumbled into some kind of war involving immigrants. If there's anything going on in that area of law enforcement, the U.S. Attorney's office would be involved. It's worth a try."

NINE

We went back to my condo and packed up. I grabbed some changes of clothes and my shaving kit. I'd stored my passport in a plastic container in the kit, and I brought it along. Jock thought that if the bad guys were using locator beacons, they might have had time to attach one to his rental. We stopped by the Sarasota-Bradenton airport and Jock switched cars with the accommodating Hertz attendant. We drove through downtown Sarasota, taking evasive actions that only Jock understood, to make sure we weren't being followed. We finally turned east toward I-75 for the two-hour trip to Orlando.

Orlando is one of those medium-size cities trying to become a metropolis. The construction crane has replaced the swan as the city's bird symbol. Steel and concrete skeletons were poking their way out of the ground, striving for their planned thirty or thirty-five floors. Soon they'd be glassed over and join their brothers on the skyline.

The Chamber of Commerce and developer types were glowing at all this tangible evidence of growth. Every day the local newspapers carried pieces about more new buildings, and this or that national company moving in to occupy them. It meant more employment, more people, more money. The power structure was happy, the developers were happy, and the people from the North looking for the good life were happy in the sunshine with their new jobs.

Nobody talked much about the lakes that looked like vats of pea soup; the ones that thirty years before had held clear, clean water, or about the ducks and coots that once lived and loved and procreated there. You didn't read a lot about the neighborhood downtown where people had lived for generations in neat clapboard and concrete block houses that were being torn down for the new civic arena. The people of that neighborhood were black and poor and had no part in the power structure.

If you cared about the land, and the water, and the trees, and the sky, and the people, you got sick of it all. I guess that was one of my reasons for bailing out, for resigning from the power structure, selling the house, and moving to Longboat Key. The rats had won the race, and I said the hell with it.

We drove out Colonial Drive to my favorite steak house. They pan fry their steaks and somehow turn out the best meat in the county. The super T-bone cooked medium rare and smothered in sauteed mushrooms is impossible to beat.

The restaurant itself was housed in one of those old concrete block buildings that were put up all over Florida in the years after World War II. It was small, divided into four separate dining rooms, each having five or six tables crammed close together. The tables were covered with red and white checkered plastic table-cloths, not in an attempt to be trendy, but because for the forty years the proprietors had been serving their steaks, they had always used them and could see no reason to change.

The place didn't take reservations, and there was always a line stretching out the door. They had a liquor license but no lounge. Waitresses would serve drinks outside while the customers waited to get in the door. It was probably technically against the law, but since the Chief of Police and the Sheriff, along with most of the rest of the area's politicians, were regular customers, there was never any trouble. Most of the patrons were locals, and on any given night the waiting line was a bit festive, with old friends gossiping, and not a little business getting done.

I'd called my law school classmate, David Parrish, from the car and asked him to meet us for dinner. He'd joined the State Attorney's office in Orlando after graduation, and after a few years had transferred to the U.S. Attorney's office. He'd risen to be Chief Assistant U.S. Attorney for the Middle District of Florida, which covers a large part of the state, extending from Jacksonville, down the Atlantic coast to Melbourne, across the state at Orlando and down the Gulf Coast from Tampa to Naples. If law enforcement suspected migrant smuggling was going on anywhere in the district, Parrish would know about it.

David was standing at the end of the line of customers when we drove up, a tall blonde man built like the college linebacker he had once been. He wore a dark suit, white dress shirt, and a printed silk tie, loosened at the collar.

"Matt, good to see you," he said, as we shook hands. "What brings you back to the big city?"

"I'll tell you over dinner, David. Meet Jock Algren."

We chatted as we worked our way up the line until we were finally seated. I explained that Jock was an old friend visiting from Texas, and that we had come to Orlando seeking some information.

Once seated and our orders taken, David looked at me and said, "Okay. What's the big mystery?"

"Are you aware of the murders over the weekend on Longboat Key?" I asked.

"Yes," he said, a look of concern crossing his face. "Don't tell me you're going to be representing somebody in that mess."

45

"No. Somebody has tried to kill me three times since Friday night." I told him the whole story, including my grisly discovery on the beach on Friday morning. "Since there seems to be some sort of Mexican connection in the murders and the attempts on me, I thought maybe you might have some insight into what's going on."

"Well, yes, I might," he said hesitantly, "but I'm not sure how much I can tell you."

"Somebody's trying to kill me, David. At the least, I need to know who and why."

"Are the police working on it?"

"Of course. But they're running blind. We can't figure out why anyone would want to kill me."

"You didn't know Dwight Conley?" he asked.

"I'd never heard of him before he was killed. Did you know him?"

"Yes. Look, Matt, I need some time to think about what I can and can't say. I might need some clearance from higher up. Why don't you and Jock come by my office in the morning, maybe around ten?"

We finished the evening with small talk. David would't discuss the Mexican connection, as I was now thinking of it. I tried a couple of times to steer the conversation back that way, but each time he simply said, "Tomorrow."

TEN

The U.S. Attorney's office was housed in the Federal Court-house on Hughey Avenue in downtown Orlando. The building also contains the social security office and several other federal welfare agencies, and there was a long line waiting to go through security. The U.S. Marshals service provided uniformed person-nel to check all handbags and briefcases. Cell phones were not allowed in the building, so I had to walk back to the car parked across the street in the public lot under I-4, taking our phones to put them with our guns. The sun was getting higher in the sky, and the warmth of the late October day was becoming a little uncomfortable as the heat reflected off the pavement.

I was dressed casually in a golf shirt, chinos and cordovan loafers. Jock wore similar clothes, and one might have thought we were headed for the course to shoot a round of golf. Our mission was a little more important, as it concerned a life very valuable to me; my own.

We were finally vetted through all the security and took the elevator to the fourth floor. A very efficient looking woman in her fifties was manning the desk in the waiting room. The aluminum and vinyl chairs arranged around the walls were partially filled with men in dark suits holding cheap brief cases. Lawyers, no doubt, come to negotiate a plea for their drug-dealing clients. None of them looked very savory. We were told to go right on back, as Mr. Parrish was waiting for us in the conference room next to reception.

The space was not large, but it held a small conference table with eight chairs set around it. David sat at the head of the table, and two men in suits sat next to each other at the end nearest him. They stood as we entered the room.

David said, "Matt Royal and Jock Algren, I'd like you to meet Rufus Harris and Paul Reich. Rufus is with DEA, and Paul is with the Border Patrol.

Rufus was a large black man, standing about six-foot-four, and weighing over two hundred pounds. As we shook, my hand was buried in his, but his grip was as soft as a caress. He was dressed in a blue business suit, white dress shirt and red silk tie.

Reich was a small white man, with light brown hair turning gray. He was about five-eight, one-hundred-sixty pounds and looked more like a mortgage banker than a Federal law enforcement agent. He wore beige pants, a blue blazer, white shirt and a blue and tan striped tie.

"I've asked Rufus and Paul to be here," David continued, "because they're involved in investigations that may have a bearing on your problem."

We took our seats. I was across from Harris and Jock sat opposite Reich. This was not what I expected. I'd anticipated a chat with David, and I was surprised by his decision to bring in two federal agents. Maybe they had the answers I was looking for.

David leaned back in his chair. "Paul did some checking in Washington," he said, "and was told that Jock could hear anything we had to say. I don't know what strings you pulled Jock, but they were powerful ones."

"Thank you for the effort," Jock said quietly.

David turned to me. "I vouched for you, Matt," he said.

"I appreciate it," I said. "Now, why is somebody trying to kill me?"

"We don't know," said Reich, "but you may have stumbled onto a drug ring. If they think you're a danger to them, they take you out."

"I have no idea what you're talking about," I said. "I've never had anything to do with drugs or drug rings. Why would some drug runner want to kill me?"

"They don't need much of a reason," said Harris. "We think there's a pretty big ring working out of the Sarasota Bay area. Maybe you stumbled onto something you aren't even aware of."

I gave it a moment. "Did David tell you about the dead Mexicans I found on the beach?" I said.

"Yes, and they might be the key," said Harris. "We think the drugs are being brought in from Mexico. The lawyer who was killed on Longboat Key was working with us."

Jock leaned over, his elbows resting on the table. "What do you mean, 'working with' you?" he asked.

Reich looked at Jock. "Conley was dirty," he said. "He was involved in providing fake identification to illegals. He had fake Social Security cards, green cards, visas, you name it. We caught him about three months ago, and made a deal with him to provide us with information on his clients in order to stay out of jail."

I grinned. "I'd say that presented some ethical problems for Conley," I said.

Reich laughed. "I don't think he's a guy who ever worried much about ethics," he said. "We couldn't use what he told us directly about his clients in a court of law, but we could and did use his information to bust up a couple of rings that supplied fake ID's. We also took down a low-level coyote we caught bringing Mexicans across the Rio Grande in south Texas."

"So," I said, "you think somebody in the people-smuggling business killed Conley. Where does the DEA come in?"

"We think there may be a drug connection to the immigrant smuggling," said Harris. "There are a lot of illegals in Manatee and Sarasota counties, working the truck farms and groves. We've also seen a rise in the drug traffic in that area. It's an interesting coincidence, but it may be no more than that. We haven't found any evidence, yet."

I shook my head. "I still don't see how this applies to me."

Reich said, "The dead Mexicans you found were probably illegals. We haven't been able to identify them yet, and the survivor is still in a coma."

Harris wiped at his eyes with both hands, the sign of a tired man. "We think Conley was getting close," he said. "His last message to us was that he had an inside source. He was supposed to meet one of our agents the morning he was killed."

I said, "You think that's why he was killed?"

"Yes."

I was quiet for a moment, thinking. "Can you connect it to the Mexicans' murders?" I asked.

"Not yet," said Reich. "But it's a reasonable assumption. The timing and location are right, and Conley was involved mostly with Mexicans. But we're at a dead-end."

Jock had sat quietly, listening, saying nothing. Then, "Is that all you have?"

Reich shrugged. "We think the Mexicans are being smuggled in by boat. They're mostly from the state of Guerrero in southern Mexico near the Pacific coast. They seem to come from an area around the town of Tlapa, but that's about all we know. It's not much, but David wanted you to have what we have."

I tried to process all this, but nothing made sense. "Any suggestions for me?" I said.

Now it was Harris' turn to grin. "Yeah," he said. "Lay low."

* * * * *

We left the U.S. Attorney's office that morning about as clueless as when we'd arrived. Parrish was apologetic about not being able to give us more information, but he assured us that we now knew everything the government did. Jock was skeptical, but then he always is.

As we were getting into the car, Jock said, "Let's go to Tlapa."

"What in the world for?" I said.

"Reich said the illegals in the Sarasota area mostly come from Tlapa, so we might find some answers there."

"How?" I asked. "Do we just place a classified ad in the local paper and wait for somebody to call us?"

"My agency has had a man in Tlapa for the past several months. He knows that area of Mexico very well."

I shrugged. "I'm game," I said. I can't get any deader in Mexico than I can on Longboat Key."

Jock had spent most of his government career in Central and South America and was fluent in Spanish. He explained that the agency he worked for had sent an operative into the mountains above Acapulco several months before. There had been some smoke wafting through the intelligence community about terrorists setting up a base camp in the rugged hills around Tlapa. Jock's agency sent in a man who would blend in with the locals, and he was still there. He and Jock had worked together in the past, and Jock was sure the agent would help us now.

I called my former paralegal, Vanessa Brice, and asked if we could leave the rental car in her garage. I didn't want to return it to Hertz or leave it at the airport in case somebody came looking for it. She told us to come on to her house.

We arrived at her home at mid-afternoon, and Vanessa fed us a late lunch while Jock made a couple of calls from his cell phone. I called Continental Airlines and made two reservations for Aculpulco. When we finished our lunch, Vanessa took us to Orlando International Airport to board a flight to Houston.

ELEVEN

The Houston skyline appeared in my window. The plane was banking to the right as it lined up for its final approach to George Bush Intercontinental Airport. The sun was low in the west, the day fading slowly into night. Jock was dozing next to me, a soft rumble escaping from his throat with each breath.

I nudged him with my elbow. "Home sweet home," I said.

"Yeah," he grumbled, waking slowly. "I was dreaming about a woman. A beautiful woman."

"Have you ever dreamed about an ugly woman?"

"Once. Didn't like it."

Our flight to Acapulco was scheduled to leave early on Wednesday morning, so we planned to spend the night in Houston. Jock lived alone in an elegant loft condo in the middle of downtown, but since we were leaving so early, we decided not to drive the thirty miles to his home.

We checked into the Marriott hotel in the terminal complex, had dinner in the restaurant and went to our rooms.

I called Anne on my cell phone to let her know I was okay.

"I wasn't worried," she said. "I know you and Jock can take care of yourselves. Where are you?"

"I'd better not tell you, sweetheart. You never know who might be listening to our conversation."

"You're right. Take care of yourself."

We chatted for a few more minutes and hung up. The tone of the conversation was off somehow, different in a way I couldn't pinpoint. Maybe my paranoia was working overtime, and I was worrying needlessly. Or, maybe I was about to get dumped.

I called Bill Lester at home, and he told me the crime lab had found a locator beacon on my Explorer and that the man in the coma, now identified as Pepe Zaragoza had not awoken. I dialed Jock's room and passed on what the chief had told me.

"That locator is a pretty expensive item," he said. "I don't think it's just some local scumbag after you."

I agreed. I read for awhile, turned off the light and fell into a deep sleep.

* * * * *

We took an early Continental flight non-stop to Acapulco, arriving in mid-morning. We cleared customs without any hassles. The Mexican customs officer referred to Jock as "*Senor* Rodriguez" as they chatted in Spanish. I figured Jock was using a passport other than his own, so I said nothing.

We left the air conditioned terminal and were immediately enveloped by the steamy air of the tropics. The sun was already climbing through a cloudless sky, generating a heat not unlike that of a Florida summer.

The pores in my skin made an emergency opening, and sweat poured out, my clothes beginning to stick to my body. The slight breeze carried a hint of the sea, its pungent smell making me homesick momentarily for Longboat Key.

A small dark-skinned man who appeared to be in his thirties approached us, grinning. "Jock, you're as ugly as ever. When are you going to get that damned hair transplant?" The man was obviously Mexican, but there was no hint of an accent to his English.

"Fuck you, *amigo*," Jock said, laughing. They embraced.

Turning to me, Jock said, "Matt, meet Emilio Sanchez."

We shook hands. Emilio said, "So, Jock tells me somebody's trying to kill you. You must be one bad *hombre*."

I laughed. "I'm just a guy trying to figure it all out, Emilio. Where do you know my bald-headed friend from?"

"Can't say much about that, Matt. But, I've known him for more than ten years, since I was in law school at UCLA."

"You're a lawyer?" I asked.

"Yeah. I'm not proud of it, but there you have it."

Jock laughed, "Emilio was born and raised in Los Angeles," he said. "Undergraduate and law degrees from UCLA. I recruited him into the agency and saved him from a life of bullshit. He owes me."

"Yes I do," said Emilio, chuckling. "He got me out of the posh downtown law offices in Los Angeles, and I get to live in a one-room shack with a dirt floor in my parents' hometown. I couldn't have done it without old Jock."

They were both laughing. I wasn't sure who the joke was on, but Jock always knew what he was doing, so I just rode with it.

TWELVE

Emilio led us to a Volkswagen bug, one of the last of its line. A plant in Mexico had continued to turn these little cars out for a few years after the Germans moved on to more sophisticated models. But even that plant had now closed, and the bug was history. I'd owned one in college, and I was a little sad to see its demise.

Jock crammed himself into the back seat, and I sat in relative comfort in the front. We drove out of the airport onto a four-lane highway, pointing east.

Emilio said, "The weapons are in the sack on the floor, Jock."

I heard a rustling of paper and then the tiny clicks of gun parts being fitted together.

Jock handed me a gun. "Nines, Emilio," he said. "You are resourceful."

"Only the best, Jock. Those clips hold seventeen rounds, and I put a couple of boxes of hollow-points in the bag. I've got more if you need them."

"Any long guns?" asked Jock.

"I've got several M4A1's in my house, with plenty of ammunition. They're yours if you need them, but you don't want to start a war up here."

I looked back at Jock. "Not if we can help it," I said. I knew the M4A1. It was the modern assault weapon for the U.S. Military, replacing the aging M-16 that I'd used in Vietnam. "I've never qualified with the M4," I said. "I'd probably kill myself if I had to shoot it."

"Jock tells me you were Special Forces, Matt," Emilio said. "I don't think you have to worry about using a weapon."

"That was a long time ago," I said. "Now, I'm just an aging lawyer relying on Jock."

Jock shook that off. "Don't let him fool you, Emilio. He's still a tough bastard."

We were climbing now, headed up the mountain range known as the Sierra Madres del Sur. The town of Tlapa is nestled in a valley at about six thousand feet, and I was beginning to have a little trouble breathing. I knew it would pass as I became acclimated to the altitude.

Soon, the road narrowed to two lanes, and was potted with holes and rocks from the mountain to which it clung. An occasional truck would pass us coming down at breakneck speed. It was a little disconcerting, but Emilio seemed to take it in stride.

We crested a peak and looked down into a valley of clustered, pastel-painted buildings, none above two stories. This was Tlapa.

There were green fields surrounding the town, and Emilio told us that the farmers grew corn and beans, chili peppers and vegetables. Most still plowed with mules, just as they had done for centuries.

"My parents left here and emigrated to California before I was born," said Emilio. "They never did become legal, but I was born in L.A., and that makes me an American citizen."

He went on to tell me that the agency had sent him back to Tlapa because he would fit in. He had cousins there, and he spoke the local language, a mixture of classical Nahautl and Spanish.

The people of the region were Nahautl Indians, proud descendants of the Aztecs. Emilio's local family simply thought he'd made enough money in California to return and live in his ancestral home without the need to work.

The largest industry in the area was the exporting of workers. The illegal immigrant to America sends an average of $300 every two weeks to his family, the money earned working for minimum wages or less in the fields and yards of *gringos*. Many of the young men and women from this region were working in the Sarasota Bay area.

"They tend to go where they have friends and relatives," Emilio said. "A generation or two ago, some of the people from this area ended up in your part of Florida picking fruit and vegetables, and now a lot of the young people head there."

We eased through the town's narrow streets, passing trucks and cars parked haphazardly, partially on the cramped sidewalks. People in colorful clothes walked slowly, all seeming intent on their journeys. We passed an open air market displaying fruit and vegetables. Large slabs of beef hung from the ceiling, flies crawling over them. A butcher was busy cutting off parts for his customers.

"I always boil the vegetables in a bleach solution," said Emilio. "My ancestors may have come from here, but my stomach comes from L.A."

As we made our way to the outskirts of the small town, I asked, "Where are we going?"

"I live in a village about ten miles from here, and almost straight up," he said. "We'll stay at my house. I've told some of the villagers that a couple of *gringo* friends of mine from Los Angeles were coming for a visit."

We drove along a dirt road, deeply rutted in places, ascending the mountain, the air getting thinner. Occasionally, an Army truck would meet us coming down the mountain, or we'd pass one going up. Each one was filled with soldiers armed with M-16s.

"What's the Army doing here in such force?" I asked.

"Nobody knows," said Emilio. "It's not a very big force, and they live in a barracks further down the mountain. They patrol the area, but I don't know why. Some Army units are in the pockets of the drug lords, but there isn't much in the way of drug trafficking around here. They might just be a show of force to make sure the local residents don't decide to join the Zapatistas."

I knew that the Zapatistas were an armed revolutionary group of mostly Mayan Indians indigenous to the state of Chiapas, located in the mountains south of Mexico City. They had challenged the government on a number of occasions, but for the most part eschewed violence.

I asked Emilio why the government would be concerned about the Tlapa area. "I thought the Zapatistas were primarily Mayan," I said.

"They are, but the government sees us all as Indians. The people around here are descended from the Aztecs, and they've never been completely assimilated. I think the Zapatistas gave the guys in Mexico City a scare. They don't want the same thing to happen in other areas of the country where there are a lot of indigenous peoples."

We were driving into a small village clinging to the side of a mountain. We crossed what appeared to be a small public square, with a church on one side and a basketball hoop on the other. Two boys, both about thirteen, wearing shorts and T- shirts, no shoes, were shooting hoops. Nearby, on a cement bench covered in colorful Mexican tiles, two teenaged girls sat watching the boys and giggling.

One-story buildings surrounded us, all painted in the pastels that seemed to abound in the area. Some were houses, and others appeared to contain stores and shops. There was a pole topped by a loudspeaker broadcasting in a language I didn't recognize.

"Nahautl," said Emilio. "That's the radio station down in Tlapa broadcasting messages to the people in the village. It's our form of e-mail."

There were no overhead wires going to any of the buildings other than the church. It appeared as if electricity had not yet reached the rest of the village.

We took a side street for about a block, and pulled up in front of a house sitting in a dusty yard. The building was one story, constructed of concrete blocks; no paint, no siding, no stucco. Just bare blocks and mortar. Every few feet, iron rebars stuck several feet above the flat roof.

We went through the front door into a tastefully decorated room with Zapotec rugs lying upon a floor of Saltillo tile. The finished walls were painted a subdued beige and adorned with framed Mexican scenes - garish oils of bullfights and peasants in the fields wearing colorful clothes. A large chandelier hung from the ceiling, rustic in appearance, with an electric candle perched on each of its branches. I could see through a dining room into a modern kitchen.

"Home," announced Emilio.

"Not exactly a dirt-floored hut," I said. "Where do you get the electricity to run everything?"

"There's a line coming in from Tlapa. Not many people here can afford it, but if you have a little money the power company will send up a truck and hook you up."

Jock, who had been quiet during most of the trip, said, "Do you own this place?"

"No. I'm renting it from a guy in the States. He works in New York in a restaurant and saves all his money. He comes home about every six months and uses his savings to build a little more onto the house. Stays with his mother when he's here."

"Why the rebar on the roof?" asked Jock.

"That's for adding the walls to a second story when he has the money."

I said, "How long have you been here, Emilio?"

"About six months. I'm going home next week. It's been pretty much a wasted trip."

"No terrorists?" asked Jock.

"*Nada*. I didn't expect to find any, but you know how Washington is these days. Everybody covers his butt on any intelligence he gets, no matter how far-fetched."

"Have you heard anything about the dead guys found on Longboat Key last Friday?" I asked.

"No. Why would I?"

I told him the story of my find on the beach, the murder of Dwight Conley and the attempts on my life. I recounted some of what we had learned at the U.S. Attorney's office and the suspicions of the police.

"The one in a coma was legal, and he was from Tlapa," I continued. "The two dead guys are probably from around here. We think there may be a connection between the people trying to kill me and some bad guys who smuggle people from this area into Florida."

We were standing in the living room. Emilio gestured with his hand to his ear, as if talking into a phone. "When Jock called," he said, "he told me he had a problem that he thought started here. We were on the satellite phone, and I'm never sure how secure that thing is unless I can scramble it. I didn't ask, so I haven't done any leg work. But, there's one guy in the area who seems to be in charge of getting people to the States."

Emilio grinned, but with no warmth behind it. "We'll go see

him after you get settled," he said.

Emilio showed Jock and me to bedrooms down a hall that opened off the living area. The room assigned to me was pleasant, holding only a single bed draped in a coverlet that looked like a serape. The walls were of plaster, painted in a pale shade of yellow, with, curiously, two watercolor prints of New York City street scenes hanging on walls facing each other. A large window opposite the door dominated the space, with a view of the dry hills rising beyond.

People had emigrated for far less reason than the building of such a congenial home.

THIRTEEN

The altitude had cooled the air, and the humidity was low, a slight breeze reminding me of late October on Longboat Key. We had lunch on a flagstone terrace behind the house. There was no grass or other greenery near the building, only the packed dirt, loosely covered with a layer of soil. Dust eddied in the air currents hovering near the ground as Emilio served us ham sandwiches and bottled water.

Jock said, "Tell us about this man we're going to see."

"I don't know much about him," said Emilio. "He lives in Tlapa and is a kind of recruiter for local labor. Everybody knows that if you want to go to America, you see Sergio Arguilles."

I swallowed a bite of sandwich. "Don't the police care that he's running an illegal smuggling ring?" I said.

Emilio shrugged. "He may be on the government payroll, for all I know," he said. "If the flow of money from the illegals in the States dried up there'd probably be a revolution here. A large part of the economy is based on the *remesas*, the remittances sent through InterMex from the workers in the States to their families here. It amounts to billions of dollars every year, second only to oil as foreign exchange. Every town of any size in Mexico has an InterMex exchange center where the money comes in."

Jock said, "So, Arguilles is probably not a bad guy."

"I doubt it," said Emilio. "He's probably just a businessman."

"How do we arrange a meeting?" I said.

"No arrangement necessary," said Emilio. "We just go to his restaurant. That's where he does his business. If you want to go to the States, you visit him there."

* * * * *

We drove back down the mountain into the center of Tlapas and parked the VW a few yards down from a restaurant that spilled its tables onto the town square. I was wearing a light windbreaker over a white golf shirt and a pair of jeans, Reeboks completing my wardrobe. Jock wore a navy blazer over a light blue cotton button down shirt, khaki pants and hiking boots. The jackets hid the weapons holstered at our waists. Emilio was unarmed.

Emilio knew Arguilles by sight, and as we neared the restaurant, he pointed him out. Arguilles was sitting at an outside table, alone, resting in the sun, a cup of black coffee in front of him. He was wearing a baseball hat emblazoned with the logo of the Houston Astros, a red shirt that passed for fashionable in these parts, and jeans. Large sunglasses covered half his face, and I couldn't see his eyes. His skin was dark, the color of the Aztecs from whom he had descended. He was as still as a statue and he looked as old as the mountains.

Jock grinned. "You think he's still alive?" he said.

"Don't let the old gent fool you," said Emilio. "He's still sharp as a stiletto."

We approached Arguilles' table, and Emilio spoke to him in the local language, pointing at us. The old man replied in almost accentless English, "Please, gentlemen, have a seat."

He gestured to the chairs surrounding his table. "What can I do for you? Do you need to a guide to take you to America?"

He laughed, a strange rumbling sound emanating from deep down in his chest, ending in a coughing fit. He pulled a large handkerchief from a pocket on his shirt, spit into it, glared at the result, re-folded the handkerchief and replaced it in his pocket. He sat back in his chair, his hands folded on his chest.

"I will order us a coffee," said Arguilles, gesturing to a waiter loitering near the door.

When the coffee came, Emilio took a sip, raised his cup to Arguilles in a gesture of gratitude and asked, "Do you know a man named Pepe Zaragoza?"

"Of course, *Senor* Sanchez," replied Arguilles, speaking in his oddly formal English. "I helped him travel to America many years ago. He has a green card now and can come and go as he pleases. He comes here to visit his family every two years, and he always comes by to have a coffee with me."

"*Senor*," said Emilio, "I'm sorry to tell you that Pepe is in a hospital in Sarasota, Florida, in a coma. The authorities think he murdered two men from Mexico, and if he survives, he will be charged."

"How did this come to pass?" asked Arguilles, his voice low, concern for a friend echoing from his words.

I told him the story of how I found the men and that someone was now trying to kill me. "We're backtracking, *Senor* Arguilles," I said "We're trying to find out who wants me dead and why. I hope you can help us."

Arguilles said, "I am sorry for Pepe's troubles, and for yours, my new friend. I have known Pepe all his life, and I do not believe he would have murdered anyone."

The old man smiled. "I also don't know of anyone who would want you dead, *Senor* Royal," he said.

65

I was not reassured. "Can you tell me how you get your people into the States?" I said.

"I do not really know," said Arguilles. "I send them on a bus to Veracruz, and my partners take over from there. I assume they go by sea to Florida, but that may not be true."

Jock broke his silence. "This appears to be a pretty loose arrangement," he said.

"It is," said Arguilles. "I am only the local contact. I spent many years in Houston, and the people here know I can get them to America. I get paid a small amount for everyone I send to Veracruz, but I really do it more as a public service."

"How does that work?" I asked.

Emilio spoke up. "*Senor* Arguilles, we wouldn't be so blunt with our questions if it weren't so important. The man who Pepe works for doesn't think he did this, and he has hired a lawyer to help him. If we can find out who's trying to kill Matt, we may be able to help Pepe, too."

"I understand," said Arguilles. "I will tell you what I know, and then I must go to Pepe's mother and try to explain this to her. I will tell her that some good men from Florida are trying to help Pepe."

He explained that his "clients," as he called them, were sent by chartered bus across Mexico to the port city of Veracruz in the state of Veracruz-Llave, southeast of Mexico City. They were met by his partner, a man named Julio Mendez, who would then have them escorted into the U.S.

Arguilles told us that we could find his partner by leaving word in a café near the waterfront in Veracruz, but he knew nothing more than that. He'd never been to Veracruz and the only contacts he'd ever had with Mendez were by phone. After Arguilles sent a busload of people to Veracruz, he'd receive his payment at the InterMex office in Tlapa.

Murder Key

We finished our coffee, shook hands all around, and took our leave. We drove back up the mountain to Emilio's rented house. The sun was setting behind the rugged hills, painting the world in a golden glow. The temperature would drop as the sun disappeared, and the night would require no air-conditioning for sleep.

We decided that we'd have to drive to Veracruz. Emilio was finished in the Tlapa area, and he'd use the satellite phone to tell his boss he was going to drive Jock and me. He'd turn the car into the consulate there and catch a flight back to Washington.

We had dinner in a small cantina in the village. There was Mexican beer to drink and one item on the menu, a chicken based stew spiced with peppers. The beer was cold and the food was delicious.

FOURTEEN

We were up at daybreak, and after a breakfast of pastries and coffee, I stashed our luggage and a duffel bag with four assault rifles and ammunition in the trunk in the front of the bug. Emilio pointed the VW east. Jock was in the passenger seat and I was crammed in the back. We'd alternate during the day, but neither of us wanted to drive the mountain roads to Veracruz. Emilio was used to them.

We came down the mountain into Tlapa and then started climbing again. The little engine strained a bit on the steep incline, but it never faltered.

After crossing into the valley of the Rio Santo Domingo the road began to climb again. It was one lane for many miles, with switchbacks taking us up and down mountains. Sometimes we were on a ridge with sheer drop-offs on either side of the road. There were no guard rails, and clouds appeared below us, blanketing the high valleys. Emilio told us that the locals were called "cloud people." It was easy to see why. For most of the year, the inhabitants of these mountains would look down to see the clouds.

The drive took us through small villages peopled by Indians. Many of the women wore *huipils,* the long woven red dresses indigenous to the area. Each village had a small church, some dating back to the sixteenth century, and an open-air market where food and dry goods were bought and sold. These were hardscrabble places, where the men plowed the fields and grew vegetables to eke out a poor living.

Occasionally, a paved two lane road would appear. We'd make good time for a while, but then just as suddenly, find ourselves back on the one-lane roads, moving at less than twenty-five miles per hour.

We passed the town of Haujaupan de Leon and the roads got better. They were still narrow and curvy, but not as treacherous. By noon, we were in Tehuacan, and stopped for lunch in a small café.

When we'd finished our meal and used the restroom, we turned onto a four-lane toll road that spanned the eighty miles from Tehuacan to Veracruz. We made it before two o'clock.

* * * * *

Jock rented a room in a small hotel, using one of his bogus passports. Emilio and I would sneak in later and sleep on the floor, if necessary. We didn't want anyone to know we were in Veracruz.

We met at a little cantina near the hotel. It was early afternoon, and the place was cooled only by circulating ceiling fans. The smell of old cigarette smoke pervaded the air. There was a bar down one side of the room and three tables scattered across a wooden floor whose boards were warped from years of spilled beer. We took a table, and Emilio ordered a beer for each of us.

Emilio said, "I called the café Arguilles told us about and told the owner I'd like to meet with *Senor* Mendez. He'll be there at four this afternoon. I was told he's a big man with tattoos on his arms. He'll be sitting at an outdoor table."

Jock shook his head. "I want to be covered on this meeting."

"I know that area," said Emilio. "I can get in place on a roof across the street from the café. If push comes to shove, I should have a clear field of fire."

"Okay," said Jock. "Matt and I'll take our pistols. That should give us enough firepower if we need it."

Emilio nodded. "I've also got back-up from the local DEA office," he said. "They've got a detachment here working with the Mexican police. They'll be in the area watching for trouble."

We finished our beers, and Jock drove through town to the waterfront. We parked in front of a small office building, where Emilio knew he could get access to the roof. He was wearing a long coat with his rifle tucked under it. I'd voiced concern that he would be conspicuous on a hot day with a long coat, but Emilio assured me that Mexicans were tolerant of those they considered a bit odd.

Jock and I walked around the block to the café. It was a small place with tables on the sidewalk. It sat across the street from the back of the building into which Emilio had disappeared. We were both wearing light windbreakers over golf shirts, our nines holstered under the jackets.

Julio Mendez was about forty and built like a pro linebacker. He was wearing a dark blue T-shirt over jeans. His forearms, resting on the table like ham hocks, bore tattoos etched into his hide. He had dark hair, worn in a buzz cut that made him at first glance appear to be bald. He was the only person sitting at a sidewalk table.

"*Senor* Mendez," I said, "may we join you?"

"Of course," he said in heavily accented English. "Please, sit down."

Jock and I sat. "My name is Matt Royal," I said, "and this is my friend John Smith."

Jock nodded, saying nothing.

"What can I do for you gentlemen?" asked Mendez.

"I'm from Sarasota, Florida," I said, "and somebody is trying to kill me."

"Why is this any concern of mine?"

"Because, I think it's related to some other murders on Longboat Key. The police think a man named Pepe Zaragoza is the murderer. He's from Tlapa. We think the two dead men are illegals from Tlapa. Your partner Sergio Arguilles thought you might have some idea about why the men from Tlapa were killed. That may help me figure out who's trying to kill me."

Mendez rose from the table. "I must make a phone call, and then I will tell you what I know." He left us.

"I don't like this," said Jock, offering a big smile to whomever might be watching. "Get your nine out and hold it under the table."

I did, resting the pistol on my lap.

In a few moments, Mendez returned. "An associate of mine will join us," he said. "I think he can tell you what you want to know."

I began to relax a little, but kept the pistol ready. We talked briefly about the beauty of the city of Veracruz, and Mendez told us he had once visited Sarasota and liked it.

Suddenly, I felt another presence near the table. I looked up into the weasel eyes of the shooter from Tiny's. He quickly sat in the chair opposite me, leaving Jock directly opposite Mendez.

The shooter grinned. "So, Mr. Royal, we meet again." He rested his right arm on the table. It was swathed from finger tips to elbow in a plaster cast. "I can shoot with my left hand, and it is holding a gun under the table pointed at your balls."

"Is this really necessary?" asked Jock, sounding as calm as if he were discussing the weather.

"*Jefe,*" the shooter said, "should I kill them?"

"Not yet," said Mendez. "We do not want to bloody up my favorite table." He laughed, snorting at his feeble joke.

Suddenly, a red dot appeared on Mendez's chest. Jock said to the shooter, "See that pretty dot on your *Jefe's* chest? Know what that is?"

"The sun?" growled the shooter, but without any juice behind it.

"Nope," said Jock, "it's a laser dot from a sniper scope attached to an M-14 sniper rifle. If you even twitch you can kiss *el jefe's* ass goodbye. He'll be dead before he hears the shot."

"That is bullshit," said the shooter.

"No, Diaz!" Mendez shouted in English. "I know about this scope. Do not twitch, for God's sake."

Jock turned to the shooter, a cold smile splitting his face. "I think what we have here is a Mexican standoff. Bring your weapon up, just one finger in the trigger guard and put it on the table."

The shooter didn't move. "*Jefe?*" he said, his voice soft.

"Do as he says," Mendez said. "Now!"

Diaz began raising his left arm from under the table, bringing his gun to the table top.

"Kill them," shouted Mendez in Spanish as he kicked his chair over backward. Even I understood that much of the language, and was beginning to react when I heard the crack of Emilio's rifle.

If you've ever heard a rifle bullet whiz close by your head, you're not likely to forget it. I knew immediately what was happening when the slug from Emilio's rifle caught Mendez in the throat as he was going over backward.

At the same instant Jock reached across the table and clamped down on the shooter's arm, effectively welding it to the table top.

I pulled my pistol from my lap and aimed it at the shooter's face.

"Be cool," Jock said, "and you might not die today."

A black SUV pulled to the curb, and the rear door on our side opened. Jock was pulling the shooter by the arm toward the vehicle. "Come on, Matt," he said. "They're friendlies."

He didn't have to tell me twice. I grabbed Diaz by his other arm, and we hustled him into the back of the SUV. The driver showered down on the gas pedal, and burning rubber, we got the hell out of there.

The passenger in the front turned and handed Jock a pair of handcuffs. "Put these on him."

It took me a minute to realize that the passenger was Rufus Harris, the DEA agent we had met in the U.S. Attorney's office in Orlando. He grinned at me.

"What the hell are you doing here?" I asked.

"I'm from the government, and I'm here to help you."

I laughed at the lame joke, relief at seeing a friendly face coursing through my brain. "Geez, Harris, what's going on?"

"I was in town looking into the Mexican end of a drug smuggling ring. Emilio's agency contacted us for help."

Harris turned to Jock, "You're not really just a civilian, are you Jock?" he said.

"Not really," said Jock, who had finished cuffing the shooter.

"What now?" I asked.

Harris reached into a gym bag on his lap. "We're going to a safe house. Put this bag over shit-for-brains' head," he said.

He handed me a large pillow case. Diaz was quiet, resigned, as I covered his head.

The big SUV rumbled over the cobblestone streets and turned onto a paved thoroughfare, picking up speed. We headed out of town, going west away from the waterfront. The driver was making good time, but staying within the speed limit.

I said, "Where are we going, Rufus?"

"The Mexican police are going to be out in force very soon," said Harris. "We've got to get out of town and ditch this truck."

I thought he was right. The local cops would probably not take kindly to one of their citizens being shot through the throat on a quiet street in the middle of the afternoon.

FIFTEEN

The house was little more than a hut, one of many gracing the side of a public dump on the outskirts of Veracruz. It seemed to have been constructed of plywood and covered over with tar paper. The door, oddly enough, was made of some kind of metal, steel perhaps.

As we entered, I noticed that the plywood was covering concrete block walls. Somebody had gone to considerable lengths to make this place look like all the other shacks surrounding the dump. But it wasn't. There was running water and electricity. The steel door was bolted into the blocks. The windows had shutters that were also of steel, and could be closed to turn the hut into a veritable fortress.

"What is this place?" I asked, as we entered.

"It's a DEA safe house," said Harris. "It's humble, but it's home. We ran sewer and electricity underground, so it looks just like all the other shacks around here."

Jock had pushed our guest of honor into a straight back chair resting against one wall of the room. He pulled a rope out of the gym bag Harris had provided and tied Diaz to the chair.

Emilio walked through the door. "That got a little dicey," he said, to no one in particular.

"Good shot," said Jock.

"We've got the see about the SUV," Harris said. "The police will be looking for it by now, and they don't like American cops in their bailiwick."

"I'll go with you," said Emilio. "I need to check in with my agency and let them know what happened. I'll leave the VW for you and Jock, Matt."

They left us in the quiet room with Diaz. "Now," said Jock, "tell me why you're trying to kill my friend."

"Fuck you," said Diaz.

Jock pulled his pistol from the holster, reached into the satchel for a silencer and screwed it onto the barrel of the weapon. He pointed it at Diaz. "Try again, *muchacho*."

"Fuck you again, *gringo*." A barely suppressed smile teased his lips.

Jock shot him in the foot, the sound suppressed into something that sounded like "*pfft*." Diaz screamed in agony, cursed, and tried to wrench his leg from the chair to which it was bound. I stepped back in shock. I had never seen anything so calculating, and I was suddenly mute. I opened my mouth, tried to speak. Nothing came out. My throat was as dry as a desicated skeleton.

There was a buzz in my ears from the scream and the shouted expletives from Diaz.

"The next one goes in your knee," said Jock, his voice low, controlled.

"I don't know anything," the wounded man said, a tremor in his voice. "I was just ordered to shoot the man."

Jock hit him across the face with the pistol. "You can do better than that."

Blood spattered from the broken nose. Diaz spit out two fractured teeth. Tears of pain welled in his eyes. Sweat had broken out on his face, and his voice, when he spoke, was

I stood there, dumbfounded. I couldn't square the casual brutality of my friend with the image I'd always had of him. This was not my junior high school buddy. This was some apparition clothed in the body of my life-long friend.

"Tell me about it," Jock said to Diaz..

"*El Jefe* called me on Friday in Sarasota and told me to go to the bar on Longboat Key and kill Royal. He told me where he would be. That's all I know."

Diaz' voice was strident, angry. He was afraid of more pain, but he wanted us to know that he was still dangerous. I could see agony etched on his facial features, but I could also see malice. He hated us, wanted us dead, was demeaned by our having the upper hand. He could be a dangerous man someday, lurking in a dark place waiting to wreak his vengeance on us.

"What were you doing in Sarasota?"

"I had come in the night before with a shipment."

"Shipment? What shipment?"

"The illegals."

"Do you ship drugs with the illegals?"

Diaz hesitated. Jock raised his pistol in a backhanded motion, as if to strike him again.

"Yes, yes, there are drugs," said Diaz, his voice rising in fear.

"Talk to me," said Jock.

"I don't know much. Cocaine comes overland to Veracruz and we load it onto a trawler and take it to Sarasota."

Diaz sounded resigned now to giving us what we wanted. He didn't want to endure more pain, perhaps was afraid that more pain would make him lose all semblance of his ignoble dignity.

I was coming back to reality. "Why carry the illegals?" I said. "The money you make must be peanuts compared to what the drugs bring."

"The illegals are cover," said Diaz.

"I don't get the cover part," I said, although it was starting to come clear.

Diaz spit out more blood. "The cocaine is put into weighted bundles and stored in a compartment between the boat's hull and the floorboards," he said. "There's a door in the hull, and the captain can open it from the bridge. If the coast Guard stops us, we throw a few of the illegals overboard and then drop the coke to the bottom of the Gulf. The Coast Guard is so busy picking the illegals out of the water that they don't see the coke."

Diaz laughed as he said it, a look of scorn creasing his pock-marked face, his fear being overcome by his innate *machismo*. "If we're arrested it's only for the importation of illegals, not drugs," he said. "Nobody ever goes to jail for that. We're sent back to Mexico, and a judge on our payroll sets us free."

"How do you get the drugs into the country?" Jock asked.

"We stop well off-shore, and small boats come out and take the drugs and the people ashore."

"Where do the small boats go?"

"I don't know. I only came in that way once, and I was dropped off at a house on a canal."

"Where?"

"I don't know. Some *gringa* came in a van and got the illegals and the drugs."

"A woman?" I asked.

"Yes, a pretty blonde woman."

"Did you get a name, any markings on the van?"

"No, nothing. Do not shoot me again. I've told you everything I know."

I said, "Describe where you were brought in on the boat."

Diaz sneered, knowing we were about finished, some of his arrogance beginning to resurface. "To a house, *mi amigo*, a big house on a canal. I don't know where it was."

"Did you leave with the illegals?" Jock asked.

"Yes. The woman let me out in downtown Sarasota, and I got a hotel room."

"Describe the trip. How many bridges did you cross?" I asked.

"We crossed two bridges, one was very tall and long. I could see the buildings of Sarasota from there. The first bridge was smaller, what you call a draw bridge. I could see many boats stacked on racks near the water."

I turned to Jock. "That sounds like Longboat Key," I said. "The first bridge would be over New Pass. You can see the Marine Max boat storage yard from there. Then they would've crossed over the Ringling Causeway Bridge to the mainland."

Jock nodded. "Anything else?"

I looked at Diaz. "Why were you there?" I said.

"*El jefe* sends one of his men on a trip sometimes. I think it's to make sure the captain stays trustworthy. I was supposed to catch a plane out of Tampa the next day and fly back to Veracruz."

"When was this?" I asked.

"I got there last Thursday night. On Friday morning *el jefe* called me on my cell phone and told me to kill Matt Royal."

"Did you kill the men from Tlapa?" I asked.

"No, *senor*. I knew nothing about that, as God is my witness." The smarmy smile came again.

"Who was the motorcyclist you were with at the bar on Longboat Key?" I asked.

"I do not know. He was just some Mexican kid. I paid him one hundred dollars to take me there and back."

"How did you get back here?" Jock asked.

"The guy on the motorcycle took me to a Mexican doctor who put the cast on my arm. I called *el jefe* to tell him that Matt royal still lived, and then I spent the night with a Mexican family that owed *el jefe* a favor. I took a taxi to the Tampa airport on Saturday morning and came home."

"Who gets the drugs in Sarasota?" asked Jock.

"I do not know," said Diaz.

Jock raised his pistol and pointed it at Diaz' knee.

Diaz' voice rose an octave. "Honestly, Sir, I do not know," he whimpered, the *machismo* giving way to fear. "I have heard some people talk about a senator, but that is all I know."

"Does the trawler have a name?" I asked.

"*Princess Sarah*," said Diaz.

Jock looked at me and I nodded my head. We were through.

Diaz was slumped in the chair, held upright by his bindings. We had gotten everything out of him that was coming. Jock and I stood in front of him, staring down at the arrogant bastard who had tried to kill me. Jock was holding his gun at his side, the silencer reaching past his knee.

Diaz raised his head, a look of sheer malevolence shooting like darts from his eyes. He knew that the questioning was over, and he had survived. His *machismo*, like an inflated balloon in the water, was again rising to the surface. He just couldn't help himself.

"You will pay for this, *gringo*," he muttered, spitting blood and saliva on the floor. "I will kill you the next time I see you. I will piss on your grave."

Jock raised the pistol and shot Diaz through his left eye.

"Good God almighty, Jock!" I shouted. "What the hell did you do?"

"Anybody stupid enough to threaten me while he's tied to a chair and I've got a gun is too stupid to breathe our air."

"That's cold, Jock."

"The bastard had it coming. No telling how many kids he's killed with the drugs he's imported."

"That's why we have courts, Jock. He gets arrested, charged, tried and sentenced."

"Yeah, if you catch him, and some smart attorney doesn't get him off. You lawyers have too many rules."

"Those rules are the only thing separating us from anarchy." I was in shock I think, and I couldn't shut up. I didn't need to give Jock a primer on the law. I was rambling, talking so I wouldn't throw up. I wasn't making a lot of sense even to myself.

"Okay, look at it this way," Jock said. " If he were coming at me with a gun, threatening to kill me, and I shot him, it'd be self-defense, right?"

"Yeah, but that's not what happened here."

"Sure it is. It's what I call a pre-emptive strike. Someday, when he came for me with a gun, or a bomb, or God knows what else, I might not be armed. I'd be dead."

"Then he could be charged with murder. You can't just go around shooting people."

"Or he might have come back to Tiny's and shot your sorry ass."

Put in that perspective, Jock's actions made a lot of sense. "Yeah, I guess you've got a point. Let's get a beer."

And that's what we did. Right after I chucked my lunch.

SIXTEEN

Emilio Sanchez and Rufus Harris were waiting for us in the bar near our hotel. We told them what had happened, and Rufus left to make a phone call.

I was still weak around the edges. I wondered if Jock had killed Diaz to protect me or himself, or maybe just in a fit of anger. I couldn't get the look on Jock's face when he pulled the trigger out of my mind. There really was no look. Jock's face had been expressionless, nothing showing, no feelings whatsoever reflected. The face of a killer.

Emilio broke into my train of thought. "Jock," he said," that was pretty nasty back there. How're you holding up?"

Jock reached over and patted me on the shoulder. "I did what I had to do," he said." the man tried to kill my best friend, and he would've come back. There was no way Diaz would take that kind of humiliation and not want revenge. He'd come after Matt someday, and he'd kill him."

I gave it a beat. "Thanks, Jock," I said.

I couldn't say what I wanted to, that I'd have taken the chance that I could live with Diaz' threat, but I wasn't sure how I'd live with his murder. That letting hm live would have been a better choice than shooting him in cold blood. On the other hand I couldn't deny the sense of relief I felt at the knowledge that Diaz would never again pop up in my life with a pistol pointed at my face.

Jock had become a hard man during his service to a nation that didn't know people like him existed. I had to understand that facet of my friend, live with the consequences, and hope never to have to be in need of that part of Jock again.

When Harris returned, he told us that the safe house would be cleaned up. He also said that the head of the DEA office in Veracruz wanted to meet with us, and that he would be along shortly.

In a few minutes, a tall man, perhaps six-feet-four, with close-cropped hair and a thin mustache came through the door. He was in his forties, and looked as if he worked out regularly. Rufus introduced us to Slade Thomas as the agent in charge of the U.S. Drug Enforcement Agency in Eastern Mexico.

Thomas ordered a rum and coke and joined us at the table. "I'm told that you guys are trying to find this end of a smuggling trail," he said. "We might be able to help each other."

I took a sip of beer. "What do you have in mind?"

"I need a man on one of the shipments. If we can follow this to the States, we can bust up that end of it. I'm not sure we'll ever get to the main men on this end. The corruption is so pervasive we'd have to take down the government to do it."

"How can we help?" I said.

"I understand you've identified the trawler, and you know where the immigration smuggling operation starts. If I can get a bug on the boat and an agent in with the immigrants, we'll be able to unravel both the drug and the people smuggling at the other end."

Emilio leaned back in his chair. "It sounds like I'm going to become an immigrant."

"Are you willing to try it?" asked Thomas.

Emilio nodded. "If my agency says okay, I can probably get back to Tlapa and get on the bus from there. I'll have to make sure that *Senor* Arguilles doesn't give me away. If he'll play ball, he can send me as just another client."

Thomas said, "I think we know where the *Princess Sarah* is docked. We'll try to get a tracking device aboard tonight. We'll hook it into the boat's power system, and it'll send a signal by satellite to the Customs Service office in Miami. We'll know exactly where you are Emilio."

Emilio laughed. "That's comforting,"he said. "I hope the device and I don't both end up in a shark's belly."

* * * * *

It was time to get out of Mexico. Harris told us there was a seven A.M. flight the next day from Veracruz to Houston. We'd change planes there for a flight to Orlando. Rufus thought it prudent for him to leave with us. Emilio would fly directly to Acupulco, and then drive to Tlapa.

Jock and I spent the night with Emilio in the hotel room Jock had secured for us. Harris left for his own accommodations and told us that he'd pick us up at 5:30 the next morning for the ride to the airport.

Rufus arrived on time, and one of his agents dropped us at the airport's departure gate. I was glad to be going home. I'd missed Anne more than I thought I would. I knew the romance was cooling, but there was still something there, and I didn't want to give whatever it was a chance to wither.

I was concerned about Jock. He had been quiet since the shooting, saying even less than usual. The flight to Houston gave me a chance to talk privately with him.

"What's the matter, old friend," I asked.

"I'm fine," he said.

"I don't think so. Is it the killing?"

"It's strange, Matt. I've been doing this for a long time, and I've never been particularly bothered by it. I only killed people who were trying to harm me or my country. There's a kind of rough justice to that, but lately it doesn't feel right. I don't know."

"Maybe you've reached your limit."

"Maybe. But it's like there are two people inside me. I don't mean like a multiple personality kind of thing, but just two sides of me. One part is fine with doing what I've been trained to do, but the other side seems softer. After an operation, I feel a sort of formless melancholy about what I did."

"Remorse?"

"Not exactly. Diaz needed to be killed. He was an evil man, and he had no qualms about killing those poor immigrants or poisoning our children with drugs. Still, he was a human being, and I'm not God. And I wonder if I killed him because he was evil or because he threatened me."

I let him be. Sometimes a man needs to think it out and make his own decisions. At some point, we all come to that ancient fork in the road of life where we have to decide which path we'll take. I couldn't help him with this one.

* * * * *

We had no problems with customs and arrived in Orlando at mid-afternoon. A taxi took the three of us to the Federal Building for a meeting with David Parrish and Paul Reich, the Border Patrol agent. Security had been alerted and a uniformed deputy marshal took us to the same conference room we'd been in only three days before. It seemed like a lifetime ago.

I told Parrish and Reich everything that had happened and

everything we had learned in Mexico, leaving out the part about Jock shooting Diaz.

"Where is Diaz now?" asked Reich.

"He tried to escape," said Harris. "He came at me with a knife and I had to shoot him."

Nobody seemed bothered or even displeased about the demise of Diaz, and I figured Harris' version would look better on the reports.

I asked, "Where do we go from here?"

Parrish shrugged. "I'll have to go to the bosses at Justice about that. Maybe this is what Conley stumbled onto and it got him killed. I still don't understand why they came after you, Matt."

"I don't either," I said, "but they're probably still out there. They might be a little pissed that we took out their boss."

Harris said, "I don't think anybody can tie that to you. I don't think we left any tracks."

I said, "If they tie me to Diaz, they might put it all together."

"Nobody will ever find Diaz' body," Harris said with a cold formality.

"What about this senator?" said Reich. "Was he a state senator or U.S.?"

"Don't know," said Jock. "All Diaz said was that somebody had mentioned a senator. We don't know who he is or what his role in this might be."

Harris rocked by in his chair. "If that stuff's coming into Sarasota, some of it's probably ending up in Central Florida," he said. "I think you need to talk to Liz Birmingham. She's one of our agents, and she has better contacts in the drug world than anybody in our division."

Parrish cleared his throat. "That's a good idea, Rufus," he said. "I'll talk to the Coast Guard in St. Pete. They'll be interested in anything coming in by boat."

Harris nodded his assent. "I'll set up a meet with Liz for this evening. Dress casually. We're going to a titty bar."

Vanessa picked Jock and me up in front of the Federal Building and took us home for an early dinner cooked by her sister Mandy.

SEVENTEEN

Orlando is the epicenter of the world of theme parks. They're clustered on the southern edge of the city, surrounded by the tourist ghettos of hotels, restaurants and gift shops. On any given day there are over a hundred thousand tourists crowding into Central Florida. Few are aware that Orlando is more than a family fun destination.

A new city has arisen from the ashes of the citrus groves that fueled the area before Walt Disney discovered it. The office towers and condos that jut upward from downtown have replaced the one and two story retail shops that were once the business center of a small city.

The tourists never see the high-end gated communities where the very rich live side by side with the upwardly mobile middle-class. Neither does the visitor see the shabby neighborhoods that house the workers, who every day willingly enter the maw of the theme park beast to earn their minimum wage paycheck.

Like every city, Orlando supports an underworld where drugs and sex are sold or bartered with an insouciance that would stun the law-abiding citizen. In Orlando, much of this business hugs a thoroughfare called Orange Blossom Trail, a name that evokes the sweet smell of citrus trees in the spring. Not anymore.

The sickly sweet odor of cannabis permeates the clubs that sell nudity along with cheap booze. Those dives line the street, their facades filled with flashing neon displays advertising naked dancing girls.

It was into this squalid milieu that Jock, Harris and I ventured shortly after dark on Friday. It occurred to me that it had been one week since Diaz had tried to kill me at Tiny's.

We were making progress, I thought, but not very quickly. I knew who had tried to shoot me and who had given the order, but I didn't know why, and I didn't know who'd told Mendez to have me killed. My life would be at risk until I figured it out.

Les Girls was housed in a square stuccoed building with a flat roof supporting a large neon sign advertising the place as a "Gentlemen's Club." I didn't think a real gentleman would ever enter the double doors that opened from the parking lot. But we did.

There was a large man standing just inside the door beside a table at which sat a young woman in a negligee right out of a Victoria's Secret catalog. She was smiling. He was scowling.

"The cover charge is ten bucks a head," said the large man. "Pay the lady."

Harris pulled out a wad of cash and peeled off three tens and passed them to the woman at the table. The big guy scowled some more, and the lady at the table smiled as if we had granted her most extravagant wish by simply walking through the door.

The room was square with enough smoke hanging in the air to gag a goat. Not all the smoke was from regular tobacco. There was a bar along one wall with a thirty-foot runway jutting at right angles into the room. There were brass poles situated at either end of the runway, anchored in the ceiling. Small vinyl-covered chairs were placed along the bar and runway.

The joint was noisy with raucous comments uttered by drunks

sitting at the runway, gazing upward, mesmerized by the hairless bodies of the dancers. Rock music pounded from large speakers along the wall, the decibels outstripping a jumbo jet on take-off. Waitresses in skimpy outfits were serving drinks and kibitzing with the customers. There were about fifty men and two women sitting around the space, intently watching a pair of nude girls making love to the brass poles.

We took a table near the back of the room. A dancer stopped by to ask if we were interested in a lap dance for fifty bucks. We declined as a waitress made her way over to us. She was tall with blonde hair falling to her waist, Her breasts pushed out of the top of a lace camisole, barely hiding the nipples. She wore high heel shoes and a pair of shorts riding low on her hips, revealing her navel with its gold stud. Her face was thin with dark eyebrows that perhaps gave the lie to her hair color. She flashed a smile, revealing even white teeth and generating so much energy that I sat back in the chair. We ordered beer.

Jock rubbed his hands together. "Now that is some hunk of woman,"

"I'll introduce you when she comes back," said Harris.

I grinned."You come here often?"

"Only on business, "Harris said, chuckling.

"Some business for a hard working government employee," said Jock. "I guess you make sure the taxpayer gets his money's worth."

"Of course," said Harris. "I'm a good steward of your tax dollars."

The waitress was back with three six-ounce glasses of beer. "That'll be twenty-four dollars," she said, "not counting the generous tip." The smile flashed again, suddenly, and like lightning on a dark night, it lit up the room. I'm not kidding.

"Sit for a minute," said Harris. "I want you to meet a couple of friends."

She sat, putting her drink tray on the table. "Hi, I'm Tiffany."

Rufus laughed. "It's all right, Liz," he said. "These are our guys."

He was talking loudly to be heard over the ambient noise. Nobody was close to us, so he wasn't divulging any secrets to anyone other than Jock and me.

Rufus put his hand on the waitress' shoulder. "Liz Birmingham," he said, "meet Jock Algren and Matt Royal. Jock works for the government, I think, and Matt's a lawyer, but he doesn't take that too seriously."

She stuck out her hand to shake with Jock and me. "Pleased to meet you," she said.

I was dumbfounded. "You're the undercover narc?" I asked.

"Yes, but that's our little secret," she said. "I've only got a minute before I have to get back to slinging drinks."

"I wanted you to meet these guys so that when they come talk to you tomorrow you'll know they're with me," said Harris.

"And they're coming back tomorrow night?" she asked.

"No, they'll meet you at the Cantina at noon. Tell them anything you know that'll help," said Harris.

Liz frowned. "If you're looking into drugs in Central Florida, you need to remember Merc Maitland. He's sitting over there."

She nodded toward a heavy-set man just getting out of a chair on the far side of the room. Maitland was about five-feet-eight and must have weighed 250 pounds. His hair was short, almost a buzz cut, blonde going rapidly to gray, probably in his early 60s. He was wearing cargo shorts, boat shoes and a golf shirt.

"That's the kingpin," Liz said. "Gotta go. See you tomorrow."

Jock looked at Rufus. "Where is this Cantina you're talking about?" he asked.

"On Wall Street, around the corner from where Matt's office

used to be," said Harris.

I didn't ask him how he knew where my office had been, but it sounded as if he'd been checking me out. I'd eaten often at the Cantina when I practiced law. It had sidewalk dining that would be pleasant on a Saturday afternoon in late October.

We had a couple more drinks for appearance sake, ogled the sweeties dancing on the bar and runway, and took our leave. Harris dropped us at the Embassy Suites Hotel in downtown Orlando, where we had taken a couple of rooms for the evening.

I hadn't talked to Anne since Houston, and I was beginning to miss her. I'd have to be careful with that. I was pretty sure our relationship was edging toward an end, and I didn't want to be left with that terribly empty feeling that accompanies lost love affairs. I called her.

"Hey, Sugar," I said. "Miss me?"

"I sure did. Who is this?"

"Awwww."

"I really have missed you, Matt. Where are you?"

"I'm in Orlando. Jock and I learned a lot in Mexico, and we'll be coming home tomorrow evening. Can you have dinner?"

"You've been in Mexico?"

"Long story. Don't mention that to anybody. What about dinner tomorrow?"

"I wish I could, Matt, but I've made other plans."

She didn't explain the plans, and the jealously monster in my brain gnawed at me to ask. I stood my ground, though. A macho man has his pride, and I'd have to learn to live with this.

"Well, I'll give you a call later, and maybe we can get together," I said.

"Are you okay?" Her voice had softened.

"Sure, why?"

"You just don't sound quite right."

"It's been a long week, Anne. I'll talk to you next week."

"Bye," she said, and I hung up.

I wanted to call Chief Lester, but it was nearing midnight. I turned out the lights and drifted off to sleep thinking about the end of an affair. It was going to be rougher than I had imagined.

EIGHTEEN

The Cantina was not crowded on a Saturday afternoon. During the week the place was full of downtown workers enjoying lunch, and at night it turned into one of those clubs where young people spend too much time ruining their tympanic membranes with loud music. The doors were always open, and pigeons joined the people for a bit of lunch.

Amber took Jock and me to a table bordering the sidewalk. Barb came by with menus and asked how I was enjoying retirement. I told her it was fine and that we were waiting for another person before ordering. We chatted for a moment and she left to take care of other diners.

I'd called Chief Bill Lester in mid-morning at home. He told me that the serial number on the transom of the small boat washed up on the beach with the dead Mexicans showed that it was a tender on a big yacht out of Ft. Lauderdale. The yacht was owned by a New York advertising agency and the tender had been reported stolen a year before. A dead end.

Pepe Zaragoza had come out of the coma the day before. He had no memory of the events on the boat and no idea how he ended up on the beach.

The last thing he remembered was leaving home on Friday

94

morning to go to work on the truck farm in eastern Manatee County where he was a foreman, overseeing the Mexicans who harvested the crops. Since there were fewer vegetables to be harvested in October, most of his crew was had moved further south and was working other fields. Pepe's job was full-time, and when there were no crops ripening in the fields, he oversaw the maintenance on the vehicles and farm machinery needed on large institutional farms.

"He's not ready to leave the hospital," said Lester, "but he'll be arrested when he's discharged."

I was relating this to Jock when I noticed a woman with short brown hair walking toward us. She was wearing navy blue slacks, a cream colored silk blouse and low heeled shoes. A small gold cross hung from a thin chain around her neck. She appeared to be in her late-twenties. Her makeup was subdued to the point that it was not apparent she was wearing any. I was idly watching her, wondering who she could be, when she smiled at me. Liz. That smile would knock me over at a hundred paces.

Jock and I stood as she approached, and I moved around to help with her chair. This merited me another high wattage smile and a thank you.

"I almost didn't recognize you," I said. "You look a little different in the daylight."

She laughed. "You liked my working clothes last night?"

"I have to tell you, I never saw a government employee dressed just like that."

She smiled again. "Push-up bras are a great invention, and a big wig just makes a girl, don't you think?"

Jock finally found his voice. "Good of you to meet with us."

"Tell me why I'm here," she said.

I told her the story of the past week, beginning with the dead Mexicans on the beach and ending with our trip to Les Girls.

"Your theory about the drugs is right," said Liz. "Most of the coke we're seeing is coming from the Tampa-Sarasota area. Our people thought it might be coming in by sea, but we haven't found anything that would help us."

"Did you ever talk to Dwight Conley?" I asked.

"No. That was all done through Rufus Harris and Paul Reich."

Jock said, "Tell us about Maitland."

"He seems to be the guy taking care of the drugs around here. I don't think he's smart enough to run the show, but he's probably the area franchisee for the Sarasota bunch. We've got enough on him to take him down, but we're hoping he can lead us up the food chain."

I said, "Do you know how the drugs get here?"

"The Sarasota people hire low-level thugs to drive the coke to Orlando. Maitland stashes the drugs in a mini-storage facility on the Trail and doles them out to his people. A lot of this stuff gets sold on street corners and a lot more in the bars all over town."

"How long have you known about all this?" said Jock.

"Since I started working at Les Girls," said Liz. "It's amazing what you can pick up hanging around a place like that. We've confirmed what I've told you, but as I said, we're hoping ole Merc will lead us to his bosses."

I shrugged. "I don't have time to wait for a slip-up by Merc," I said. "Not if I want to keep breathing."

"Do you know where he lives?" asked Jock.

"Yes, but I don't want you guys busting up a project we've been working on for months," she said.

Jock was quiet for a moment, thinking. "What if he thinks we're another group trying to muscle in on his territory?" he said. "Couldn't we get what we need out of him without tipping DEA's hand?"

"Possible," said Liz. "But you'd have to be very careful. And you'd have to let me in on what you learn."

"We will," said Jock.

I said, "What else can you tell us about Maitland."

"Not much. He served state time up at Raiford, but he's pretty much a quiet guy. I don't think he made any waves up there."

I nodded to Jock. "We need to make a run at him. We'll report in, Liz, as soon as we know something."

"Deal," she said, and gave us Maitland's address. And smiled.

NINETEEN

Merc Maitland lived in a gated community that sprawled around a lake on the western edge of Orlando. The gate guard would want proof that we belonged there or we wouldn't be let in.

It's one of the conceits of the rich and nearly rich that a minimum-wage gate guard would keep criminals out of their neighborhoods. A common burglar would be slowed down, or maybe even defeated in his designs, but the real criminals probably lived among the ever-so-pompous denizens of these newly minted fortresses.

We stopped at a military surplus store and bought identical sets of clothing; work boots, gray long sleeved shirts, matching gray pants. We changed into the clothes in the dressing room. Our old clothes went into a plastic bag. We got two plain gray baseball caps, paid cash and left.

"We need a truck to go with these uniforms," said Jock. "Let's see what we can find."

We drove by the yards of several industrial companies, but found their trucks either too big for our needs or locked up behind chain link fences.

We stumbled onto a local cable TV company's maintenance yard, filled with panel vans left haphazardly in the parking lot.

"Looks like the Saturday crew left in a hurry," said Jock. "Let me out."

I stopped the rental car and Jock got out carrying a small leather packet and a slim jim, a flat piece of metal that will fit between the window and door frame of a vehicle. He was into the van in a second and bent over under the steering wheel. The van started, and Jock sat up and wheeled out of the parking lot. The whole thing had taken less than a minute.

We drove to a shopping mall called West Oaks Center and parked the rental. We'd pick it up later. I climbed into the passenger seat next to Jock and we headed for Maitland's house.

* * * * *

The gate guard came out of his air conditioned hut, smiling. "Somebody having cable trouble?" he asked.

"Nah," said Jock, "it's the whole neighborhood. We gotta check all the nodes until we find the problem. Great way to spend a Saturday afternoon, isn't it?"

The guard laughed. "Know what you mean. Go on in."

He hit the button to raise the red and white pole that guarded the entrance road.

We drove to the address given us by Liz. "Got your piece?" asked Jock.

"Yep. You?"

"Always."

"Ready?"

"Yep."

"Let's go."

We went, Jock carrying a tool box from the van in his left hand.

The house was large, built in a style often called McMansion, because of its ostentatious appearance. It was a two-story with a triple garage opening onto the driveway in front of the house. The lot was small, and the houses on either side crowded in. The double doors at the entrance were inlaid with beveled glass, stained so that we couldn't see inside. I knocked on the door and then, as an afterthought, pushed the bell button set into the facing. In a moment a large black man appeared.

"Can I help you?" he asked. He was wearing shorts, athletic shoes and a white T-shirt.

"We've got to check out the TV cable," I said, gesturing back to the van emblazoned with the logo of the cable company.

"We don't have a problem with the TV," he said.

I looked at a notebook from the truck, holding it so that the man at the door couldn't see anything written there. "A Mr. Maitland called about a problem," I said.

"Hold on," he said. Then turning to the interior he called, "Merc. Cable guy's here."

"What cable guy?" A scratchy voice came from what I presumed to be the family room.

"Said you called them," said the black guy.

"Coming," said the voice, and a moment later Merc Maitland waddled into the foyer. He looked just like he did the night before, and he was wearing the same clothes.

"What's this about a cable problem?" he asked.

Jock and I pulled our pistols from under our shirts. "Back into the house," I said.

"What the hell!" roared the black man.

Jock grabbed him by the front of his shirt and stuck the nine millimeter up under his nose. "Just be quiet. Anybody else in the house?"

"No. Just us," said Maitland, his voice quivering. "You're not the cable guys?"

"Duh," said Jock, grinning.

Jock produced two pairs of handcuffs and placed them around the men's wrists, hands behind them. Jock was always prepared. We moved them into the family room and told them to sit on the sofa. Jock went to search the house, while I held my gun on the men. He came back in a few minutes to tell me that we were alone.

"Jock," I said, "I'd rather not shoot these people if we can help it."

"Okay. Did you bring the cattle prod?"

"Cattle prod?" said Maitland. "What do you need a cattle prod for?"

"It's electric," said Jock. "It'll help you think."

"I don't need any help," said Maitland, his voice rising in panic. "Just tell me what you want."

I pointed my gun at the black man. "How about Dufus here?" I said,

"Jeep don't know a damn thing," said Maitland. "You can shoot him if you want."

"Merc!" yelped the black man. "Don't be talking like that."

"Well, it's true," said Merc. "You don't know shit."

"See?" said Jeep, looking at Jock. "Ain't no need to be shootin' me. I don't know shit."

"I'll get the cattle prod," I said.

"No! Wait," said Merc. "You don't need that. What do you want to know?"

"Where do your drugs come from?" I asked.

"Drugs? What are you talking about?" said Merc, a slight tremor audible in his voice.

I turned toward the door. "I'm going for the prod," I said.

"No, wait," said Merc. "Who are you guys?

Jock grinned, mirthlessly. "We're your new competition."

"What do you mean?" asked Merc.

"Our boss in Miami is getting a little pissed about you squeezing him out of Orlando," said Jock.

"I'm not squeezing anybody," said Merc. "I'm just helping out some friends."

"Which friends?" I asked.

"I can't tell you that," Merc said reasonably. "They'll kill me."

I pointed the automatic at him. "I think you've got a choice to make. If you don't tell your friends about our little discussion, you'll be all right. But if you don't tell us what we want to know, you'll be dead in a few minutes."

"What about him?" Merc said, pointing to the black guy named Jeep.

"We'll kill him, too," I said.

"No, I mean, if I tell you anything, he'll know and rat me out."

Jock grinned again. "Then you'll both be dead," he said. "You guys are tied together, and if the senator decides to kill one of you, he'll kill both of you."

Merc blanched at the mention of the senator. "Oh, shit," he said, "I don't know who they are. People bring me the stuff and I give them cash and they go away again."

"How does it work?" asked Jock.

"They bring me a bunch of the stuff and I pay them for the last bunch they brought. It's kind of a consignment thing. I make a few bucks profit on each deal."

"What happens if you don't pay for the last shipment?"

"I don't want to know," said Merc. "One day this dude comes by the house carrying a big garbage bag. He tells me that a guy I know in Melbourne didn't come up with the cash like he was supposed to. I said, 'What's that to me?' He opens the friggin' sack and the Melbourne guy's head's in it. I ain't gonna miss no payments."

Now, I grinned. "Who's the senator?" I asked.

"I don't know, I tell you," mumbled Merc. "I've just heard about the senator, but not a name. All these guys live in Sarasota."

"How did you get involved with these people?" I asked.

"Well, you see, I did a little time in prison."

"How little?" Jock said.

"Thirty years."

"That's more than a little," I said. "Were you selling drugs?"

Merc shook his head. "No, nothing like that."

"What were you in for?" I asked.

"Murder."

"Murder? Who did you kill?" I said.

"My wife."

"Why?" I asked.

"She was doing drugs and I wanted to put her out of her misery."

"Never mind," I said. "How did you get involved in this deal?"

"I met a guy named Charlie Peters at Raiford, and when we got out he helped set me up. He knew the Sarasota guys from somewhere."

"Where can we find Peters?" I asked.

"I don't know. The last time I saw him, all I saw was his head in a garbage bag," Maitland said.

"The guy from Melbourne," I said.

"Yeah." Merc said.

"Go get the prod," said Jock.

"Why? I'm cooperating," said Merc, his voice rising again.

"You're holding back," said Jock. "I need a name."

I put the barrel of the gun under the black guy's nose. "If you don't give me a name now," I said, looking at Merc, "I'm going to shoot your friend, and then I'm going to shoot you."

"Don't," said Jeep. "I know a name."

"You don't know shit," said Merc.

"Merc works for me," said Jeep. "He just don't know it. Thinks he runs things around here."

"Shiiit," said Merc. "Go ahead and shoot him."

"What's the name?" I asked.

"Jimmy Wilkerson,"said Jeep.

"Who is he, and where can we find him?" asked Jock.

"He's some Cracker lives over near Duette in Manatee County," said Jeep. "I think if you ask around some of the bars out east of Bradenton you'll find him." His English had suddenly improved substantially.

"Who else?" I asked.

"Nobody else," said the black guy. "Jimmy is my connection. I don't know who he reports to, or where he gets his merchandise."

I removed the gun from under Jeep's nose. "What does Jimmy look like?" I said.

"I don't know," Jeep said. "I've never met the gentleman. My only dealing with him was on the phone."

"How do you know where he lives, then?" I said.

"For some reason, he mentioned it in the one phone call I had with him."

I said, "He's your connection, but you only talked to him that one time?"

"Yes. Some other dude, a real bad-ass, brings the stuff in. He was the one who brought Peters' head by."

Jock pointed to Merc. "What in the world are you doing with this idiot?" he asked.

Jeep laughed. "He's so stupid he can't find his dick in the dark. If he ever gets caught by the feds he's not going to be able to tell them anything. You probably noticed it doesn't take long to figure out he's dumber a Georgia pine stump."

Merc sat quietly, chewing on what he had heard. "You mean I'm not in charge?" he asked.

"I don't think so," said Jock. "What do we do with these two geniuses?"

"Let's leave them," I said. "Unhook them and let them go about their business."

I looked at the handcuffed men and said, "If I find out you've alerted Jimmy Wilkerson or anybody else that we're looking for them, I'll come back and shoot your dumb asses dead. Understood?"

They both nodded their heads, and we took off the handcuffs. Jock pulled a roll of duct tape out of his tool box and we bound their hands in front. By the time they got out of the tape, we'd be out of the gate and gone. If anyone found them in the house tied up, it'd raise too many questions. We were flying under the radar and wanted to keep it that way. It was time for the hunters to become the hunted.

TWENTY

We were in the rental chasing the setting sun west on I-4. Jock had dropped me off at the mall where we'd left the rental, and I followed him back to the cable company's parking lot. He wiped down the van, destroying any fingerprints, and crawled in beside me.

"They'll probably never know it was missing," he said.

The sun hovered above the road ahead, a giant orange ball starting its daily disappearing act. I pulled down the visor and put on my sunglasses. We were still wearing the gray uniforms.

"I want to get home to my own bed tonight," I said. "This has been one hell of a week."

"That it has, my friend, that it has. Let's go straight to your condo. I think we'll be safe for the night. Park the car in a visitor's spot, and nobody will know you're home."

I nodded. "If they come, they'll have to come through the front door. I think we've got enough firepower to cover ourselves."

We drove through the slowly descending darkness, not talking, listening to a smooth jazz station on the radio. I wasn't sure what to expect when we reached Longboat Key. I knew the people trying to kill me hadn't given up. The chief had told me there were no leads on either the Mexicans' deaths or Conley's.

I hoped that we could find Jimmy Wilkerson and begin to unravel the thread that would lead us to the senator, whoever he was. The eastern parts of Manatee and Sarasota counties were full of Crackers, and that was how Jeep had described Wilkerson.

More than two thirds of Floridians live in the coastal counties, most of whom crowd near the beaches. The vast interior of Florida south of Orlando has relatively few people. A little more than a hundred years ago most of the interior was controlled by the cow catchers, a rough breed of pioneering men and women who pulled wild cattle out of swamps and drove them to Punta Rassa near present day Ft. Myers for shipment to Cuba. The Spanish-American war at the end of the nineteenth century and the advent of fenced land gutted that industry.

There are over ten million acres of working farmland in Florida, producing seven billion dollars a year in revenue. Florida leads the nation in the production of snap beans, bell peppers, tomatoes, cucumbers and squash. Florida ranks twelfth nationally in the production of beef products, supplying almost a million head of cattle annually to Midwest feed lots.

The great prairies of inland Florida have been chopped up by strip miners digging out the phosphate discovered in the late nineteenth century. There's still a lot of land given over to cattle, however, with ranches running into the thousands of acres.

This is a Florida most tourists never see. The people of the vegetable and cattle growing regions still consider themselves Southerners, and their accents confirm it. Many are the descend-ants of the pioneering cow catchers and farmers and have lived on their land for five generations or more.

The cowcatchers were rough men whose exploits rivaled those of the Old West as told in the movies. Most carried long rawhide whips for driving cattle and, on occasion, fighting each other. The loud cracks made by the whips gave a name to a whole culture; the

Crackers.

Some of their descendants had retained their rough ways and their accents. It was probably from this group that Jimmy Wilkerson had sprung. I'd start looking for him the next day.

The Cracker bars of east county would be running at full blast on a Sunday afternoon, the men letting loose after sitting in church for two hours at their women's insistence. There was only so much fire and brimstone a Cracker-man could take before he heard the siren call of Jack Daniels or Jim Beam. They knew in their guts that real men don't drink scotch.

At Tampa, we turned south on I-75 and headed for Longboat Key. The sun was gone, and I switched on the headlights. An hour later we crossed the Intracoastal on the Cortez Bridge, and I opened the windows to enjoy the subtle scent of the sea. I was home and glad of it.

A gibbous moon was hanging over the Gulf as I came to the dead-end of Cortez Road, the beach in front of me. A luminescent swath seemed to grow out of the moon, spreading ever more widely on the surface of the water as it closed in on the shore, ending abruptly at the parking lot of the Beach House Restaurant.

Groups of satisfied diners were ambling out of the restaurant, heading to the parking lot or across the main road, that ran along the beach. I turned left onto Gulf Drive and drove south, enjoying the sea air and the full moon.

I crossed Longboat Pass Bridge and a mile further turned into my condo on the bay. We parked in the visitors' lot and took the elevator to the second floor.

We drew our guns as I keyed the lock. Jock went in first, staying low. I stood at the side of the door covering him. He disappeared into a bedroom, called "clear" and went into the other bedroom.

He came out, his gun tucked into his belt. I engaged the safety on my nine and relaxed. "Well, at least nobody was waiting for us," I said.

"Got anything to eat?" asked Jock.

"No, but we can order a pizza from A Moveable Feast," I said.

"Do it. No anchovies. Put it in my name, so if anybody's paying attention they won't know you're home."

I called the restaurant and ordered the pizza. Twenty minutes later Jock went to get it.

TWENTY-ONE

The land was flat, sere, pocked by strip mines and mounds of phosphogypsum rising five hundred feet above the ground; small mountains of mineral waste that appeared in the distance as desert hillocks. Nothing moved in the still air. The mid-afternoon sun was hot, its rays reflecting off the moonscape left by the raping of the earth.

A huge crane sat in the middle of a dug-up field, idle on a Sunday afternoon, waiting for the next workday, to begin wrenching phosphate out of the earth. White dust covered the equipment and the road, each particle a radioactive speck. Air sniffers sat at the end of the occasional driveway, guarding the modest homes against the minuscule threat of contamination. No tourist brochure ever carried a picture of this part of Florida.

Jock and I had come out-east, as the coastal inhabitants called this desolate place. It was near the point where Polk, Hardee and Manatee counties joined, a place where workers daily dug out the minerals that would be turned into fertilizer to sustain the crops of vegetables planted in the fields to the west and the south.

We were in separate cars, Jock running a little ahead of me. We drove a two lane asphalt road running straight as an arrow between the pits from which the miners dug their daily bread. I came to a building surrounded by a gravel parking lot. The structure was old, built long ago, the wood weathered by time and heat, topped by a rusting tin roof. A painted sign advertised it as the Vagabond Bar.

The vehicles in the parking lot were mostly pick-ups with a few ancient cars scattered about, their rust-pitted hulks showing the signs of life in a harsh environment. I spotted Jock's rental and pulled in next to it. We had come looking for Jimmy Wilkerson.

I'd borrowed Logan Hamilton's car for our plunge into Cracker country. The Vagabond Bar was our third stop of the day. We'd driven north on I-75 and east on Highway 62 until we found a narrow two-lane paved road shooting north into the mines.

Jock and I had worked out a plan. He'd arrive at one of the local dives about thirty minutes before I did and take a seat at a table with a view of the bar. When I came in, I'd sit at the bar, order a beer, and ask the bartender if he knew Jimmy Wilkerson.

Jock was there for backup if I needed it. We weren't sure how Jimmy would react if we found him, nor were we too sanguine about the possible reaction of the rough men who frequented these bars.

This was certainly not a scientific approach, but we couldn't come up with anything better. Bill Lester had gone to the office that morning and run a fruitless computer search through the National Crime Information Center for our friend Jimmy. Either he wasn't in the system, or the man we were looking for was using an alias.

I walked into the Vagabond Bar and lost half a century. I was sure the place looked just like it did when it was first built, and a sign over the bar announced that it was celebrating its fiftieth anniversary. The rectangular room was large, with a bar of chipped and dented walnut running the length of one wall, a mirror taking up the entire space behind it. Four pool tables were clustered in one corner. Most of the rest of the space was filled with small tables with chairs arranged around them. The air conditioning unit cooled the place, and the fans hanging from the ceiling stirred the thick smoke drifting from lighted cigarettes sitting in half-full ashtrays. There were about thirty people in the bar, half of them hard-looking women.

I spotted Jock at a table near the center of the room. He was still wearing the gray uniform shirt and pants, washed the night before in my washing machine, and a baseball cap with a Caterpillar Tractor logo. I had on jeans, a white T-shirt and a Pittsburgh Pirates ball cap. I took a seat on a stool at the bar about twenty feet from Jock.

The bartender took my beer order. When he returned I asked if he knew Jimmy Wilkerson. He shook his head and walked off. I'd had no better luck in the previous places we'd visited. Maybe the only thing I was accomplishing was drinking a little beer. While that wasn't bad, I'd rather do it on Longboat Key than in this wasteland.

A body slid onto the stool beside me. I studied him in the mirror, seeing a thin man with a three-day growth of beard and matted dirty brown hair tucked under a baseball cap. A scar ran from his right temple, across his eye and down to his cheek. Alarm bells were going off in my head.

I'd seen this man before, at Taggarts, the bar we visited just before the Vagabond. Was he following us or was this just a co-incidence? I didn't have time to answer my own question before I heard the nasal twang of the Cracker in my ear.

"Heard you been lookin' for me," he said.

He was sitting close, and I felt the barrel of a gun poking me in the ribs.

"Are you Jimmy Wilkerson?" I asked.

"That would be me, Mr. Royal."

"You know who I am," I said.

"Yessir, the man who won't die." He cackled, a high-pitched sound that reminded me of a great heron's mating call. "I think we can fix that now, don't you?"

"Are you the one trying to kill me?" I said.

"Sorta."

"What does that mean?"

"It means I'm sorta involved. If I'd been in that bar on Longboat Key last week we wouldn't be having this conversation. You'd be dead."

"Why?"

"It don't matter why."

"Do you know?

"Nope. Ain't none of my business. Let's go," he said, poking me harder with the gun barrel.

"I'm not going anywhere with you," I said. "I don't think you'll shoot me here with all these witnesses."

"Mr. Royal, every one of these people will swear you tried to kill me and I had to take you out in self defense. Now, let's go." He poked harder.

I'd seen Jock leave, and hoped he wasn't just taking a bathroom break. I slid off the stool, and we walked toward the entrance, the pistol boring a hole in my back.

I pushed open the heavy oak door that led to the parking lot, the man close behind me. As I stepped down the one step to the concrete pad that served as a porch, I saw a flash of gray to my right. Instantly, Jock had his gun poking my would-be killer in his right ear.

"Don't move, Tonto, or you're dead," I heard Jock say in a low rumble. "Drop the piece."

"Whoa, there," said Jimmy, dropping his weapon. "Careful, now."

I turned, grabbed Jimmy by the shirt front and pushed him against the wall. "You son of a bitch, why are you trying to kill me?" I said.

"I don't know," said the thin man.

"Look, Jimmy," I said, "You're in deep..."

"I ain't Jimmy," he broke in.

"Right," I said.

"No, look in my pocket. I got ID."

"Let's go, Jimmy," I said, taking him by the arm and heading for Jock's car.

"No shit, man, I ain't Jimmy."

Jock waved the pistol in the man's direction. "Then, who are you?" he asked.

"I'm Byron Hewett. I just followed you when I heard you were looking for Jimmy. Check my ID."

I reached into the hip pocket of his dirty jeans and retrieved his wallet. There was about twenty dollars in small bills, two small notes that meant nothing to me, folded to fit into the wallet, and a Florida drivers' license that identified the man as Byron J. Hewett of Myakka City.

I looked at Jock. "His names Byron Hewett, according to this license."

Jock said, "Things are sure screwy around here."

I grabbed the man by the shirt again. "Why are you after me?" I asked. "And how did you know my name?"

"Jimmy and me was in Taggarts when you came in. He told me who you were and to come get you and bring you to him. I wasn't going to kill you."

"Where are you supposed to take me?" I asked.

"Man, he'll kill me if I tell you."

I gave him my coldest stare. "I'll kill you if you don't," I said.

"Okay, okay. We was supposed to meet at a closed-down mine

over near Mulberry."

Jock motioned with his pistol. "Let's go, shithead."

"Where we goin'?" asked Byron.

"To meet Jimmy," replied Jock.

TWENTY-TWO

We drove through the heat, the sun's glare bouncing off the white detritus of man's need to feed himself. I was driving Byron's king cab pickup with Byron sitting next to me, his hands bound behind his back. Jock was in the back seat, a gun pointed at Byron's neck.

Hewett directed us to a dirt road running eastward off the narrow blacktop we were following. We had seen only a couple of cars since we left the Vagabond.

We came to a gate anchored into an eight-foot tall chain link fence.

"It ain't locked," said Byron. "Just pull the chain out from around the posts."

I got out of the truck, nervous, exposed to anyone who might be watching for us. I unwrapped the chain that held the gate closed and swung it open. I got back into the truck, and we drove through, not bothering to close the gate behind us. We might need to make a quick exit.

We continued on the dirt road for a couple of miles and came to a small building, a shed of corrugated steel that looked like a World War II Quonset hut, hidden among mounds of phosphate waste.

There were no trees, no grass, no birds or other wildlife. Just the piles of waste and the hut. Byron told us to pull over.

"I don't see his car," said Byron.

Jock asked, "You're sure this is where you were supposed to meet Jimmy?"

"Yeessir," said Byron.

I said, "We'll wait."

We sat for fifteen minutes, the truck idling to keep the air conditioner blowing cool air. Hewett was visibly sweating, the cold air not making a dent in his fear. The time dragged by. We sat quietly watching for the dust cloud that would signal the approach of a vehicle.

"He ain't comin'," said Byron. "He must've seen you take me at the Vagabond. He's smart like that, you know."

"Where does he live," I asked.

"Don't know," said Byron. "He calls my cell when he needs me, and I meet him at a bar somewheres."

Even the Crackers had embraced technology.

Jock asked, "What do you do for him?"

"Sometimes he needs help with the Mexicans," said Byron.

"What kind of help?" asked Jock.

Byron shrugged. "You know, kinda slap 'em around sometimes to keep 'em in line," he said. "Sometimes they get to thinking they can do better working somewhere else and we got to change their minds."

"Who does Jimmy work for?" I said.

"I don't know, and that's the gods' honest truth," said Byron.

Jock asked, "Is Jimmy in the drug business?"

Byron shook his head. "If he is, I don't know nothing 'bout it. I just work with the Mexicans."

"Which Mexicans would those be?" I said.

"The ones what lives in the labor camps Jimmy runs."

"Who do the Mexicans work for?" Jock asked.

"I don't know. Jimmy hires them out to farmers around here when there's pickin' needed to be done. He runs a lot of them south for the season down there, and then upcountry when he needs to."

"Is Jimmy Wilkerson his real name?" I asked.

"Guess so," said Byron. "It's the only one I ever knowed him by."

"How long have you known him?" I said.

"'Bout three years. Met him at the Vagabond. I was gettin' damn tired of working the phosphate."

I didn't think Byron had any more to give us. I glanced at Jock, who nodded.

Jock waived his pistol at Hewett and pointed toward the car door. "Get out of the truck," he said.

"Now wait a minute. What you fixin' to do?" said Byron, fear making his high pitched voice climb several notes. "I told you everything I know."

Jock placed the barrel of his pistol against the back of the agitated man's head. "Get out, now, or so help me your brains are going to be all over this truck."

Byron opened his door and climbed down from the cab. Jock walked him about fifty feet away and told him to stop.

"Oh, shit, man, don't shoot me. I wasn't going to shoot your buddy. I ain't never killed nobody in my life. All I ever did was rough up a few Mexicans, and that don't count for nothin'."

"Shut up," said Jock, as he untied Byron's hands. "We'll park your truck at the Vagabond."

"You're not leaving me way the hell out here, are you?" Byron whined.

"Either that or I can shoot you," said Jock.

"Okay, mister, okay. I don't mind the walk."

"You can probably catch a ride when you get to the hardtop," said Jock. "If I ever see you again, I'm going to shoot your sorry ass. Understand?"

"Yessir. Don't worry. You won't see me again."

We drove off, leaving Byron standing alone in a landscape as desolate as any I'd ever seen.

TWENTY-THREE

We left the truck at the Vagabond and drove our cars back to Longboat Key. Logan lived in Bay Isles in a large condo overlooking Sarasota Bay. A few months before he'd sold his unit on the beach where his girlfriend Connie had died and moved to the new place.

The gate guard came out of the gatehouse as I pulled up. He recognized me from my regular visits and said, "Good evening, Mr. Royal. Go on through. I'll let Mr. Hamilton know you're on your way."

"Thanks, Bill. The guy behind me is with me."

"No problem, Mr. R."

We drove through the gate and down a street lined with shrubs, most still blooming in the fall. In about a half-mile we came to Logan's condo, parked and took the elevator to the fifth floor. The door was open.

"Come on in, guys. You look like hell. Where've you been all day?"

We sat and sipped bourbon on the rocks, telling Logan about our day. "It was pretty much a bust," I said. "We didn't find Jimmy Wilkerson, but we did let the bad guys know I'm back."

Jock rattled the cubes in his tumbler. "That might not be such a bad development," he said. "Now that they know we're closing in, somebody's going to get itchy. They'll come looking for us, and we'll be ready."

"I've canceled my week," said Logan. "I might be able to help you guys."

I took a slug of my drink. "I'm pretty much out of ideas. Jimmy knows we're looking, but I've got no clue as to how to find him. That name's probably an alias anyway."

"If we stay holed up on the key he'll have to come here," said Jock. "Just think of yourself as bait."

I laughed. "That's comforting. I'd rather be moving, taking the initiative. I just can't figure out how."

Logan poured himself another drink. "Let's look at what we've got," he said. "We know the drugs and the illegals are connected. We know they're both coming in by trawler from Veracruz, and from what Diaz told you, we can pretty much count on Longboat Key being the drop site.

"We don't know who the Mexicans on the beach were," Logan continued, "nor do we know why they were killed. There's got to be a connection, but we can't see it yet."

Jock shifted on the sofa. "I think the lawyer, Conley, must have been using one of the Mexicans Matt found on the beach as a mole in the smuggling operation," he said. "Probably the legal one. Somebody caught on and took them both out."

"But why kill the other two illegals?" I asked.

"Maybe it was nothing more than an attempt to cover up Pepe's murder," Logan said.

"Then why try to kill me?" I said.

"Somebody thinks you knew more than you do," said Logan. "The loose ends are Jimmy Wilkerson and the senator. Jimmy is working the illegals, and maybe he has some connection to drugs. If he's in the distribution end of it, there has to be some central location where the drugs are shipped from. And where do the illegals go once they hit the ground?"

I thought about that for a minute. "Jeep, in Orlando, said Wilkerson was their guy," I said. "That means he's into the drug business. Byron said Jimmy hired him to keep the Mexicans in line. So, Jimmy is the one person we know at the intersection of the drugs and the illegals."

Jock nodded. "Don't forget the senator," he said.

"He's probably the guy pulling all the strings," I said.

Logan smiled. "We've got to find Jimmy," he said. "But we knew that yesterday. We haven't accomplished much."

I said, "I called Bill Lester from the car and gave him the tag number on Byron's truck. He checked it out, and it is registered to Byron, with an address in Myakka City. The chief's going to see what else he can dig up on Hewett. Maybe that'll give us a shot at Wilkerson."

Jock said, "Yeah, but Wilkerson's only a gofor. If Emilio can get aboard that trawler, and we can track it, we might be able to find the head of this monster."

Jock leaned forward on the sofa. "If the boat's headed here, it'll take her six days," he said. "That'll give us some time to stir the pot. Maybe we'll shake something loose." Mixed metaphors are fun.

Logan said, "If we can find where either the illegals or the drugs go when they come ashore, we'll be ready when our ship comes in."

Jock and I both groaned at the bad pun.

I said, "I think our best bet is to follow the drugs and the immigrants after the boat gets here."

They both nodded in agreement.

Logan grilled steaks on his balcony overlooking the moonlit bay, and we enjoyed a quiet evening as we ate. The moon was up, casting a soft glow on the still water. Occasionally, we'd hear a sea bird grumble from the rookeries where they slept at the edge of the bay. We discussed our options, and none of us could come up with anything to get us closer to the senator before the arrival of the *Princess Sarah*.

TWENTY-FOUR

Monday morning dawned comfortably. High cumulus clouds seemed to be on fire with the reflected colors of the rising sun. The temperature was in the high-sixties and would climb into the mid-seventies by the afternoon. I was sitting on the balcony overlooking Sarasota Bay, reading the morning paper, a cup of black coffee in my hand. Jock was still asleep in the guest room. The phone rang.

It was Paul Reich, the Border Patrol agent from Orlando. "We picked up an interesting illegal yesterday down in your neck of the woods. He tells us that he escaped from what sounds like a slave labor camp," he said.

I said, "Slave labor? What's that all about?"

"Don't know. The illegal's name is Juan Anasco. He said he came in by boat from Veracruz and was taken to this camp and put to work on a truck farm. Says the laborers are all kept locked in the camp when they're not working."

"Do you know where the place is?"

"Not exactly. From the way Juan described things, we think it's in Merrit County. We've got a confidential informant down there, but he's playing it close to the vest. We don't even know his name. We know there's a camp, but we don't know its location.

We're putting together a task force to look for it."

"What about the sheriff's office? Those rural cops usually know what's going on in their counties."

"We're not too sure about the sheriff's department down there. There are only three deputies, and one is a bad-ass named Casey Caldwell who likes to beat up on the Mexicans."

"Did Anasco know where he worked?" I asked.

"No. All he could tell us was that it was on a farm."

"Anything else?"

"He told us how he came into the country. It sounds like it was the same route you turned up in Mexico. Through Longboat Key. He said some young blonde woman drove them to the camp."

"Thanks, Paul. Jock and I may do a little looking around. We'll let you know if we turn up anything."

"Be careful," he said and hung up.

Jock had come out onto the balcony with a cup of coffee as I talked to Reich. I related our conversation.

Jock sipped his coffee. "Where's Merrit County?"

"Southeast of here. It's a big ranching and farming area. More cows than people."

* * * * *

We drove south on I-75 to Port Charlotte, and then followed a two-lane state road due east for twenty miles before crossing into Merrit County. In another ten miles we came to the county seat, a small town whose ancient one-story buildings advertised its precarious existence. The highway ran through the town and kept going until it ended at Lake Okeechobee. We weren't going that far.

I'd called Logan to brief him on what we were doing. I wanted somebody I trusted to know where we were. Logan wanted to go with us, but I reminded him that he was still recovering from the heart surgery he'd undergone in the summer, and he didn't need to be involved in any rough stuff. He reluctantly agreed.

We pulled into a McDonald's for coffee. It looked to be the only building constructed in the town in the past fifty years. Jock and I were wearing jeans and polo shirts, his white and mine forest green. We were shod in running shoes.

The teenaged girl behind the counter appeared Hispanic. Jock said something to her in Spanish. She gave him a sullen look and a short reply in English.

We got our coffee and sat in a booth next to the windows looking onto the parking lot. Next door was a building that seemed to be the courthouse, dilapidated and uninspiring. There were few people on the street, and most of them were Mexicans.

Jock locked his hands around his styrofoam cup. "I asked her if she knew where the farm workers lived around here," he said. "She told me she didn't know."

"I'm sure she does."

"Yeah, but if they're part of a slave labor deal, there's bound to be some muscle around to keep them all in line."

"I guess so."

Just then, an old school bus, painted blue, rumbled down the street in front of the restaurant. Jock looked up. "I bet that's a labor bus."

We took our coffee and hurried to Jock's rental car in the parking lot. He swung out behind the bus, which was about three blocks in front of us. We followed it east, driving out of town, then north on a county road. Citrus groves crowded the highway on either side. Rows of trees ran perpendicular to the road, standing straight and even, like silent soldiers in formation.

When we had gone about ten miles, the bus turned left onto a dirt road heading west. Jock kept driving for about a mile and then turned around on the shoulder. We parked and sat, trying to decide what to do next.

Jock said, "When in doubt, just knock on the front door."

"We could try that. At least we'll get a look at the place."

"Of course, this might not be the right place. There are probably lots of labor camps around here. Lots of farming."

"True," I said, "But since we're here, we might as well take a look."

* * * * *

The dirt road ran for about three miles. The groves petered out, and we were driving between plowed fields that had not been planted. In the distance we could see buildings.

As we got closer, the camp came into sharper focus. The place looked like an aging army bivouac, set in the middle of a dusty field. Five long barracks constructed of wood, sat on short brick pilings. The buildings were whitewashed, with grime showing through. A lone electric line ran from the poles along the road to the end of each building. No grass had the temerity to grow in this desolate place.

A chain link fence about ten feet high, topped with barbed wire, angled inward, enclosed the sorry dwellings. This was a fence to keep people in, not out.

A few shoeless children played on the bare ground, laughing in their ignorance of how harsh their lives were.

We drove up the road to the gate, manned by a large white man in a khaki uniform. A small guardhouse shielded him from the elements, and a sturdy gate blocked our way.

"Can I help you?" asked the man as we came to a stop next to the little building.

Jock rolled down the driver's side window. "We're just here

for a visit."

"No visitors," said the guard, his Cracker accent forming around the wad of tobacco lodged in his cheek.

"Juan Anasco invited us," said Jock.

The guard shrugged. "It don't matter who invited you. Ain't no visitors allowed. You just need to back up and turn around and be on your way."

We did as we were told.

Jock rolled up his window as we left the gate. "Seems more like a prison than a labor camp."

"Maybe it is," I said.

We turned off the dirt road onto the paved county road, heading south. Jock was driving at the posted speed limit, looking in the rear view mirror every few minutes. There was no other traffic.

Then, "Uh oh," he said. "I think we've got company."

I turned in my seat. A police cruiser had turned off one of the dirt roads stretching into the groves, and was now behind us, his blue lights rotating. The driver tapped the siren, and Jock pulled over onto the shoulder.

The cruiser pulled in behind us. Jock rolled down his window and sat rigid, both hands on the steering wheel. "Don't make any sudden moves," he said. "The cop has his gun out."

A deputy sheriff came to the driver's side. He leaned down and said, "You, driver, come out of the car real slow-like. Keep your hands up."

He looked at me. "Stay where you are until I tell you to get out."

Jock eased his way out of the car, the deputy standing back, pointing his gun at him. "Lean against the trunk and spread your legs."

I could see the deputy in the rear view mirror. He patted Jock down and pulled the pistol out of its holster, dropping it to the ground. Then, taking Jock's arms one at a time, the deputy cuffed them behind his back.

"I'm going to walk around to the other side of the car," he said, looking at Jock. "You try anything, I'll shoot you."

The deputy came around to my side of the car, still pointing his pistol at Jock. "You," he said, glaring at me. "Out."

I've got out. "I've got a gun," I said. "Left side of my waist. I've got a permit, too."

"Put your hands on the car and lean over. Spread your legs," he ordered.

I complied. He patted me down, took my weapon, and cuffed me. "Get over there by your buddy."

Jock and I were standing next to each other on the grass shoulder of the road. No cars had come by since we were stopped. It was a lonely place.

The deputy stood in front of us, a scowl on his face. He was not a big man, maybe five-feet-eight, but he appeared fit. His green uniform shirt was tight across a barrel chest. He wore a badge, but no name tag. I could see the little holes where it had been pinned to his breast pocket. I didn't think that his removing his identification was a good sign.

He smiled, showing yellow teeth, with the right eyetooth missing. "Now, who are you and what are you doing in my county with guns?"

I spoke up. "I'm Matt Royal and this is John Algren. We've both got permits for the guns. Why are you arresting us?"

"I ain't arrested you."

"Then why are we in cuffs?" I asked.

"Let's just say I've detained you boys. You gotta learn not to be messing around in other people's business."

I smiled. "So, you're Deputy Caldwell."

He unconsciously reached for the place where his name tag had been removed, stopping his hand in mid-air. "How did you know my name?" he asked, menace in his hard voice.

Jock spit, the glob of saliva landing near the deputy's boot. "We heard that the dumbest fuck in the county was named Caldwell," he said, "and we just put it together."

Caldwell began to pull the billy club from his equipment belt.

A low raspy voice, menacing and confident, escaped from Jock. "If you're planning to use that on us, you'd better do some re-thinking," he said. "You'll be dead before you can hit me. If you get lucky and connect, I'll come for you another day."

A look of rage danced across Caldwell's face. "I'll kill you, you smug son-of-a-bitch," he said.

Jock's voice grew quieter, more menacing. "And if that happens, some very bad men will come and kill everybody in your family out to second cousins. You'll be the last to go."

The deputy hesitated, then grinned. He had decided not to believe Jock's threat. After what had happened in Mexico, I pretty much believed it.

The billy came out. Caldwell swung it one-handed back over his shoulder like a tennis racquet wielded by a poor player, and then started his swing toward Jock's head. Jock pivoted on the ball of his right foot, turning inside the billy's swing radius and ended up with his back to the deputy, close in, as the club swung around harmlessly.

As Jock started his pivot, I whirled to my left, turning three-hundred-sixty degrees, and slammed my left foot into the side of Caldwell's left knee. I heard the ligaments snap under the impact, and at the same time, was aware that Jock had butted the back of his head into Caldwell's face. Blood flew from the battered man's shattered nose, and a hoarse scream erupted from his throat.

The deputy went down on his back, with Jock on top of him. Caldwell was holding his broken nose with both hands, moaning softly, not even aware of his ruined knee.

I sat on the ground next to the deputy, my back to him. I reached for the deputy's key ring with my cuffed hands. I wanted the key to the handcuffs.

Jock saw what I was trying to do. "No, we'll leave the cuffs on," he said. "I want the man in charge to see that we're harmless. Take his gun, though."

Jock walked over to the cruiser and sat in the driver's seat. "Let's get the law out here," he said.

"Do you think that's a good idea?'

Jock was quiet for a moment, his brow wrinkled in thought. "Maybe not," he said, "but we can't just leave this like it is. See if you can get dipshit's keys and unlock my cuffs. I'll hold my pistol behind my back while you show whoever comes that you're cuffed. If there's a problem, I'll take care of it."

That sounded like a plan. We walked back to the wounded deputy and retrieved his keys. I unlocked Jock's cuffs, and he retrieved his pistol.

Jock went back to the cruiser and picked up the radio microphone. "We've got an emergency on county road 496 A, about two miles south of the turn-off to the labor camp," he said. "Get somebody out here right now."

The radio crackled with static. "What kind of emergency? Who are you?"

Jock looked at me and grinned. "Ignore that. Somebody will be on the way in a very short time," he said.

The radio crackled again as we got out of the car. We walked over to the deputy who was writhing on the ground, aware now of the pain in his knee. We leaned against the cruiser, waiting.

Within minutes we heard sirens. Two sheriff's vehicles, one an SUV, screamed to a stop behind Caldwell's car. A young deputy got out of the first one, his gun drawn, pointing at us. He walked over to Caldwell, still on the ground, moaning, blood seeping from his nose, his knee at an odd angle.

A tall man with brown hair and a round face climbed out of the SUV and came toward us, gun drawn. He appeared to be in his late thirties and was wearing chinos and a green golf shirt with a gold sheriff's badge embroidered on the left breast pocket.

"Who is it, Bobby?" he asked over his shoulder.

The young deputy was upset. "It's Casey Caldwell, Sheriff. He's hurt bad."

"Call an ambulance. I'll take care of these two."

I said, "We're handcuffed, Sheriff. We can't give you any trouble." I turned slightly to show the man my bound hands. Jock stood still, his hands behind him.

I said, "Deputy Caldwell cuffed us and then tried to take us out with his billy club. We resisted. He had no reason to try to rough us up, other than sheer meanness. He never told us why we were stopped."

"Who else was involved?" the sheriff said.

"Just us, Sheriff," I said.

The sheriff looked skeptical. "You did all this damage while you were in handcuffs?"

Jock spoke up. "We've had some training," he said.

The sheriff looked at Jock. "What're your names?" he said.

"I'm John Algren and this is Matthew Royal, a lawyer."

Jock could have left that last part out. I didn't think this sheriff was going to be intimidated by the fact that I was an attorney, and sometimes cops make it tougher on lawyers, just because they can.

"I'm Sheriff Kyle Merryman. Tell me what happened."

I related the events since arriving at the labor camp. I didn't want to get into any detail about why we were there.

I added, "Once we were stopped, the deputy seemed to go berserk. Told us he was going to teach us not to mess around in other people's business. That's when he took a swing with the billy club."

"Why didn't you get Caldwell's keys and uncuff yourselves?" the sheriff asked.

Jock said, "We didn't want anybody to think we were dangerous. In an officer-down situation, trigger fingers sometimes get a little twitchy."

The sheriff nodded and turned to look south as the distant wail of a siren pierced the air. "You two stay put," he said, and turned to walk to where Casey Caldwell lay on the ground moaning softly.

I could hear a whispered conversation between the sheriff and the young deputy as they stood over Caldwell, but I couldn't make out what they were saying. Then, the sheriff squatted on his haunches next to the injured cop, and they had a discussion.

Merryman rose and walked slowly toward us, a look of determination on his face. The siren had gotten louder, and the ambulance appeared in the distance, coming toward us at high speed.

The sheriff planted himself in front of Jock and me, and said, "My deputy says you attacked him first. I suspect he's lying. Did you attack first?"

I said, "No, Sheriff, he had a gun and we'd been disarmed."

The sheriff looked at me quizzically. "Mr. Royal, where are you from?"

"Longboat Key, now, Sheriff. But I practiced law in Orlando for a long time."

The ambulance pulled over onto the shoulder of the road, its siren abruptly dying. The young deputy waved the medics over to Caldwell. Merryman ignored them.

The sheriff took a deep breath, exhaled. A brief expression crossed his face, disappearing too quickly for me to read it. He breathed again and slapped at a small insect crawling up his neck.

133

I could hear the rattle of the leaves on the citrus trees as they were disturbed by a light wind blowing out of the west. The hum of insects living in the brush beside the road gently assaulted my ears.

The sheriff was staring at me, not moving. Everyone else was still. Even Caldwell's moans had ceased. It was as if time had stopped, and we were actors in a tableau vivant staged in a bizarre setting.

Probably no more than a second had elapsed, but in retrospect it seemed longer. The sheriff shifted his weight to his left leg, and looking directly at me, asked, "Do you know Jimbo Merryman?"

TWENTY-FIVE

Did I know Jimbo Merryman?

A long time ago, in a faraway place called Vietnam, a team of U. S. Army Special Forces troops, the toughest fighting men on the planet, eased its way single-file along a jungle path. It was December, 1972, and the Americans were withdrawing, tasting the bitter fruit of defeat. Apparently, nobody had bothered to tell the North Vietnamese troops we were leaving, because they were still trying to kill us.

A nineteen year old soldier was at the head of the column, alert, scared, waiting for whatever was going to happen. That was me. A kid with a rifle. I'd been in-country for several months, and I had been in battle. The firefights always started without warning, rifles going off, men grabbing the ground, sighting on the enemy, pulling triggers, killing and wounding each other.

And that's the way it happened that hot day in December.

* * * * *

I'd joined the Army the day after I graduated from high school, and during the summer of 1971, I had enjoyed the hospitality of basic training at Ft. Jackson, South Carolina. I was offered a slot in Officer Candidate School if I could pass the entrance exams, and after I finished my advanced infantry training, I was sent to Ft. Benning, Georgia, to the Infantry OCS to learn how to be a leader and a gentleman. Six months later, some Colonel pinned gold bars on the epaulets of my dress khaki uniform, and I started Ranger school. From there I went to Special Forces training at Ft. Bragg, North Carolina.

The boys in green berets taught me how to eat lizards, navigate in a jungle, climb up or down mountains, kill with rifle, pistol, machine gun, mortar, knife and bare hands. They had a ceremony and put a green beret on my head an assured me that I was one mean son-of-a-bitch.

They put me on a big jet airplane with 150 other kids and took me off at a place called Thon Son Nhut airport in the city of Saigon, in that showpiece of democracy, the Republic of South Vietnam. They herded several of us onto a helicopter and dropped us off in a pigsty called Base Camp O'Conner in the mountains that traipse across the waist of the Indochinese peninsula.

I was introduced to a ragged group of boys and a man about forty years old. This was my A team. Together, we were supposed to kill all the little yellow men we could.

There were eleven of them. With the exception of the older man, the sergeant, their age averaged mine. They were good at their job. The lieutenant I replaced had been mailed home in a box.

The sergeant was on his second tour and was a wise man indeed. Back in OCS, a sergeant-instructor had told us that we should never let those little bars go to our heads; that we should cozy up to a sergeant and learn everything we could from him. It might just keep us alive. I took that advice and learned a lot from Master Sergeant Jimbo Merryman. That knowledge saved my life more than once.

We scurried about in the jungle for eight months, killing a few sad looking little fellows, and then getting shot at by the ones that replaced them. America was fighting a limited war, but the enemy wasn't. We'd blow up an ammunition dump and get choppered back to Base Camp O'Conner. After a few days of boredom, we'd get choppered back to blow up the same dump again and kill a few more of the same guys we'd killed the week before.

We'd been in the boonies for about four days on some long-forgotten and unimportant mission when what seemed like the whole North Vietnamese Army jumped us. We were snaking down a trail in jungle so thick we couldn't see four feet on either side. The overhanging branches, like an inverted sea of shaggy green with cerulean highlights and scudding whitecaps, gave us an occasional peek at the sky. By then we were so attuned to the jungle that we were like the animals that lived there. We could walk for miles in the stifling heat without making a sound.

We had become immune to the insects that took their daily meals out of our hides. We didn't even bother the animals anymore, and the buzzing and crackling in the bush became just background noise to us, like that droning music in elevators that you are subliminally aware of, but don't hear.

Suddenly, there was a shot, and Myers, the point man, fell. He was about ten yards ahead of me, and I could tell he'd never get up again. He dropped with a looseness of the body that only the dead achieve.

I hit the ground and rolled into the brush beside the trail. There was a lot of gunfire, all of it the distinctive bark of the Chinese-made AK-47 automatic rifle. I saw two more of the good guys fall. One was completely quiet, but Abernathy, a big blonde kid from Arkansas, was screaming and rolling on the trail holding his gut. All the firing was coming from ahead of us, near the clearing we had been making for. I knew that three were hit, but I couldn't see the other eight. They had been spread out at ten yard intervals when the shooting started. I hollered for Jimbo.

"I'm hit, Lieutenant," he called back.

"How bad?"

"In the shoulder. I can make it."

"How about the others?"

"Smitty and Kines are down. I think they're dead. Cate is with me. I can't see the others."

"Sing out!" I said, hoping that most of them would answer.

"Galis."

"Sims."

"Craft. I can see Sandifur, Loot. He ain't movin'. Looks like he got it in the head."

"Beemis," I yelled. "Are you okay?" No answer. "Can you see the bastards, Jimbo?"

"Nossir. But they're all over the place. We're getting fire from all sides."

"Aber's hit. I'm going after him. Cover me," I said to no one in particular.

The kid was about twenty yards behind me, lying near the middle of the trail. Little puffs of dirt were exploding around him. He was still screaming. I strapped my M-16 across my back and began to crawl toward him, staying as close to the cover of the trees as I could. The jungle was so thick in places I had to crawl onto the trail, and the little puffs of dirt would begin to explode around me. One was close enough to splatter gritty sand into my eyes.

By the time I reached Abernathy, he had quieted down and was moaning in little short gasps. I rolled him onto his back and stuck a compress over the hole in his belly. I laid on my back on top of him, my rifle between us, put his arms around my neck, and rolled onto my stomach.

I started crabbing to the nearest cover, about ten yards in front of me. I felt Aber twitch once, and then he was quiet. When I reached the trees he was dead. He had taken one in the back. It entered his side just below his right armpit and came out on his left side about waist level. I was sticky with the boy's blood.

I laid him on his back. He was staring at me accusingly, but he wasn't seeing anything. I closed his eyes and started shaking, uncontrollably.

Suddenly, all the months of futility and terror, the dead and the maimed, the terrible waste of it all, overwhelmed me. I was hyperventilating, gasping in shallow breaths, not getting enough oxygen. A part of my brain told me to snap out of it, but I had no control over my body. It was as if I were standing to one side watching my body dessert me for the first time ever.

I told myself to slow down, to get hold of my panic. I'd been in situations this bad before, and I'd always handled them. I prided myself on never panicking, no matter what the danger. I told myself that I was in charge, and I owed these guys some leadership. Nothing worked. I couldn't get control of the panic. It was overwhelming me, and I knew, with absolute and terrible certainty, that it would kill me.

I remember thinking that this was a lousy place to die. I wasn't ready yet. I had about fifty more years to live according to the insurance tables. I was scared. Bone-shaking, teeth-rattling scared. I curled up in a little ball and said goodbye to the world.

I wondered how my mother would handle the memorial service. I saw my name on the little plaque that hangs in the main hall of my high school, announcing the names of the alumni who had died in every conflict since World War One.

Jimbo was shaking me and hollering loud enough to be heard by the staff in Saigon. "Goddammit, Matt. You chickenshit little wimp. You no good goddam shavetail asshole. You crap out on me now, and I swear to God I'll kick your sorry ass all the way back to Florida and feed the alligators a meal of chickenshit lieutenant."

I was still standing there, outside my body, watching the sergeant bring me back. It was like one of those stories you read of near-death experiences, except that I was only near-death emotionally. I wasn't even hurt, not in the physical sense.

I've read of aborigines in Australia who have been boned. A shaman points a bone at one of them and tells him that he is going die. The man, even though in the peak of health, dies within a few days, because he believed in the power of the shaman. He had willed himself dead. Maybe that's what I was trying to do. I never figured it out, and I never had another similar experience.

I began to pull out of it. I gulped lungfuls of air. I was as tired as I'd ever been. The lack of oxygen in the shallow breaths of the hyperventilation had taken its toll.

Suddenly, I was back in my body. "I'm all right, Jimbo," I said. "Thanks. Lets figure a way to get the hell out of this." I was lucid and in control and figured I had at least a fighting chance of surviving this mess.

The big sergeant grinned. "That clearing is about a hundred yards in front of us," he said. "It's big enough to bring in choppers if we can get there. We've still got the radio. I hope the chopper boss hasn't stopped monitoring it."

I got the men into a circle, firing into the trees on all sides. The guys were mad and doing their damndest to earn their pay. In the process they were shooting up one hell of a lot of Uncle Sam's ordinance.

The little radio was working, and I called the chopper boys. Our group was code-named Riding Hood for some unknown reason. Probably a little joke dreamed up by the staff boys back in Saigon. I called for Bald Eagle, another ridiculous name, but one that could save our butts if they were listening, and if they were in position as they were supposed to be.

"Riding Hood, this is Bald Eagle. What are your coordinates?"

I gave him our map coordinates and told him that we were up to our asses in Charlies. I described the situation and asked for a lot of fire power to be laid in between us and the clearing. I suggested he have a gun ship make a pass and then hold off until we called again. We'd move as soon as the chopper passed, and we'd come out shooting.

I told the men that as soon as the area was strafed, we'd move ahead about ten yards firing everything we had in all directions.

The gun ship came in low, firing all those big machine guns. As he was angling up, our little group, still in a tight circle firing on all points of the compass, moved ten yards down the trail. On the fourth move my leg went out from under me. As I hit the ground I felt the hot pinpoint of pain in my calf. I reached down and brought back a bloody hand. The bone seemed all right. I got back to my feet and could walk, but every step felt as if a hot poker were being stuck into my lower leg.

Suddenly, we were at the edge of the clearing. Jimbo was next to me, and Galis and Sims had their backs to us firing into the jungle.

"Where are the others?" I asked.

"Dead," muttered Sims.

"Are the choppers still with us?" I asked.

"I saw one of the gun ships go in," said Jimbo. "He took a direct hit from some sort of heavy weapon."

I grabbed the radio. "Bald Eagle, we're on the edge of the clearing. If you can get a slick in, we can make a run for it. There're only four of us left."

The radio crackled. "That's a mighty hot LZ," said the helicopter unit Commander. "I've lost two guns and another is heading back to base with a shot up crew and a smoking engine. I'm gonna put a slick in there, but you guys better be aboard before he sets down or you ain't gonna get out. Bald Eagle three, see if you can get those boys out of there."

Bald Eagle three came lumbering down at a sharp angle. We burst from cover, running full-out for the place where our ride home would set down. He was about twenty feet off the ground when he exploded in a huge red fireball. He flipped over on his side and bounced off the ground like a gut-shot turkey. Bald Eagle three wasn't going home.

As we started back to the cover, Galis fell. He was a little guy, about five foot six and 130 pounds, prematurely balding. I was six feet, one-hundred-eighty pounds at playing weight and had spent four years of high school running up and down a field with a football. As I ran by Galis I leaned over and scooped him up like a fumble. I don't think I even broke stride. The coach would have been proud of me.

It didn't do any good. Galis was dead. I later wondered how I did that with a bullet hole in my calf. Funny, I don't even remember feeling the leg. I was scared, and the old adrenaline was pumping. I guess there is some ancient memory we all have that reminds us to forget everything else and get away from the carnivore as quickly as possible. Whatever it was, I didn't spend much time in that little clearing thinking about my leg.

The radio was talking as I laid Galis on the ground. "Riding Hood, on your word Bald Eagle two is going to take a shot at you. Same drill."

This chopper boss didn't give up easy.

I remember thinking that those pilots were one bunch of heroes. They kept coming for us, and they kept getting it up the ass from Charlie. There were already more dead air crewman in that little bit of hell than there were dead grunts.

I gave the word, and in came another chopper. Sims, Jimbo and

I were running as fast as we could toward the spot where the helicopter would land. Suddenly, machine gun fire was plowing into the aircraft. I saw the door gunner take one in the face and fall forward, his safety harness holding him half-in and half-out of the side door. The chopper veered up. I learned later that the co-pilot had taken a slug through the chest and was as dead as the gunner. The pilot caught one through the shoulder and another through his thigh.

We could see Charlie or the North Vietnamese, whoever they were, coming out of the jungle. We couldn't go back. The three of us fell behind a coconut log in the clearing.

Bald Eagle came on the radio. "Riding Hood, we can't make it in. It's too hot. We can't get you."

There was an ineffable sadness in his voice, and a tinge of resignation at the imminent death of men he had so desperately tried to save.

"This is Bald Eagle two. I'm going back in."

"Take your position Bald Eagle two. There's nothing else we can do," said the air boss.

I saw the chopper that had made the last try coming our way. His door gunner was still hanging out the door. The pilot was coming toward the clearing at a sharp angle, bow down.

"Goddammit, Scholfield, get back up here. Do you hear me, Scholfield? I'll have your ass Scholfield," screamed the little radio.

I guessed the pilot of Bald Eagle two had to be Scholfield, and he wasn't paying a whole lot of attention to his flight leader. Scholfield dumped his shot-up chopper right in the middle of the landing zone, about twenty yards from us. Bullets were flying toward the aircraft, tracers, even in the daylight looking like Fourth of July fireworks at the big shopping center back home.

We were running at a speed that would have awed Walter

Payton. I'd completely forgotten the little devil sticking the pitchfork in my leg. Jimbo was in the lead, holding his wounded left arm close to his body, then Sims. I was tail end Charlie. Sims took a hit in the back, ran two or three steps, stumbled, and went down. I stopped to pick him up.

Jimbo was on the chopper and got the machine gun in the door working. He was spraying in a ninety-degree arc and hollering at me to keep my head down. I began to sidestroke my way toward the chopper, pulling Sims in a life-saving grasp that I had learned a long time ago in the Boy Scouts. I don't think they recommended it except in the water.

As I reached the helicopter, Jimbo climbed down to help me load Sims. I got in and was tugging on his arms. Merryman was on the ground using his good arm to push on the wounded man's backside. Suddenly, Jimbo dropped. He had taken a shot in the back. The chopper was no more than ten feet off the ground.

In the microsecond it took me to think it out, I saw my mother meeting me at the airport and taking me home for one of her fried chicken dinners. I'd probably attend the memorial service for Jimbo, and tell his wife and kids what a great guy he had been. Maybe I'd even tell them how he saved my ass back there when I was so scared I 'd caved. I could tell them about all he'd taught me, and how I was alive today because of him.

I dropped the ten feet to the ground. I put Jimbo's head in my lap, and for the second time in an hour, waited to die. Then I saw that ridiculous looking shot-up chopper with the maniac driver crab over and land not ten feet from where we were sitting.

I grabbed Jimbo under his arms and started backing toward my taxi as fast as I could. His feet were dragging, and he wasn't moving at all. I got under him and loaded him onto the chopper and started to climb aboard. I heard the pilot scream over the roar of the engine. He was taking the old bag of bolts up. I had my knees on the edge of the door frame when a sledgehammer hit me in the side, and suddenly there was nothing.

* * * * *

I came swimming up out of a black pit. I could see a haze, gray with tinges of red. I tried to wipe it away, but couldn't move my arms. If this was heaven, it sure wasn't like the Baptist preacher of my childhood had described it. I smelled orange blossoms, reminding me of those soft Florida evenings in the warmth of early Spring when the trees are in bloom and the air is saturated with the sweet scent of citrus blossoms.

A soft lady voice told me to take it easy. She told me everything was going to be all right. The blackness returned.

* * * * *

I was staring at a fluorescent light. The orange blossoms were back in bloom. A face came into focus, a soft face with the deepest blue eyes I'd ever seen. It was surrounded by soft red hair, cut short. It had a mouth of full lips with a trace of lipstick. The nose was short, turned up, with a fine spray of freckles across the top. The mouth was moving.

"Can you hear me, Lieutenant?"

"Am I in Florida?"

"No. You're in Saigon. In the 97th General Hospital."

"I smell orange blossoms."

"Oh, it's just that silly perfume one of the men gave me."

"I can't move my arms."

"We've got them taped down, Lieutenant, so you won't tear out the I.V."

"Is Jimbo dead?"

"I don't know any Jimbo."

"He was my sergeant."

"If you mean that big bald headed brute with six stripes named Merryman, he's alive and well and driving everybody nuts. He apparently doesn't think we know how to take care of you. He's in here every hour or so telling us what treatment you need."

"Thank God. I want to see him."

"You get back to sleep now. You can see him tomorrow."

I felt a prick in my shoulder, and the blackness returned.

* * * * *

When I awoke, the morning sun was streaming in the window, and Master Sergeant James B. Merryman was sitting by my bed. He was dressed in a crisp green class A uniform with five rows of ribbons between his breast pocket and the paratrooper jump wings. He was a squatty man, about five feet eight inches and 200 pounds of muscle and bone. His hair was brown, turning to gray and receding up his skull. His remaining hair was cut a quarter-inch off his head. He assured us all that baldness was a sign of virility, and in that department his wife was the envy of every NCO wives club she had ever joined. I always figured he spoke the truth.

He was grinning. "It's about goddamned time you woke up, you sack rat. How are you, kid?"

"I feel like the whole Miami Dolphin defense fell on me, Top," I said, using the title all U.S. Army first sergeants were given by their men.

There was a look of tender concern in that beat up old face. "You're going to be okay, son. I have it on good authority that you're going to be good as new. That pretty little Lieutenant Sloan said you'd be playing football in a few months."

146

"How long have I been here?"

"Two weeks yesterday."

"What happened?"

"Best I can piece it together, when we were trying to get Sims in the bird, I caught one in the back. It was a clean shot and didn't hit anything of importance. That slug had to have come from a long way off and was about out of juice when it got me.

"When I fell, I cracked my old noggin and got knocked out. That crazy pilot was taking off, and you come jumping outta that crate and picked me up. Scholfield set her back down, and you dragged me over and put me in. While you were loading me, you caught one. Except yours was hot, and it kinda tore up your insides. Nothing that can't be fixed, though.

"Then that crazy Scholfield brings that shot up crate back to O'Conner and bounced us around pretty good getting it down. The medics loaded you and me an Sims in a Medivac along with the crazy pilot and flew us down here. The gunner and the co-pilot bought it."

"What about the other two?"

"Sims made it, but he's gonna spend the rest of his life in a wheelchair. Scholfield's over in the next ward with the other Warrants trying to figure out how to screw some of the nurses."

"We lost some good men, Top. Maybe they'll let us go home now. Any word on when we can get out of here?"

"Well, Sir, I guess some good comes out of all the shit. Scholfield got hit in the leg and shoulder, and just as he was pulling out of there, he got one in the gut. It wasn't as serious as it could have been, but I sure don't know how he got us back. Mine wasn't bad at all, and I'll be going back to duty.

"The Army must figure my number's coming up, because they're sending me back to Bragg as an instructor. A year in Korea in '52 shooting at Chicoms and two tours here, I think they're right.

" I've only got two more years before I can take my pension and quit. Scholfield will be going home for discharge, and in about two weeks they're gonna send you back to the world to a real hospital. And while you were laying around here doing nothing you got promoted to First Lieutenant, and next week they're cutting orders promoting me to Sergeant Major. With any luck, I'll retire in a couple of years and move to Florida."

My war was over. After a couple of months at Letterman Army Hospital in San Francisco, I was discharged from the service and came home to Florida to start college.

I kept up with Jimbo Merryman for a few years, and then, for no reason I can think of, our correspondence just drifted off. The last I heard from him was that he was planning to retire to Florida. It's a shame to lose contact with old friends, but it happens too often.

Yeah. I knew Jimbo Merryman.

TWENTY-SIX

"I know him," I said to the sheriff.

"Uncuff them," said the sheriff. "This man won the Distinguished Service Cross in Vietnam. Do you know what that is?"

"No, Sir," the deputy replied.

"It's the second highest award the U.S. Army gives for valor in combat," said the sheriff. "Take those cuffs off."

"But, Sheriff," said the deputy, "these guys almost killed Caldwell."

The sheriff scowled. "He won that medal saving my dad's life. Unhook 'em."

"Okay," mumbled the deputy as he went about unlocking the cuffs.

Jock held up his hands, grinning, his pistol pointed toward the sky. "Sorry about that, Sheriff," he said. "We weren't sure what kind of reception we'd get."

The sheriff nodded.

I was too stunned by what the sheriff had said about my old sergeant to say anything. Jock looked at me and said, "You never told me about the medal."

"It didn't seem important," I said. "I lost most of my team that day, and that's not hero stuff."

I turned to the sheriff. "Are you really Jimbo's kid?" I asked.

"Yes, Sir."

"How is Jimbo?"I asked.

"He's fine. He lives here in Merrit County. He'll be glad to see you. I grew up on stories about how you saved his life."

"Did he tell you that he saved mine?"

"No, that never came up."

"I'm not surprised," I said. "But he did. Ask him about it."

I introduced him to Jock, explaining that Jock was an old high school buddy visiting from Texas.

* * * * *

We were sitting in the sheriff's office. He was behind a big desk, Jock and I in side chairs facing him. There were no windows, and fluorescent lighting gave the place the feel of a hospital waiting room. There were no pictures on the walls, no plaques or certificates. Just a bare room with a minimum of furniture. Jock and I had dictated statements to a secretary who was typing them up in the next room.

Sheriff Kyle Merryman leaned back in his chair. "Caldwell is finished. I've heard rumors that he was quick with that billy he likes to carry, but I've never been able to prove it. Your statements will give me the leverage I need to fire him."

I nodded. "Why have you kept him on until now?"

"His dad's on the county commission, and I have to go to them every year to fund this office. Caldwell senior is a bully, and he won't like that I've fired his boy. It always just seemed easier to go along to get along. I keep Caldwell junior, and the commission gives me the budget I ask for."

"What about now?" I asked.

"I don't think there'll be a problem. The other commissioners will go along with me when they get proof that Caldwell is abusing citizens. They kind of looked the other way when it was just Mexicans."

Jock grinned. "Sounds like a nice little county you got here," he said.

The sheriff thought about that for a minute. "It's not all bad. This was a quiet little place until old Senator Foster started buying up property. Turned a lot of good ranch land into truck farms and started bringing in the Mexicans to work them."

"Senator?" I said.

"Used to be," said the sheriff. "He served in the state senate forty years ago, and he likes to use the title. Everybody just got in the habit of using it, too."

"What can you tell us about him?" I asked.

"Not a whole lot. Why? You interested in buying some vegetables?"

I laughed. "Not exactly."

I was about to tell him what I'd heard about the senator when the office door burst open.

A big man from my past came through the door. "Matt, you shavetail son-of-a-bitch."

I stood to shake Jimbo Merryman's hand, and he grabbed me in a bear hug. I hugged back. The years had been kind to my old sergeant. He was still fit, his hair now completely gray, and what little was left was still worn in a buzz cut. His voice was undiminished, loud and brash and southern.

"God, it's good to see you," he said. "When Kyle called, I couldn't believe it. I thought by now some jealous husband would've shot your ass dead."

"It's good to see you, too, Jimbo." My voice cracked; tears were welling in my eyes. Shit. I couldn't break down here. Not in front of the two toughest men I'd ever known. What the hell was wrong

151

with me?

I disengaged from the big soldier, quickly wiped my face on my shirt sleeve, and mumbled. "Got something in my eye."

The others pretended not to notice.

I introduced Jimbo to Jock. "This tub of guts saved my ass in the Nam."

Jock stared at Jimbo. "Could've saved us all a lot of trouble if you'd just left him there."

"I would've, except the brass kind of frowned on us losing lieutenants. I was just trying to make rank."

Jock chuckled. "I hear you, Sergeant Major," he said. "I hear you."

Jimbo said, "I guess you know he saved my life that day in the bush."

"He never mentioned it," said Jock. "Not once, and I've known him his whole life."

Jimbo grinned. "Not surprised," he said. "When you all get through here, Kyle's going to bring you by the house for supper. I'll tell you the whole story."

"I'd love to see Molly," I said, "but we don't want to just show up on short notice."

"Too late. Molly's already cooking. I'll see y'all at the house."

When Jimbo was gone, the sheriff turned to me. "Now, tell me why you're interested in the senator."

I sat quietly for a moment. "Kyle," I said, "I don't know if I can trust you. You've kept a corrupt cop on your payroll for your own benefit. You've got what appears to be a slave labor camp in your county, and this rogue deputy is obviously protecting the people who run it. He had no other reason to stop us or to try to rough us up. Tell me why I should trust you."

The sheriff leaned back in his chair and used both hands to massage his temples, all the while looking straight at me. "I don't know if I can trust you either, Matt. A lot of water has gone under the bridge since you and my dad were in Nam together. Show me a card, and let's see how the hand plays out."

I looked at Jock. He nodded. "Okay," I said. "Somebody's trying to kill me. We think it's tied up with illegal immigrants and drugs. A Border Patrol agent who's been working with Jock and me told us about a camp here in Merrit County."

"What's the Border Patrol guy's name?"

"Paul Reich."

The sheriff reached into a drawer in his desk and pulled out a cell phone. "Did you know you can buy these little phones at convenience stores over in Ft. Myers?" he said. "They have a limited number of minutes to use, and then you throw them away. They're completely anonymous. Untraceable."

He dialed a number, and then said into the phone, "This is Viper. Let me talk to Reich."

Then, after a moment, "Agent Reich, this is Viper, authentication code Friar Tuck. I'm about to blow my cover, but I need you to vouch for me."

Kyle handed me the phone. "Tell him what you need to."

"Paul?" I asked.

"Yeah. Who's this?"

"Matt Royal."

"Good Christ, Matt. How did you find Viper?"

"Actually, he found us. Your Viper is Sheriff Merryman."

"Holy shit! You're sure?"

"Jock and I are sitting in his office in the courthouse. Turns out his dad's an old friend of mine."

"Viper's been giving us good information, but we haven't been able to figure out who he is. I'll be down there this evening. We need to talk."

"Here's the sheriff," I said. "See you soon."

I handed the phone to Kyle. He told Reich to come to his dad's house and gave directions.

I told Kyle about the attempts on my life and our trip to Mexico, and what we'd turned up.

The sheriff frowned, and was quiet for a moment. Then, "I know about the camp. I didn't know how the Mexicans got here. I knew Caldwell was hooked into the bad guys, and I think his dad is, too, but I can't prove anything. Casey is the enforcer. He makes sure the Mexicans don't get out of line, and he scares off anybody who looks too closely."

Jock said, "Who else has been looking?"

The sheriff said, "We get some immigration advocates coming around sometimes, and Caldwell just stops them and suggests they leave the county and don't come back. I've gotten a couple of complaints, but they're anonymous. I guess folks don't trust anybody in our department."

I asked, "How long has this been going on?"

"About a year now, maybe a little less. I got the first complaint from a farm worker advocate in January. It was an unsigned letter telling me that there was a labor camp in my county, and that the people were virtually slaves. Apparently this person had been told to leave the county by a deputy."

"What did you do?" asked Jock.

"I made an anonymous call to the Border Patrol office in Tampa. I have a small force, and I didn't know which deputy was bent. I did know that the Mexicans were working for the senator, so I figured he must be involved.

"I didn't know whether anybody at the Border Patrol might be on the payroll. Never heard back from them, so I became Viper. Turns out they were concerned about the Sheriff of Merrit County. I've ben running my own investigation and, as Viper, keeping the Border Patrol posted."

I asked, "What have you found out?"

"Not much. I think a guy named Jimmy Wilkerson is running the camp, but that name is probably an alias. He has no record of any kind in any of the data bases. Not even a record of his birth."

"We know about Wilkerson," I said, and related the events in Orlando and in eastern Manatee County. "Tell me about the senator. His title keeps coming up, but we've never heard a name until now."

Kyle smiled. "The senator. He's an odd duck."

The sheriff told us that the senator, whose name was Conrad Foster, was in his late seventies, and, as a young man, had been elected to the state senate. He left after one term because of some improprieties that were never made public. He liked being called "Senator," so people still accorded him the courtesy title.

He had grown up in eastern Sarasota County on a large truck farm owned by his father. Once he inherited, the senator, with a little help from his political cronies, expanded the holdings until he was one of the largest land owners in the state of Florida. His holdings included cattle ranches, citrus groves and truck farms.

He employed a lot of people, most of them Mexicans, and most of them illegal. He'd never been charged with any labor law violations himself, but once in a while the Border Patrol would sweep down on his farms and arrest some of the illegals. It didn't happen often, and the number of arrestees was small enough not to make a dent in the senator's operations.

There had been rumors for years that the senator paid off the politicians to keep his operations solvent and keep the flow of labor unimpeded. No one knew anything for sure, and there had never been an investigation.

Kyle leaned back in his chair, his booted feet on the desk. "A couple of years ago, the senator bought up several small cattle ranches in Merrit County, plowed them up and planted crops," he said. "The old Cracker cowboys moved on, and the Mexicans started showing up."

Jock said, "And nobody's doing anything about the illegals."

The sheriff grimaced. "No. The big farmers and the big construction companies don't want to lose the cheap labor, and they put a lot of political pressure on the Border Patrol. They'll make a show of raiding some small farmer from time to time, but the senator doesn't get bothered much. I think once in a while he'll lose a few workers, but that's planned. Don't want it to look like he's getting any special treatment."

"Where does Paul Reich fit in?" I asked.

"Far as I can tell, Reich is straight as an arrow. He's probably got some juice in Washington, so the locals don't mess with him. If we can find the proof, he'll take the senator down, and the hell with the consequences."

Jock leaned forward. "Then that's what we'll do," he said.

TWENTY-SEVEN

Jimbo Merryman lived in a small ranch house situated on a large lot facing a short dirt road that ran off the main highway, out near the edge of town. No other houses were visible as we parked in his driveway.

A large banyan tree shaded the front yard, and azalea bushes filled the beds on either side of the front stoop. A well tended lawn of emerald green grass surrounded the house like a thick carpet. An ancient citrus tree sunned itself at the corner of the home. Spring would bring brilliant color to the flowering trees and hedges, and the smell of citrus blossoms would sweeten the air.

Jimbo had come home from the wars, at last.

We trooped up the sidewalk, the sheriff in the lead. Suddenly, the front door burst open, and out came a large lady, moving at full speed. She was wearing a mumu in a bright floral design, big red flowers nestled on a sea of yellow. Her gray hair was in a bun at the back of her neck, her large blue eyes hinting at the beauty she had been when she was young.

She rushed passed Kyle, whooping with joy. "Matt, you rascal. God, I've missed you."

She enveloped me in a bear hug, then leaned back, hands on my shoulders. "You're still a handsome devil," she gushed. "I don't think you've changed at all. Still got all your hair and there's no gray. When old Jimbo croaks, I'm coming for you."

I laughed. "Jock Algren, meet the inimitable Molly Merryman, the woman who finally domesticated the Sergeant Major."

"Not completely," she said, chuckling. "Kyle, don't just stand there. Get our guests inside and find them something to drink."

"Yes, Ma'am," said the sheriff, grinning as he led us into the house.

Jimbo was coming in through the sliding glass doors that led to his lanai and screened pool. "Got the charcoal going," he said. "The steaks will be ready soon. The Border Patrol guy called for directions. He should be right along."

Kyle was rattling around in the kitchen, the sound of ice dropping into tumblers reaching out to the family room over-looking the pool. "Name your poison, gents," he called out.

Jock and I both ordered bourbon on the rocks. Jimbo asked for a scotch, and told us to make ourselves comfortable. Kyle brought the drinks and joined us. We sat in the overstuffed furniture and sipped our whiskey, Jimbo telling us about his quiet life in a small town. He needed action, and was looking forward to the next few days. The old soldier was ready to join up and help us take down the bad guys.

The sheriff sat quietly, watching his dad, concern etching his face. Molly had excused herself and was making salads in the kitchen.

"Dad," said Kyle, "tell Matt about the heart attack."

"Nothing to it," said Jimbo. "Docs fixed me right up."

Molly coughed from the kitchen doorway. "No, they didn't," she said, "not all the way. He has to take it easy, Matt, so we need to keep him out of this mess with the Mexicans."

"Ah, Mol," said Jimbo, "I can take care of myself."

"He's like an old fire horse," said Molly. "The alarms go off, and he's ready to run, pull the wagon, get smoke in his nostrils. He doesn't understand that he can't do that any more."

I raised my drink. "Top, you're the best soldier I ever met, or even heard of, but you're only a Sergeant Major, and Molly's the General."

Turning to Molly, I added, "We'll follow orders, ma'am."

"Thank you, Matt," she said, and returned to her kitchen.

Jimbo frowned, and then smiled, and waived his drink in a dismissive gesture. "Okay, okay, I know when to retreat," he said. "I'll stay out of it, but keep me posted on what's going down."

A car door slammed. "That'll be Paul Reich," said Kyle, getting up and moving toward the front door.

When introductions were made, and he had a tall scotch and water in his hand, Paul began to talk. He was excited about what we'd put together so far, but he was concerned about a leak in his operation. He hadn't told any of his people that he'd contacted me about Juan Anasco, nor had he ever told them about Viper. No one knew he'd come to meet us, and he wanted to keep it that way.

"We've known about the leak for some time," Paul said. "That's why I was brought in from D.C. The people at the top gave me a blank check on this one. I can get pretty much anything I want.

"A lot of the information that comes directly to me stays with me. I never told anybody about Viper, because he was giving me good intelligence, and I was afraid somebody would leak the information to the bad guys. If that happened, they'd shut down before we could get to them.

"Jock, you and Matt turned up at just the right time. I was able to use you for intelligence gathering when I couldn't use my own people. I've kept David Parrish in the loop, and Rufus Harris has been a big help. He's clean, but we're not sure about his people. The leak may be in DEA instead of in our shop."

Jimbo settled himself deeper into his chair, and said, "Matt, what about this guy Logan Hamilton? You've kept him in the loop. Is he good people?"

I nodded my head. "He was a chopper jockey in Nam, Top. Won a silver star for pulling some grunts out of a bad situation. Got shot up doing it, too. I think he was a lot like our old buddy Scholfield. I'd trust him with my life."

"Good enough for me," said the Sergeant Major.

Kyle rattled the ice in his glass, took a last sip of gin and said, "You know the problems in my department. I'll be taking some heat in the next few days over that idiot Casey Caldwell. His old man is going to stir up a shit-storm with the County Commission."

Reich frowned. "How's that going to affect what you do?"

"It won't," said the sheriff. "I got more votes in the last election that any of the commissioners, and they won't screw with me too much. It'll all die down in a few days."

Jock nodded. "We may not have a few days."

"I know," said Kyle. "I'll be here for whatever you need. Just keep in mind that the only manpower I can provide is myself. I'm down to two deputies, and I wouldn't trust them either of them right now on this thing."

Reich said, "Actually, I think we do have a few days. If we want to bust both the immigrant and the drug rings, we need to wait until the *Princess Sarah* gets to Florida. She hasn't left port yet, and Emilio is still in Tlapa waiting for the bus."

Jock grinned. "So," he said, "Emilio pulled it off."

"Yeah," said Reich. "He's made contact with Arguilles and is in the next group to be taken to Veracruz. Apparently Arguilles was contacted by Mendez' replacement, and he's still in business. Arguilles is pissed about Pepe and the two dead guys, so he's cooperating."

Jimbo had been quiet during the entire conversation. Now he

said, "Does anybody have any idea when the trawler will start toward Florida?"

Reich turned to Jimbo. "The DEA folks think they'll time their arrival to coincide with the new moon," he said. "That'll happen next Wednesday night, so we're betting the boat will leave Veracruz on Wednesday or Thursday of this week. It'll take six days to make the crossing, so they'll get here just as the moon goes dark."

"So," I said, "We've got nine days to get everything ready. How're you going to set this up?"

Reich said, "We'll put together a task force. I'll have either the Customs people or my folks in Miami send us some agents on a need-to-know basis. We'll keep everything under wraps until the day of the bust, so there'll be little chance of a leak. We'll involve Longboat Key PD and the Coast Guard, but they can come in at the last minute. Rufus and I'll be the only ones in the Tampa and Orlando offices to be in on it."

The rest of the evening was given over to quiet talk, good steaks and one more drink. Some of us had to drive. Jock and I would head back to Longboat Key, and Paul Reich was going to make the three hour drive to Orlando.

TWENTY-EIGHT

On Tuesday morning, Jock got a call on his cell phone from Emilio. He'd be boarding the mini-bus in Tlapa that afternoon, headed for Veracruz. Everything was going well, so far. Jock told him to be careful.

On Tuesday afternoon, Jock left for Houston. We couldn't do anything more until the trawler arrived off Longboat Key, so he was going to get a little work done in his office.

Logan had decided to go about his business, and left that morning for Atlanta.

Life on the key settled back into routine. I began jogging on the beach at sunrise, but I drove to a different spot on the island each day and ran on part of the beach that was not my customary route. It didn't hurt to be careful.

On Wednesday morning, Anne Dubose called and asked if I could have lunch with her at the Sport's Page Bar and Grill on Main Street in downtown Sarasota. She said we needed to talk. I agreed, and drove there with much the same enthusiasm as that of a condemned man shuffling toward the gallows.

I was early and took a seat at the bar to wait for Anne. I ordered a diet coke and told the bartender that I'd be having lunch as soon as my friend arrived.

I was focused on the TV above the bar, watching the noon news on a local channel, when Anne came in. She tapped me on the shoulder, and as I turned, she kissed me on the cheek.

"Hi, Handsome," she said.

She was wearing medium heels, a beige linen dress adorned with small embroidered flowers. She was carrying a briefcase, looking very much like a lawyer.

"You look great," I said. "I've missed you."

"Can we get a table?"

"Sure," I said, and led her across the room to a table in the corner.

I didn't think for a minute that she hadn't heard me tell her I'd missed her. She just flat hadn't missed me. I'd been around long enough to know that when a guy's significant other mentions the need for "talk," some bad stuff is about to fall in on him.

I helped her with her chair, and then I sat. The waitress showed up and took our drink orders, a diet coke for me and a glass of Chardonnay for Anne.

I raised my eyebrows. She didn't usually drink until the evening, and then not very much.

"Oh," she said. "I'm taking the afternoon off. I've been in court all morning."

"I've missed you," I said.

"You already mentioned that."

"It's been over a week since we went to Egmont."

"You were in Mexico."

"For part of the time."

She frowned. "Are you being difficult?"

"Sorry. I don't mean to be."

The waitress brought our drinks and took our food order. Anne asked for a small salad with vinaigrette dressing, and I ordered a Caesar.

I sat quietly, waiting. Whatever Anne had to say would be said, and I didn't want to prolong things. When you know somebody is about to stomp on your heart, all you can do is take it and get on with your life.

She was quiet, too, not wanting to get into it. I'd wait her out, I thought. She raised her wine glass to her lips, thought better of it, and put the glass back on the table. "I've met someone," she said, finally.

The shoe had dropped, and I could feel the pain dancing at the edges of my soul, building in intensity, threatening to overwhelm me, to burst out in anger and calumny. But I didn't have the right. Anne didn't belong to me, and she was now slipping inexorably beyond my grasping need for her, a need I had not fully appreciated until that very moment. I'd anticipated her leaving, but I hadn't expected the searing pain that was even now coursing through my consciousness.

"And?" It was all I could manage, and my voice cracked on that single syllable.

"And I think we shouldn't see each other any more. Not like that, is what I mean. Of course, we can see each other as friends, but not lovers. I don't want to lose the friendship."

She was rambling, trying to put a good face on an ugly event. Then she was quiet again.

I let her stew for a beat. "Who's the guy?" I said.

"You don't know him. He's a stockbroker here in Sarasota."

I was quiet, trying to marshal an argument to convince her to stay with me. It was fruitless, and I knew it in my gut. I just sat there.

"Well," she said, finally, "say something."

I pushed back my chair and stood. I dropped a twenty- dollar bill on the table. "I love you, Anne," I said, and I walked out of the restaurant.

The October sun was blinding as it reflected off the cars parked along the street. I was making a fool of myself, and I was well aware of it. I would have to apologize to Anne later, but I couldn't continue this conversation at that moment.

I started walking west, toward the bay. This was the same pain I'd felt when my former wife Laura told me she was leaving. Only, I hadn't seen that one coming. I had been so absorbed in myself that it never occurred to me that Laura wanted more than I was willing to give.

I knew what was coming with Anne, but that knowledge did nothing to blunt the pain of the reality. Suddenly, my arm was caught in a tight grip.

"Matt, you bastard," Anne said. "You can't tell me you love me and then just run off."

I stopped walking and turned to face her. "I'm sorry, Anne. I just can't handle this right now. I've been swimming in a tub-full of crap for the past ten days, and now this. It's just very bad timing."

"Matt, you don't love me. You've never told me that before. We've had something pretty wonderful, but we both knew it wasn't forever."

"I know, Anne, I know. I'm sorry I said that. I guess I was trying to make you feel bad about this, because it does hurt."

"I know, Baby, but we've got to move on." She leaned in and kissed me lightly on the lips. "Call me next week."

I mumbled something that must have sounded like "yes" or "okay," and she turned on her heel and walked off, her pretty butt swinging down Main Street like she owned the place. And maybe she did, in the way that beautiful young women can make an otherwise drab place light up just by being there. They make the place theirs, and they may not even know it.

Then, she was gone. We both knew I wouldn't call. And the

rottenest surprise of all, was that in that moment I understood that I did love her.

* * * * *

On Thursday, I got a call from Rufus Harris. The *Princess Sarah* had put to sea at midnight. Emilio was aboard.

TWENTY-NINE

On Wednesday afternoon, a week later, I was sitting in Bill Lester's office, a cup of black coffee in my hand. I sipped it, while Bill worked his phone, talking quietly to the people he needed to reach.

The key had been quiet during the last week. In a fit of caution, I'd changed my routine again, doing my jogging on the sidewalk that ran along Gulf of Mexico Drive. I hadn't heard from Anne, and I didn't think I would.

Logan had flown in late on Thursday, and the next evening we had a few at Tiny's before I headed down the island to the Colony, my regular stop on a Friday evening. The smooth voice of Debbie Keeton, the jazz singer who performed in the Monkey Bar on weekends, was the best way for me to wind down a week.

Logan always had some adventure to relate, and the one for this week was worse than most. It seems that he'd been to a barbeque with his boss on Thursday evening, and he'd consumed a lot of baked beans. His flight from Atlanta to Sarasota late that night was in a small regional jet, and he was crammed into a seat next to a fat elderly lady who smelled of gin and moth balls.

The beans were doing their dance in Logan's stomach, causing the usual rise in gaseous pressure. He would quietly release the gas

167

as he pretended to sleep. The old fat lady would grunt every time he let go. Finally, she took to elbowing him, which, according to Logan, only increased the effusion of noxious odors.

When they landed, Logan smiled at the lady, and said, "I hope you enjoyed the trip, ma'am." He left the woman sitting in her seat, sputtering in her rage and stabbing futilely at the flight attendant call button

That image brought a chuckle, and the chief looked sharply at me, bringing me back to the present. Finally, he hung up the phone, rousing me from my revery.

"What's so funny?" he said.

"Nothing. I was just thinking of a story Logan told us Friday night."

"Okay," Bill said. "The Blue Lightning Strike Force is up and running. We'll meet here tomorrow afternoon at five. You and Jock are welcome. Logan will be your liaison with Sheriff Merryman."

"Tell me about this Strike Force," I said.

Bill told me that some years before, in a rare spirit of co-operation, the U.S. Customs Service had set up a joint command structure with local police that could be activated on an ad hoc basis. Each local department would cross-designate a few officers as U.S. Customs agents. After training, in which the locals learned about boarding practices, space accountability, detention on the water, and other duties not normally encountered by them, they were certified as customs officers. This gave local law enforcement agencies jurisdiction in federal and international waters.

Bill laughed ruefully. "Most of the time, the feds just leave us out. It's a money thing," he said. "If we confiscate a boat or other property used in the crime, we sell it and the money goes into the Asset Forfeiture Fund. That money is then divided among the agencies involved in the take-down. The fewer the agencies, the more money each gets."

"So, crime does pay," I said.

Bill smiled, "Pays us, sometimes," he said. "They can't really cut us out when we initiate the bust. Like now."

* * * * *

It was late afternoon when I left the police station. Jock had flown in from Houston, and Logan picked him up at the Sarasota-Bradenton airport. We'd agreed to meet at the Bridge Tender Inn in Bradenton Beach for a drink, so I pointed the Explorer north.

When you cross the Longboat Pass Bridge onto Anna Maria Island, you leave New Florida and pass into Old Florida. The state has changed drastically in the past twenty years, and what's left of the Florida of my childhood is sequestered in little enclaves like Anna Maria Island.

The big condos have not yet invaded, and there are still places where working people can afford to live. The bars are not as trendy, and they're louder, more real somehow. Small motels run by the same owners for a generation cling to the beaches, their guests returning year after year.

But taxes keep rising, and the mom and pop places are beginning to dry up. For some reason, not apparent to the average person, Florida mandates that property be taxed at a rate that reflects its highest and best use. If a forty year old motel with twenty rooms could legally be turned into a high-rise condominium with twenty units, it'll be taxed at the condo rate.

This obtuse tax philosophy was driving the mom and pop beach motels out of business. All along the coast, the owners were selling their property to condo developers. Fewer hotel rooms meant fewer tourists, and the gift shops and restaurants that depended on visitors for their livelihood were being forced to close.

The reality of the onerous tax structure is that it signals the imminent death of the Florida of my childhood. It's turning the state into Baby Boomer Heaven.

Reality is not something that Florida politicians recognize, so Old Florida is slowly dying, its demise hurried along by developers and the tax man. It'll all be gone soon, and those of us who love the state will be poorer in spirit.

The Bridge Tender Inn takes up space at the foot of Bridge Street, across from the city pier in Bradenton Beach. Jock and Logan were at the bar, Jock sipping a beer from its bottle and Logan nursing a scotch and water. I pulled up a stool and ordered a Miller Lite.

Jock tipped the bottle toward me. "How did it go?"

"We're in," I said. "The chief has set something called the Blue Lightning Strike Force in motion. It'll be a joint effort by Sarasota PD, Customs, DEA, and the Longboat police. We're going along as observers. Logan, Bill wants you to go to Merrit County and be our contact with the sheriff."

Logan said, "When?"

"Tomorrow night. We're meeting at the Longboat Police station at five tomorrow afternoon. The Blue Lightning people in Miami told Bill that the trawler is moving northeast and should be in position off Longboat by then."

"I hope Emilio's all right," said Jock.

I raised my glass in silent agreement.

Logan pointed to a couple at a corner table. "Isn't that Marie Phillips?" he asked.

I hadn't seen Marie since the evening at Pattigeorge's, but there was no mistaking her striking good looks. She was seated across from a man who appeared to be in his late thirties or early forties. He was wearing a Hawaiian shirt hanging loose over khaki pants.

Marie was in shorts, golf shirt and sandals. A casual night on the island.

I said to Logan, "Do you know who her date is? He looks familiar."

"I'm not sure, but isn't he one of the Sarasota County deputies who came to the Hilton the night somebody shot at us?"

"That's it," I said. "I wonder what he's doing with a woman whose monthly condo fees are more than he makes."

Nobody had an answer.

We ate at the bar, talking quietly about things that had nothing to do with the pending operation. Night had fallen, and we could see the twinkling of mast lights on the sailboats moored in the bay in front of the restaurant and the colored lights of the nearby Cortez Bridge. At some point Marie and her deputy slipped out without our noticing.

"Nobody's tried to kill me in over a week," I said. "I wonder if I should be insulted."

Jock chuckled. "Probably, you just aren't worth killing."

I laughed. "That's a sad state of affairs," I said.

"I'm serious," said Jock. "Whoever was trying to take you out probably wanted to stop you from talking to the cops. Since they didn't get you early on, they must have figured you didn't know anything, or if you did, you already told the police."

"Makes sense, I guess."

"We're not letting our guard down, though. You never know."

THIRTY

The conference at the Longboat Police station was packed. Rufus Harris and Paul Reich were there drinking coffee from Styrofoam cups with the Starbucks logo. Two uniformed Sarasota police officers, the Longboat Key marine cop dressed in shorts and a golf shirt, a tall thin man in a black suit, white shirt and black tie, and Bill Lester had the other seats. Introductions were made by the Longboat chief.

Pointing to the black suited man, Bill said, "This is Abe McClintoc from Customs. He'll be in tactical command."

McClintoc nodded. "Let's get to it, then," he said. "We've got a delicate operation here. We need to get the go-fast boats in and unloaded, and the immigrants off the premises before we bust the drugs. We'll have the Coast Guard standing by to intercept the trawler after everything else goes down. We don't want somebody shooting or dumping the immigrants because they find out we're onto them. And we've got an agent aboard the trawler posing as an illegal."

A Sarasota cop raised his hand. "Do we even know which island they're going to?" he asked.

McClintoc shook his head. "No," he said, "but we know they'll be coming into Sarasota Bay. At least that's what they've done in

172

the past, and they're on course for Longboat as we speak. I'll explain the surveillance in a minute. We'll find out where they're going and then take it from there.

"We'll have a P-3 surveillance aircraft out of Jacksonville flying cover, and it'll have the trawler on radar. We also have a tracking device on the trawler that's being monitored through satellite downloads to our operations center in Miami. In case everything else fails, the Florida Marine Patrol platform and its hundred-mile radar will be anchored off Casey Key.

"If they surprise us and veer off to Siesta or Casey Keys, we'll make adjustments."

The platform he was referring to is a sixty-foot sport fisherman confiscated a couple of years before in a drug bust. It bristled with radar and other electronic gadgets, and was used by the authorities when they didn't have the P-3. This time, it would be back-up.

McClintoc continued. "We're pretty sure the go-fasts will have outboards. If they're going up a canal at night, those big inboards with the thru-hull exhausts would make too much noise."

The Customs agent turned to the wall behind him, from which hung a large chart of Sarasota Bay and the adjacent coastal waters. "We think they'll have several boats and they'll come in at different passes. One will come in here, at Passage Key Inlet."

He pointed to the area just north of Bean Point, the northern-most end of Anna Maria Island. "He'll have to come into the channel to get across the Bulkhead. That's a very shallow sandbar across the mouth of Anna Maria Sound. He can then turn in short and run into Bimini Bay.

"If he doesn't do that, he'll have to cross underneath the Manatee Avenue Bridge. We'll station a fully equipped Customs boat there, and that boat can let us know if he veers off before getting to the bridge." McClintoc pointed to a bit of land known to the locals as Gilligan's Island, that hunkered just above the water near the eastern side of the narrow channel over the Bulk-head.

"We'll have a man in the bridge tenders' shacks on both the Manatee and Cortez bridges. If the go-fast bears off to his left into Palma Sola Bay, we'll know it when he doesn't get to the Cortez Bridge. If he goes under Cortez, he'll have to follow the channel south, inside of Jewfish Key.

"We'll have another boat tied up at Moore's restaurant to let us know where he heads after he clears Jewfish. This boat will also keep tabs on anybody coming in Longboat Pass. And we'll have a man in the tender's shack on that bridge. Any questions, so far?"

The Longboat marine cop stirred. "Just to make sure, we're not to follow them or make any approach to them," he said.

"No." said McClintoc, "It's impossible to follow somebody on the water without being seen. The Customs boats all have radar and will be able to track them without moving."

"Why doesn't the P-3 just keep tabs on them?" asked one of the Sarasota officers.

"Ground clutter," answered the Customs agent. "The P-3 will probably be able to keep tabs on the boats, but this other is all just back-up in case there's a problem."

"What about the other passes?" Bill Lester asked.

McClintoc took a sip of his coffee. "Okay," he said. "We'll have a boat in Big Pass. I'll be on that one, and Jock and Matt will ride with me. We'll have to be very careful not to be found out.

"If the boat comes in the channel he'll either have to pass under the Ringling Causeway Bridge, or he can cut off into that little channel that runs between St. Armand's and Bird Keys over by the Sarasota Yacht Club. We can put a man on the Ringling Bridge, but the little bridge just past the Yacht Club has 'no fishing' signs posted on it. We don't want them getting suspicious.

"We'll have to keep tabs on that boat with our radar and heat detecting gear. If one of them goes up the little channel, we'll move out into Sarasota Bay. He'll be visible to us when he comes back out into New Pass.

"We'll have a man on the New Pass Bridge, and the Longboat police boat anchored close into the mainland at mid-bay to keep anything moving that way on radar."

Bill Lester stood up. "Sounds like a plan. Any questions?"

There was silence.

"Okay," said Bill, "We'll see you guys tonight."

THIRTY-ONE

Low clouds scudded across the dark sky, their passing evidenced only by the winking on and off of stars. The new moon hung between the earth and its life-giving star, its orb dark without the sun's reflection. The tide was ebbing, and the water flowed languidly toward the Gulf. Black water lapped gently against the boat's hull, the only sound in the enveloping quietness of the wee hours.

Jock and I were passengers on a Customs Service boat, a 32-foot Intrepid powered by twin 250 horsepower outboards. The boat was equipped with a gyro stabilized heat detecting night vision array that could detect something as small as a crab trap float a mile away. The radios had frequencies that connected us with all the other partners in the Blue Lightning Strike Force. Our radar would pick up any boats within a fifteen-mile radius.

We were anchored close in to shore on the Lido Key side of Big Sarasota Pass. Large sandbars have crept into the inlet over the years, blocking much of it. The boat channel ran from the south along the beach on the northern edge of Siesta Key before turning east into the pass itself. It then hugged the shore of Siesta Key on the south side of the inlet before easing into mid-pass as it made its way into Sarasota Bay. We were nestled on the northern side of the waterway, far enough west so that a boat turning into the channel running to the Sarasota Yacht Club wouldn't see us.

Our boat was painted black, and if the bad guys had radar, we'd be lost in the clutter of the Australian pines that lined the beach. Our job was just to observe and let the other agencies know if any of the boats came our way.

Two Customs agents wearing military fatigues and carrying M-16s rested on the pull-down seats in the stern. McClintoc was at the helm. Another agent manned the radios, earphones strapped to his head so that no noise escaped. The engines were shut down, and conversations were carried on in whispers.

Sixteen thousand feet above us, the Customs Service's P-3 aircraft circled, its radar tuned to the trawler and its pups. The aircrew could search a 200,000 square mile area every eight seconds. Tonight, it was centered on the action off Longboat Key.

The Blue Light Operations Center in Miami, or BLOC as it was known to the law enforcement community, advised that the target trawler had gone stationary about twenty miles offshore of Longboat's mid-key area. The P-3 added that five small boats had been waiting in the area for an hour or so.

The radioman coughed quietly. "He's dropped anchor. They'll begin off-loading soon."

We waited. I could feel the tension emanating from the agents. Jock seemed unconcerned. He and I were both armed with our nine millimeters. I didn't think we'd need them, but they gave me a sense of security.

Time crawled, the minutes creeping by in slow motion, tension building in my chest. I was ready for action, any action, but we sat silently as my mind wandered over the landscape of the last few days. I thought about Anne, wishing she were home waiting for me, and imagining her in the arms of somebody else. I thought I had prepared myself for the end of the relationship, and I was surprised at how much it hurt. I had the fleeting thought that her life was moving on, and would be peopled with a husband, children and friends I'd never know, while my life stood still, a lonely man swirling in the eddies of years dwindling down toward oblivion.

And the dead came to visit, as they often do in the night. Ghosts of lost soldiers danced around the edges of my consciousness, reminding me that I lived and they didn't. My grandmother's frying chicken crackled in my memory banks as she stood at the ancient stove in the small house where I grew up, her dark hair tied in a tight bun at the base of her neck. I thought of other friends, too; gone now into the unknowable world of death, my memory of their sojourn in life receding like the wake of a passing boat.

The radioman's whisper broke the silence. "They're moving in every direction. Three are coming this way. They'll be fast with the flat sea tonight."

Silence again, then from the radioman, "The P-3 advises the ones coming this way are hitting fifty knots. They'll be here in about twenty minutes. The heat signatures say outboards, so we might not hear them until they're on top of us. Those new four stroke engines are quiet."

The silence gathered again. We sat, each man lost in his own thoughts.

I looked over at Jock. He smiled, and whispered, "We're back in action, Podner."

More minutes passed. The radioman spoke, "P-3 says one of the boats is headed for New Pass. The other two are coming this way."

Adrenalin, my old friend, began to leak into my tissue. My heart rate went up. The night seemed even quieter, more intense. My ears took on an acuity I had not known since the war. I could hear birds rustling in the bushes that lined the beach just behind us. An owl cried nearby, its mournful sound signaling doom for some unsuspecting rodent. Then, far out, I heard the faint sound of powerful outboard engines.

"They're coming," I said.

"Heads up," said McClintoc. "Turn on your night vision equipment."

The radar screen on the dash showed blips racing down the Gulf, heading south to pick up the Big Pass sea bouy and the channel. The heat detecting equipment was lit up by the outboards churning away at top speed.

The blips made a sharp turn into the channel, hugging the Siesta Key shore, running northeast into Big Pass. As they came onto a more easterly course toward the bay, we could see them in the night vision goggles.

I said, "I see a lot of people in the second boat."

"Got 'em," said McClintoc. "There's only the driver and a rifleman in the lead boat."

The boats were on plane, running at top speed, the whine of their big outboards now buzzing in my ear, drowning out the sounds of the night birds. They were dark, no running lights visible. The vessels were identical, about thirty feet in length, center consoles, with big twins hanging off their transoms. No T-tops or biminis - these were stripped down boats.

As they came abreast of us, I could see about a dozen people, sitting on the deck of the trailing boat, their heads poking above the port gunwale. A rifleman stood in the stern behind the pilot, the stock of his M-16 resting on his hip, the barrel pointing toward the sky.

Their wakes rolled under us, tossing us a bit and straining the anchor rode. The second boat peeled off, crossing the wake of the lead vessel, running on a diagonal toward the entrance to the

Yacht Club channel. The first go-fast maintained a heading for Sarasota Bay.

McClintoc put his hand on the radioman's shoulder. "Tell Chief Lester that we're moving into the bay, and to watch out for two coming his way from the south."

The big Mercs on our boat came to life, and we eased quietly out into the main channel. We could still see the lead boat heading east into the bay. Suddenly his running lights came on.

"What the hell?" I said.

McClintoc shrugged. "He'll draw less attention to himself with his lights on."

We eased slowly into the bay itself just as the lead boat ran under the Ringling Causeway bridge at full speed.

The radioman spoke up. "Chief Lester has them both on radar and the P-3 is still tracking. The boat with the people slowed at the yacht club to clear that short bridge. Now, he's around the City Island point and turning in tight on the channel that runs close in on the bay side of Longboat Key."

"Good," said McClintoc, as he pulled the throttles back to idle position. "Let's sit for a spell."

I turned to the boss. "What do you think?" I asked.

McClintoc ignored me. Speaking to the radioman, he said, "What about the other boats?"

After a moment, he responded. "The Passage Key and Longboat Pass boats are in the main channel coming south. They just passed Sister Keys and are turning east across the top of the bay."

McClintoc turned to me. "I think we have four decoys. The one with the people in it is probably the one we want. Looks like he's headed for one of the canals on Longboat. We'll know soon."

McClintoc put the boat in gear, and we headed slowly under the Ringling Bridge, making our way to the intersection of New Pass and the Intracoastal channel.

The radioman said, "Boss, the boat with the people turned into a canal in Country Club Shores. The other four boats are sitting idle at marker 15 in mid-bay. The P-3 still has the boat in the canal."

"Okay," said McClintoc. "Let me know when it stops."

A minute of silence, two, then, "Boss, the P-3 says the boat is docked at the third house in on the south side of the canal."

"Are the police moving in?"

"A Longboat officer is on routine patrol in the area. He'll drive down the street and report back."

More silence. The two agents in fatigues hadn't said a word since we got on the boat.

The radioman pumped his arm once in a victory salute. "Yeah! The patrolman says it's a pretty big house with almost no lights showing. No cars in the driveway, but there's a twenty-foot boat on a trailer parked in front of the garage. As he was leaving, a white van turned off Gulf of Mexico Drive into the neighborhood. We got 'em."

"That we do," said McClintoc, with the first smile I'd seen. "Let's head in. Tell the chief to round up those boats at marker 15."

THIRTY-TWO

We pulled into Marina Jack on the Sarasota waterfront, moored the Customs boat in its slip, and climbed into a black Chevy Tahoe. The radioman and the two fatigue-clad Customs agents stayed with the boat.

I was in the front passenger seat, and Jock sat in the back. McClintoc drove.

I asked, "What now?"

"We wait," said McClintoc.

He drove over the Ringling Bridge, cut down Washington Street and crossed the New Pass Bridge. "We'll park in the Chart House's lot and see what happens," he said.

The Tahoe was equipped with several radios, and I could hear the chatter from all the units involved in the operation. The P-3 reported that its infrared scanners were picking up bodies moving about the yard of the house where the go-fast was moored. The van was in the driveway, parked next to the boat resting on its trailer.

I heard Bill Lester check in with his dispatcher. They had taken custody of the decoy boats and were taking them into the Holiday Inn Marina in Sarasota.

Murder Key

A Customs Service Blackhawk helicopter had been positioned at the Sarasota-Bradenton Airport just across Highway 41 from the bay. It would be only minutes from Marker 15 and the assembled boats. Bill later told me that he'd alerted the chopper as he and two Sarasota police boats started moving toward the idling go-fasts.

The Blackhawk was on the decoy boats before they knew what was happening. A strong spotlight beam illuminated all four craft, and an air crewman used a loudspeaker to tell them not to move, or he'd blow them out of the water.

One, perhaps a little braver or stupider than the others, shot the juice to his engines and was starting to come on plane when the door gunner on the chopper cut loose with his M-60 machine gun. Tracers pinged into the water just off the bow of the bad guy, and he immediately cut his engines and raised his hands.

When the chief and the Sarasota boats got to the runners a couple of minutes later, the crews were all standing in their vessels with their hands raised. Bill put a cop in each boat, and had the bad guys, eight in all, handcuffed, placed in life jackets and stashed on the sole of his boat. They started the short trip to the Holiday Inn Marina.

We sat in the Tahoe, waiting. Jock coughed, and the silence settled on us again, the only sound the low murmur of far-off voices slipping from the radio receivers.

The radio came alive with a transmission from the P-3. "The van is loaded with people and moving. The beacon's been activated, and we have a fix on it."

We watched for a minute, and then saw the van coming south on Gulf of Mexico Drive. As it passed under a street light, I could see the drivers head, framed by long blonde hair. We let it go.

"Emilio must be all right," Jock said. "He activated the tracking beacon."

I was surprised. "How did you get a tracking beacon to Emilio?

Wouldn't the immigrants have been searched?" I said.

"It's about the size of a penny," said Jock. "Very powerful, but the battery is only good for six hours or so. It was taped to the back of Emilio's scrotum. Doubtful anybody would look there. All he had to do to activate it was to pinch the sides of the transmitter."

"He's probably damn glad to get off that trawler," said McClintoc.

"He's been on the boat for a week," said Jock. "That beacon is probably uncomfortable as hell by now. He's supposed to stick the bug to the underside of a seat in the van."

We sat silently again, waiting for something to happen. Then, the disembodied voice of the P-3's radioman filled the Tahoe. "A vehicle from inside the garage is moving. We think he's hooked up to the boat trailer in the driveway. Turning south on Gulf of Mexico Drive."

McClintoc stirred. "He's coming our way," he said. "What the hell is that all about?"

He picked up the radio microphone and called the Sarasota PD liaison. "Can you get an unmarked to follow a vehicle pulling a boat and trailer that'll be crossing the New Pass Bridge in about two minutes?" he said.

The reply came immediately. "No problem. I've got a car stationed on St. Armand's Circle."

McClintoc keyed the mic again. "He's just passing us now, headed for the New Pass Bridge. It's an older model Ford pickup towing a twenty-foot aluminum jon boat with a small outboard. He's got fishing rods in the holders on the gunwales. I don't know what this is all about, maybe nothing. Don't stop him, but don't let him get loose."

The radio crackled. "Ten-four," the Sarasota cop said. "We'll follow, but won't intercept without your word."

Such a boat would not draw much attention after it left Longboat Key. There were thousands just like it all over the west coast of Florida. They were cheap, and workingmen who liked to fish could afford them.

Jock said, "I wonder if they're using the boat to haul the drugs. Diaz said they used the illegals as cover on the trawler. Maybe they're keeping the drugs and the illegals separate now."

McClintoc said, "You may be right, Jock. We'll see how this plays out at the other end."

We sat quietly again, waiting for some word from the various parties tracking the van and the pickup. Time dragged slowly, and the Tahoe's seat was getting uncomfortable.

It was two in the morning, and nothing seemed to be happening. I was getting restless. "What now?" I said.

McClintoc turned toward me. "The P-3 can stay up for several more hours," he said. "We'll track the van, but my guess is it's headed for Merrit County. I don't know about the pickup and the boat. We'll just hope for the best on that."

Jock said, "If we don't have to stay here, why don't we see if we can round up some coffee."

McClintoc cranked the SUV. "Good idea," he said. "There's a McDonald's on Tamiami Trail that has twenty-four hour drive-up service."

We crossed the New Pass Bridge again, rounded the circle and headed east on John Ringling Boulevard. McClintoc was back on the radio with the P-3, who advised us that the van was headed east on Fruitville Road toward I-75.

We got our coffee at the drive-thru and parked, waiting to find out whether the van turned south or north on the Interstate. We sipped our brew, blowing on it to cool it enough that it wouldn't blister our mouths. Jock went inside the McDonald's to use the restroom. He came back. We sat some more.

The radio came back up, loud in the silent space of the SUV. The van had turned south on I-75. We headed south on the Trail to Bee Ridge Road, turning east and driving toward the Interstate.

I called Logan. "They're headed south on Seventy-five, probably toward you. I'll let you know as soon as they turn off and head toward Merrit County."

"I'll tell the sheriff. Jimbo's here in the office. Said to tell you he didn't trust this operation to a shavetail."

I laughed. "Tell him to keep his head down," I said. "His big ass, too."

Logan hung up. The vehicle was quiet, the hum of tires on asphalt and the occasional murmur of the radio the only sound. We drove south, staying just below the speed limit. McClintoc didn't want to have to explain anything to a Highway Patrol Trooper.

Soon, the P-3 advised us that the van had exited the Interstate at Port Charlotte and was running east on the state road toward Merrit County. I called Logan again. He answered on the first ring, and I told him that the van was on its way.

He acknowledged the information and said, "You never told me about the damn medals. You're a hero."

"I lost my team that day, Logan. The only heroes out there were Jimbo and that chopper jock. Gotta go." I hung up.

As we were nearing the Merrit County line, BLOC came up on the radio to tell us that the pickup pulling the boat had gone out Fruitville Road and picked up Highway 70 east-bound. It had just turned south onto Highway 27. The Sarasota cops had several cars following the pickup at various times and intervals. They didn't think they'd been detected.

McClintoc grinned. "Sounds like they're headed to Merrit County, too," he said. "Let Logan know what's going on, Matt."

I called Logan again and filled him in. While I was talking to him, the P-3 came back on the radio to tell us that the van had passed through town and turned north on the county road that Jock and I had taken the week before. It was headed for the labor camp.

McClintoc picked up the microphone again. "BLOC, we're going to stop at the sheriff's office," he said. "Call me on my cell when the van gets to the labor camp. And keep me posted on that pickup. Tell the Sarasota cops that if it turns off onto a dirt road, not to follow it. They can come on into town to the Sheriff's office."

We pulled into the courthouse parking lot, parked, and walked toward the sheriff's office.

THIRTY-THREE

The sheriff's small office was full of men. Rufus Harris, Paul Reich, Logan, Jimbo and the sheriff sat drinking coffee.

Kyle Merryman stood as we entered. "Gentlemen," he said, "coffee pot's in the corner."

I introduced McClintoc, and Jock and I poured cups of coffee for ourselves. The Customs boss declined. We filled the group in on what had happened during the long night.

I said, "We think the pickup with the boat is headed to the labor camp. I'm not sure what that's all about."

The sheriff looked tired, a man with too little sleep. "I think the drugs are in the boat," he said. "If the van with the illegals got stopped, there wouldn't be any drugs to find. Transporting illegals is nowhere near as serious as running drugs. A pickup pulling a boat headed to Lake Okeechobee wouldn't arouse any suspicions."

McClintoc looked up. "Good call, Sheriff," he said. "Jock had the same idea. You're probably right."

The Customs agent's phone rang. He answered, and listened, then hung up. "The Sarasota cops said the pickup and boat turned off on a dirt road. The GPS coordinates are for the labor camp road. BLOC sent the cops home."

Jimbo stood and walked to the coffee pot in the corner. "Sun'll be up soon," he said. "You got a SWAT team coming in, Mr. McClintoc?"

"Not yet. They're on alert in Miami, with a helicopter standing by. They can be here in an hour or so. Can't use them tonight, though. I'll go back to Tampa tomorrow and try to get a Federal Magistrate Judge to sign a search warrant. Then I'll call in the team. It'll take a couple of days."

Kyle leaned over his desk. "By then," he said, "the drugs will be gone."

I looked at my watch. Almost four. We had about two-and-a-half hours before the false dawn chased the darkness out over the Gulf.

I said, "There's no reason a couple of civilians can't sneak in and look around. If we find something, it won't be ruled inadmissable because of the lack of a warrant. The exclusionary rule only applies to the government."

McClintoc sat quietly for a moment, pondering. "Can you and Jock get in there, Matt?" he asked.

"I think so," I said. "Logan can drive us almost to the labor camp, and then we can walk in. Shouldn't be any traffic out this time of the morning."

Jock had been sitting quietly since we arrived at the sheriff's office. "We can do it," he said. "Logan?"

"I'm game," said Logan. "I'm tired of sitting around."

We hatched a plan. It wasn't brilliant, but with a little luck it'd work. Logan would use an old pickup the sheriff owned to drive Jock and me to within a mile of the labor camp. The vehicle wouldn't attract much attention even if somebody saw it. It looked like a hundred other farmers' trucks in the county.

The plan was for Logan to drop us on the dirt road, and we'd go across the open fields and slip over or under the fence. Logan would wait while Jock and I reconnoitered. With no moon, and

189

dark clothes, we should be just about invisible. We thought.

Jock and I took our nine millimeters, stuffed into holsters on our belts. The sheriff provided us with dark green windbreakers and hats. I was wearing the sneakers I had come in. Jock had traveled in what looked like a pair of paratrooper boots. They were a lot more utilitarian than my old Reeboks. Logan wore a pair of jeans and a green golf shirt with the logo of Lynches' Pub and Grub on the pocket. He'd be staying with the truck, but he borrowed a handgun from the sheriff's armory.

We took our cell phones, with McClintoc's number fed into our fast dials. We were ready. It was 4:30, and we had about two hours to get in and out.

* * * * *

Logan dropped us off according to plan, and Jock and I started the slog across the open fields. It took us fifteen minutes to get from the courthouse to the drop area, and we figured it would take us about the same amount of time to get to the fence. We could poke around for an hour, and make it back to the truck and out of the area before dawn.

We were moving at an easy lope. At this rate, we'd be ahead of schedule. We were running at a diagonal to the road, so that when we reached the fence, we'd be several hundred yards from the gate house. I hoped neither of us stepped in a hole.

We made it to the fence, and had just crawled under it, when the area was lit up like daylight. Four men in fatigue uniforms rose from their cover, not ten feet from us and pointed M-16s in our direction.

The light was coming from a spotlight on an Army surplus two-and-a-half ton truck, the one soldiers called a deuce-and-a-half. I could see other men outlined in the glare from the beam.

"On your knees, gentlemen. Hands up," called out a voice, heavy with a Cracker accent. We dropped to our knees, hands in the air. One of the men in fatigues frisked us and took our weapons and phones.

"Restrain 'em," came the Cracker voice.

Two men came forward with plastic ties like the police use in place of handcuffs. Our hands were bound behind our backs.

"Stand up," the Cracker said. "You're two of the dumbest college men I ever did see."

The man came into the light, and I could see his face. It was Byron Hewett.

"I'm Jimmy Wilkerson," he said.

"I'm confused," I said.

He laughed. "You boys had me and didn't know it," he said. "Jimmy Wilkerson don't exist. I just use that name to confuse folks."

Jock spoke up. "How did you know we were coming, Byron."

"Electronics," he said. "We've been tracking you all the way across the field. We got sensors all over the place. A rabbit moves, we got him."

Jock said, "Then you'll know when the SWAT team gets here.

Byron laughed. "Bullshit," he said.

Jock said, "Other people know we're here, Byron."

Hewett spit tobacco juice onto the ground. "Right," he said. "You guys just don't know when to quit. We've been expecting you ever since you busted up my favorite deputy. Thought you'd have been here before now."

"We're part of a federal task force," said Jock.

"Cut the shit, man. There ain't nobody here but you idiots. Don't you think I've got what you might call sources in the feds? Get in the truck."

Jock and I were led to the deuce-and-a-half and helped into the back of it. As I climbed over the transom, I was pushed from the rear and sprawled onto the bed of the truck. I felt a prick in my upper arm, and then blackness enveloped me, like the night sea closing over a diver.

THIRTY-FOUR

I came slowly awake. My head felt like a Roman Legion was marching over it. Pain shot through my temples like lightning through the dull throbbing in my brain.

I tried to sit up. My hands were tied behind me, my legs bound at the ankles. I couldn't see anything, and for a moment I was afraid that I was blind. Panic was setting in, and I willed it down somewhere into the pit of my being. *Just stay there until I can get my bearings*, I told the fear. I knew from experience that panic could be deadly.

Time to take stock of my situation. The plastic ties were tight around my wrists, and something else bound my legs at the ankles. There was no way I could break them. I turned over on my back, feeling with my hands. I was on a dirt floor. I couldn't see the stars, and I sensed that I was in a structure of some kind. I stretched out my legs and rolled to the right. I made two complete turns, and bumped into a body. It was warm, but still.

"Who's there?" I said, more in a groan than a whisper.

"Matt." A hoarse voice came from across the room. "I'm over here."

"Jock?"

"Yeah."

"Somebody's over here, but he's not moving. He's still alive."

"Stay where you are. I'm going to roll myself over to you."

I could hear in the small grunts he made the effort it took Jock as he moved toward me. It seemed to take forever, but I'm sure it was only a minute or two before he bumped against me.

Jock said, "Can you get to my boot? The heel is hollow, and there's a knife in there."

I moved around, positioning myself by feel and sound, until I was lying on my side, my hands even with Jock's feet.

"If you can get hold of the heel, just twist it. Be careful. The knife isn't very big."

I fumbled twice, but finally got my right hand on the heel of his boot. "Is this the right one?" I said.

"Doesn't matter. Both of them have knives."

I twisted the heel slowly and felt an object fall out of the hollowed-out receptacle. I felt around in the dirt until I located what felt like a small pocket knife.

Jock moved his legs out of the way. "Can you open it?" he said.

"I'm trying."

I was able to use both hands, or at least the thumbs and forefingers of each hand, and got the knife open. The blade folded onto itself so that when it clicked into place, it was longer than the typical small knife.

I said, "I can't cut myself lose. Can't get the leverage. I'm going to move up and cut your ties."

I eased myself around again, putting my back to Jock's back. I found his hands and then the ties on his wrists. I started sawing. Jock was quiet, conserving energy.

The ties came loose. Jock pulled his arms around in front of him. "Give me the knife," he said, "Let me get my legs free."

I heard him sawing on something with the knife. "They've put twine on our legs. I'll have you loose in a minute," he said.

Just then, I heard a noise that was all too familiar to me. The whirring of helicopter blades, and the winding down of the turbine that kept the ship aloft. It was coming in for a landing very near us.

"Helicopter," I said.

"Yeah."

Jock cut my bindings, and I sat for a moment letting the blood begin circulating in my arms and feet. The chopper had set down, but I could hear its engine turning at idle speed.

Jock was moving now, on his feet. "I wish I could see who this is," he said, apparently having found the other body in the room.

A groan escaped from the area where the person lay. "Matt? Jock?" It was Logan.

I heard Jock say, "What the hell are you doing here?"

"Where are we?" Logan wanted to know.

"Hell if I know," replied Jock. "Let me cut you loose. How did you get here?"

Logan sighed. "You and Matt hadn't been gone long when two guys with M-16s showed up at the truck," he said. "They put me in another pickup and must have shot me with some kind of drug. All I remember is a pricking sensation in my arm and then, just now, hearing your voices. I've got a hell of a headache."

"He's loose," said Jock. "Let's find out what kind of place we're in. Matt, let's walk slowly to a wall, and then you go one way and I'll go the other. We'll count paces until we meet up and see what we have.

When we were finished, I told Logan that the room seemed to be about twelve feet square and made out of rough concrete block. "There's a door in the middle of one wall. Based on the feel of the facing, I think it opens inward," I said.

Jock had taken the other small knife out of his boot heel and given me one. "Someone's coming," he said. "This can't be good.

Matt, get behind the door. Logan, get back on the floor and try to look like you're still tied up."

I heard a rattling outside the door, like a padlock was being opened. I slipped to the side of the door, so that when it opened I'd be behind it. It opened, and the small space was flooded with the light of early morning.

A man loomed in the doorway, an assault rifle carried at port arms. I could see him through the crack between the jamb and the opening door. "Wake up, shitheads," he said. "We're going for a little helicopter ride and a swim in the Gulf."

Jock and Logan were on the dirt floor facing me, hands behind their backs. I hoped our intruder wouldn't notice that their legs were no longer bound.

He stepped through the door, and as he cleared the leading edge, I took a step, grabbed his chin with my left hand, pulled his head back, and ran the knife blade into his larynx. It was so quick he didn't have time to make a sound, and as my weapon carved up his vocal cords, he lost the ability to utter even a croak. I brought the blade further around, severing his jugular vein and carotid artery. There truly are things you learn in the military that can be applied in civilian life.

Blood erupted like a geyser, coating my hands and the dirt in front of the dying man. I let him go, and he slumped to the ground.

Jock grabbed the dead man's rifle, and I pulled a pistol out of the holster at his waist. Logan was up and moving, but a little unsteady on his feet. He'd never completely recovered from his heart surgery, and I could see the strain in his face as he came into the light splaying in the door.

"You okay?" I said, reaching over to give him a hand.

He shook me off. "I'm fine," he said. "Let's get the hell out of here."

Jock was standing at the door, peeking out. "The chopper

pilot's standing over by his ship, smoking a cigarette," he said in a low voice. "There's a big house about a hundred yards to the left of us, and men with rifles milling around about a hundred yards the other way. Looks like they're eating breakfast. Maybe half a dozen of them.

"Logan," he said, turning from the door, "can you fly that thing?"

"Bet your ass," answered Logan.

I wasn't too sure about that. "When's the last time you flew one?" I said.

"Vietnam. But it's not something you forget how to do."

Jock said, "There's got to be people in the house, and if we try to make a run for it, they, or the guys on the other side of the chopper, are going to have clear shots at us. Our only chance is the helicopter. It's bout 20 yards from us, and the engine's idling. It's ready to go."

"What about the pilot?" I said.

Jock lifted the M-16. "I'm going to take him out. The shot will alert the bad guys, but so will the pilot as soon as he sees us. The tail of the chopper is facing us. I know this rig. It's a Bell 206. The rear passenger door is on the left."

He gestured toward the aircraft. "Matt," he said, "go left when you get there. Take the front seat. The rear door's open, and that's where I'll head. Logan will be going to the right for the pilot's seat. Y'all go, and I'll hang back. As soon as the pilot notices you, I'll take him out and come on the run."

I looked at Logan. "You ready?" I asked.

He grinned. "As I'll ever be," he said. "I gotta stop hanging out with you guys."

"Go," said Jock.

Logan went first, with me right behind him. We were almost to the helicopter when the pilot noticed us. "Hey," he yelled at the top of his lungs. That was his last word in this life. I heard the crack of the M-16, and the pilot's head exploded with the impact of the heavy lead entering it.

Logan was at the pilot's door on the right side of the chopper, and I was heading to the left. I saw the men across the field getting up from their breakfast, lifting their rifles, looking around in confusion. They'd heard the shot, but they didn't know where it came from. I could hear Jock coming at a run behind me.

I crawled into the seat next to Logan. He was already turning switches and pouring gas to the engine. The chopper was getting light on its skids when I heard Jock climbing into the back seat.

"Go," he said, and we lifted off, Logan screaming in sheer joy, or perhaps fear. I never did ask him.

I saw little flights of fire coming from the muzzles of the guards' rifles. Jock was pounding away with the M-16 on full automatic, taking short bursts, holding down the guards. I saw one grab his chest and fall, and several others hit the dirt.

Logan had the nose of the aircraft pointed up at such an angle I thought we were going to fall out of the sky. The rotary wings did their job, taking us higher. We passed over the building where we had been held. It was a small concrete block structure with a tin roof, just a shed. It might have been a place to hold workers who resisted the conditions in the camp.

I looked back in time to see a car racing out of the camp gate. We were too far away to tell the make of it, but the driver was hauling ass.

Then we were out of range, flying over barren fields and then citrus groves.

I turned in the seat. "You okay back there?" I asked Jock.

"Yeah. Close call. Logan hasn't lost his touch."

I was still feeling the adrenalin rush, antsy as hell, but relieved. "Do you know where we are?" I asked Logan.

"Yeah. This thing has a GPS system just like in my car. Sure could've used this in Nam."

"Well, where the hell are we?"

"We were in the labor camp. We'll be over the courthouse in a minute. You want me to put this thing down?"

"No, let's swing out and try to contact McClintoc. What time is it?"

"Seven o'clock. Unless we've lost a day, we haven't been gone long," Logan said.

"No, they were going to kill us," I said. "They wouldn't have taken a chance by leaving us alive for a full day. It's still Thursday."

"Hey," said Jock from the back seat. "Guess what I found? Now I know how they move the drugs from the labor camp."

"How?" I said.

"I've got a box full of it on the floor back here. At least I've got a box full of white powder. It's probably coke."

I turned back to Logan. "Can you radio McClintoc?" I said.

Logan handed me a phone. "I can do better than that," he said. "The pilot left his cell."

I didn't know McClintoc's phone number and I had no idea how to contact BLOC in Miami. I took the phone and called the Longboat Key Police Department. I identified myself and asked the dispatcher to patch me through to Bill Lester.

"Matt, where are you?" Lester said when he answered. "We've got the calvary scouring the woods around the camp."

"I don't want to talk on the radio, Bill. Give me your cell phone number and I'll call you right back."

When I got the chief on the phone, I explained what had happened. He told me a Customs Service SWAT team was about to raid the labor camp. They were going in without a warrant, because three citizens, us, were believed to be held there against their will. They'd waited until the busses took the laborers out for the day's work. They didn't want to kill any more people than they had to.

I said, "I don't think you're going to find the ringleaders there. We left some dead people, and there were a few guards still shooting at us when we pulled out. We've got the cocaine. They'd loaded it into the chopper and were going to drop us in the Gulf on the way to wherever the drugs were going."

"I'm on the state road, headed for Merrit county. I can be at the sheriff's office in about five minutes. Can Logan land that thing anywhere near the courthouse down there?"

"There's a McDonald's next to the courthouse. Have the sheriff clear the lot and we can put down there. We ought to have some firepower standing by in case the bad guys are tracking us somehow."

"I'll see to it. Give us about ten minutes." He hung up.

"Logan, can you find the courthouse?" I asked.

"Didn't I hear you say that once about a lawyer? That he wasn't smart enough to find the courthouse, let alone try a case?" Logan was still high on adrenalin, or maybe just the sheer joy of being in control of a helicopter again.

I gave him my stoniest look. "Can you?" I said.

"You find it, and I'll land this thing."

"Fair enough."

I could see a road below us, but I had no reference points that would tell me which road it was or which direction it ran. I was straining to see in front of us, hoping to catch a glimpse of the county seat, or a church steeple, anything to give me some perspective.

Logan chuckled. "Hey, Sherlock," he said. "Look at the GPS in the dash. It gives you highway numbers and everything."

I slapped my forehead, which only reminded me that my head

still hurt. I could tell we were about five miles north of the courthouse. I told Logan that we needed about ten minutes more and then we'd head south. By then, the sheriff would have cleared us a landing zone in the McDonald's parking lot.

Logan swung the chopper toward the east in a sharp banking turn. We approached Lake Okeechobee, and our pilot went down on the deck, skimming just above the water. Birds began to rise from the surface, frightened by the noise of the jet engines powering our ride. Logan was having the time of his life.

Finally, as we approached the Port Myakka lock on the east side of the lake, Logan took us back up and set a course for the county seat. We had seen a demonstration of an extraordinary flying skill, undiminished by the passing of years.

We came in low over the town, and I could see the blue lights of a police cruiser parked on the road next to the McDonald's. The cars had been moved out, and there were people standing by them, munching on their breakfast and sipping their coffee. A team of fatigue-clad figures, about five-strong, was placed around the perimeter of the lot, their rifles at port arms.

Jock finally stirred in the back seat. "Don't crash this thing," he said.

"Looks like a hot LZ," said Logan. "We're going in fast."

"Shitfire," said Jock.

"Just kidding," said Logan. "I'll put her down nice and easy." And that's what he did.

Kyle and Jimbo Merryman came running over as I opened my door. Logan was busy shutting down the big machine.

"Hey, Loot," Jimbo said over the dying whine of the turbo, "Looks like a chopper jock pulled your ass out of the fire again."

I laughed. "Wasn't the same without you, Top."

Kyle winked at me. "Appreciate the helicopter, fellows. It was used in a crime in my county, and now it belongs to me."

McClintoc strode up. "Not so fast, Sheriff. This is a federal task force. We get the chopper."

Bill Lester had driven up and gotten out of his car. "Whoa. We started this thing. It belongs to Longboat Key," he said.

Logan came around the front of the aircraft. "Like a bunch of pirana going after a hog in the river," he said, shaking his head.

Kyle laughed. "I got a feeling this will get sorted out later," he said. "Do you want the drugs, Agent McClintoc?"

"Yeah," said McClintoc. "I'll have one of my people inventory it and put it in an evidence locker."

McClintoc's phone rang, and he walked off to the side, talking quietly into it. We stood silently, letting the adrenalin subside. Logan was still a little giddy from the flight, but I only knew that because he couldn't stop grinning.

I was trying to blot out the image of a dying man whose throat I'd just sliced open. I looked at my hands, and was startled to see the blood stains still there. I wiped them on my pants, but it didn't help. I'd wash as soon as I could, but I thought those stains would likely stay for a lifetime.

I poked Logan lightly on the arm. "Good flying, buddy," I said. "You saved our bacon."

"Man, I'd forgotten the thrill of taking one of those babies up. Bad guys shooting at you, pulling out of a hot LZ. Just like the old days. Straight up and fast."

Jimbo laughed. "I always said you chopper jocks were nuts," he said.

McClintoc re-joined us. "That was the SWAT commander," he said. "They've got the camp cleared and about twenty men under arrest. There are a few women and some small children left. All the others are in the fields. Border Patrol will round them up and decide what to do with them."

I said, "What about the van and the boat?"

McClintoc shrugged. "The van and the boat and the pickup pulling it are at the camp," he said.

Jock said, "Did you find Emilio?"

"I asked," said McClintoc. "He's apparently in the fields somewhere. Border Patrol will find him. They know he's one of ours."

I told them about Byron Hewett. "Did your guys find him?" I asked.

"No," said McClintoc. "I'm willing to bet that Byron Hewett is an alias, too. The big guys must have left right after they got you and Jock. Probably figured we were closing in. Didn't want the drugs to be found on them if they got stopped, so they arranged for the chopper."

Jock was frowning. "Don't tell me the pilot was just some slob who happened to be in the wrong place at the wrong time."

"No," said McClintoc. "Our guys identified the body from his driver's license. He's been running drugs for years, and Miami-Dade PD thinks he's good for at least three murders. Did some state time up at Raiford on drug charges, but we haven't been able to pin anything on him in years. Nobody's going to miss him."

Jock looked relieved. "Okay," he said quietly.

I knew his ghosts were hovering nearby, whispering to him of remorse and regret. Eventually, because of those fears, he'd hesitate to act when he needed to, and that would prove fatal. But, his icy performance at the labor camp was done without equivocation, and it had saved our lives. He still had time to get out alive. I'd talk to him, soon.

I was bone tired. I hadn't slept in twenty-four hours, and the knock-out drugs were still circulating in my body.

THIRTY-FIVE

I came awake with a start, my body jerking. I smelled frying bacon and fresh coffee. I didn't know where I was for a moment, and then I remembered. I was in Jimbo Merryman's guest room, and Jock was next door.

I looked at the clock on the bedside table. Five o'clock. The afternoon sun was creeping through the drawn drapes. I'd been asleep for most of the day. I got out of bed, slipped into my jeans and a shirt that smelled like Sasquatch had slept in it, and headed toward the kitchen.

Jock, Jimbo and Emilio were sitting at the table, talking quietly. "Ah," said Jimbo, "here comes the sack rat."

I found a cup and poured it full of coffee. "Emilio," I said, "I'm damn glad to see you."

"And I'm damned glad to be here," he said. "Every time Jock shows up, something bad happens to me."

"Any news?" I said.

Jimbo spoke up. "I just talked to Kyle. The Coast Guard boarded the trawler a couple of hours ago. They've got the crew in custody and they're taking the boat to the St. Pete Coast Guard Station. Nothing else on the others. Hewett, or whatever his name is, has disappeared."

"Where's Logan?" I said.

"Headed for Longboat," said Jimbo. "He and the chief spent the day sleeping in a hotel room in Port Charlotte, and then headed home. McClintoc left for Miami with the drugs. The helicopter was stolen in Orlando, and the owner sent a pilot down today to pick it up."

"What are your plans?" I asked Emilio.

"I'm headed to Miami too, as soon as the agency gets a chopper here to pick me up. I'll spend some time with the task force guys getting debriefed, and then back to D.C."

I joined them at the table. "Can you tell us about your cruise?" I asked Emilio.

"Lousy food, bad accommodations," he said. "I wouldn't recommend it for a honeymoon."

Emilio had gone back to Tlapa and met with Sergio Arguilles. The old immigrant handler was distressed to hear that some of the people he was sending to Veracruz were ending up as virtual slaves in Florida. Emilio didn't tell him that Mendez was dead.

"I only started dealing with Mendez about a year ago," the old man told Emilio. "The man I had worked with for years died, and Mendez took over. Now, somebody else has replaced Mendez."

Emilio told him that the authorities in Sarasota had identified the two dead men found with Pepe. Arguilles had sent them to Mendez, and he felt a personal responsibility for their death. He was willing to help Emilio put the smugglers out of business.

Emilio boarded the mini-bus in Tlapa with three other young men. There was an air of excitement among the group, which grew to twelve as the bus stopped in two other villages along the way to Veracruz. They were going to America, and for the first time in their lives, they were experiencing a feeling of something like hope.

The group arrived in Veracruz late at night and was taken

directly to the dock where the *Princess Sarah* was moored. They were each given a bunk in the hold of the small ship, and told not to come topside during the day, and only with express permission from the captain at night.

The bunks were stacked three high in four tiers on either side of the hold. There was a small table in the middle, between the bunks, that was used for card games and eating. The food was mostly fish and a few potatoes, but there was plenty of it.

The immigrants were told that if the boat was boarded, they should go quietly with the Coast Guard. If they didn't say anything about the men who brought them this far, they'd get a free ride on the next trip. A money-back guarantee.

The crew consisted of the captain, a mate and the cook who doubled as a deck hand. They were pleasant enough, and didn't abuse the passengers in any way. There was no hint that drugs might be aboard, until the night the men were loaded into the go-fast boat off Longboat Key.

Emilio told us that all twelve immigrants were put into the one boat, and then a duffel bag was handed over by the trawler's captain. It was taken by a man with a rifle and stowed in the stern of the go-fast. If Emilio hadn't known about the drug smuggling, he would not have picked up on the transfer as anything but innocent.

Once in the house on Longboat Key, the immigrants were given bottled water and a sandwich and loaded into the van driven by the blonde woman. Emilio had removed the tracker beacon from his scrotum when he relieved himself in the house. He attached it to the underside of the back seat in the van when he boarded.

"There was no water for showers on the boat," he said, "so we pretty much stank when we got there. I didn't mind that so much, but that damn beacon taped to my balls was about the worst thing I've ever been through."

Murder Key

The men were told by the blonde woman, in passable Spanish, that they were going to their new home and would be introduced to the labor boss the next morning. They'd be put to work in the fields, and would have to remit part of their salary each week to the labor boss to pay for room and board and their passage on the *Princess Sarah*. She did not tell them that they would be held as slaves, or that the payments to the boss would never be enough to pay off the debt, which rose incrementally with the interest tacked on each day.

They were driven to one of the barracks in the labor camp and told to get a shower and settle in and get some sleep. The building was one story and held fifty single beds, twenty-five to a side. There was a locker beside each bed for personal belongings. A bathroom took up one end of the building, with a large shower stall and several lavatories and commodes.

"They got us up at dawn," said Emilio, "even though we'd only had two hours sleep. They told us we'd have to work off our passage before we could leave the camp. One of the men who came over with me told them that his family had paid Arguilles. This big Mexican guy holding a baseball bat told us that there were some other charges for the boat, and we'd have to work that off."

Emilio talked to some of the other workers as they were waiting to leave. He was told that some of the men had been held for a year or more. They had to buy their food and clothing from a store in the camp, and the cost was deducted from their pay, as was the rent for the bunkhouse. Most of them were charged more than they made, and the interest was building at a high rate. Many of them had decided they would not get out of the camp alive.

They were taken in an old blue school bus to the fields about five miles from the camp and put to work harvesting a late crop of tomatoes. They were there when the Border Patrol found them.

Emilio laughed. "I"ve never seen a bunch of Mexicans so glad to see the U.S. Border Patrol," he said. "They were free, and knew they'd be deported to Mexico. They also know they'll be back in Florida within a few weeks."

Kyle poured himself another cup of coffee. "What do you think happened to the man Arguilles had been dealing with before Mendez came into the picture?" he asked.

Emilio said, "I think Mendez showed up at the same time the drug shipments started. Until then, they were probably just shipping illegals into Sarasota. Mendez probably killed Arguelles' contact in Veracruz, but we'll never know for sure."

"Kyle," I said, "what do we know about the house on Longboat where the drugs were coming in?"

"Bill Lester called about that a little while ago. Turns out it's owned by an elderly couple who live in Traverse City, Michigan, and they only use it during the winter months. They leased it to some guy, who probably doesn't exist, for the months of April through December. The renter paid the whole thing up front and in cash."

I drank some more coffee. "I guess that about wraps it up," I said, "but I still don't know who's trying to kill me."

Jock finally stirred. "Wilkerson or Hewett or whatever his name is, is the one who knows," he said. "He's on the run. The feds will get him sooner or later. I think it's over as far as you're concerned."

"Then," I said, "let's go home."

* * * * *

Sheriff Kyle Merryman had one of his deputies drive Jock and me to Longboat Key. I called Logan to see about dinner, but he said he was too tired to move.

We decided that eating in would make more sense than going out for dinner. I ordered a pizza, and we sat in the living room eating it and discussing our adventure. As we called it a night, it occurred to me that it had been exactly three weeks since Diaz had tried to kill me in Tiny's.

* * * * *

Jock left on Saturday morning, headed back to Houston. I dropped him at the airport and swung back by Lynches for lunch with Logan.

We re-hashed the events of the past few days. I hadn't told him about Anne, so I recounted what I'd begun to think of as the "great dumping." Logan was sympathetic, but not much concerned.

Most of November had slipped by without my noticing. There was a little chill in the morning air, hinting at the colder days to come. Thanksgiving was less than a week away, and Logan was planning his annual feast. He always invited the singles and older couples who had no family in the area. He'd have The Market cater it, and there'd be more food than we could eat. I always went, and I always felt a little more like a member of our island family after the event.

Logan was headed home for a nap, still tired from his ordeal, not yet fully recovered from his heart surgery only a few months before. I was antsy, a withdrawal symptom from the flood of adrenalin that had suffused my body for several days. I went to Mar Vista for a beer, looking for a little conversation with the regulars. I found more than I expected.

Cracker Dix was at the bar. An expatriate Englishman who had lived on our key for years, he was a popular figure on the North End. He was bald and wore a closely trimmed beard. He was dressed in jeans and a T-shirt advertising a pub in Dorset. His voice still carried the accents of his homeland. "Matt," he said, "somebody's looking for you."

"Who?"

"Don't know. He was around at lunchtime asking if you ever came in here."

"Can you describe him?"

"Hispanic guy. About five-eight and wiry. Had a crew-cut. Know him?"

"I don't think so, Cracker. If you see him again, give me a call. He may not be friendly."

"I've seen him hanging around for the past couple of days. He shows up at odd times, both here and at some of the other places on the North End."

I didn't like the sound of that. Somebody was stalking me.

Cracker said, "I heard about all the crap coming down on you. I didn't even tell the guy I knew you. You sure must have pissed somebody off."

"Wish I knew who," I said, but I thought I knew the answer to that.

Some of the early snowbirds had returned to the key and were taking the sun while they lunched on the patio overlooking the bay. Halyards on sailboats anchored just offshore rattled in the light wind huffing its way toward us. A bowrider, with two small children in front and mom and dad at the helm, idled toward the Mar Vista dock. A tranquil autumn day in our version of paradise.

Cracker and I sat and talked for a while, letting the afternoon wind down. I stopped to pick up a sandwich at Whitney Beach and went home. I entered my condo slowly, ready to bolt if anybody was there. I had my pistol in my windbreaker pocket, and I'd use it if I had to. The place was quiet, and I wondered if the Hispanic guy looking for me was benign. I didn't think so.

Murder Key

* * * * *

On Sunday morning, I jogged on my usual stretch of beach for the first time since I'd found the dead Mexicans. Things were getting back to normal, and I couldn't see any reason not to resume my routines.

A northwest wind brought cooler air tumbling off the Gulf, a reminder that what passed for winter in these latitudes was coming.

I kept a steady pace, running south, the hard-packed sand left from the previous night's high tide providing a sturdy track. The sea was dead calm, not a ripple on its surface. The tide had left globs of seaweed in its wake, and sea gulls were pecking at the tiny crustaceans mired in the damp masses of brown plant matter. A lone pelican skimmed the water fifty feet off the beach, looking for breakfast. Sandpipers scurried out of my path, their tiny feet leaving no tracks in the sand.

The quiet was broken by the sound of unmuffled marine engines. I glanced over my right shoulder and saw a blue go-fast boat approaching at high speed, running in close to shore. A rifleman was setting up in the bow, trying to gain some purchase on the gunwale.

Geez, I thought, *these guys never give up.* I turned to my left, accelerating into a sprint. The beach wasn't wide at this point, and I ran toward the seawall of a condo complex. I knew the area, and if I could make it to the buildings, my pursuers would never find me. I didn't think they'd come ashore, but one can never tell.

I zigged and zagged, and heard in my mind's ear the long-ago shouts of a drill sergeant in Ranger School. "Goddamit it, Sir, zag, don't zig. Charlie will shoot yore ass off."

I could hear the crack of the rifle and see spurts of sand kicking up around me. I was at the seawall and decided to take the four steps up rather than jump. Bad decision, but I made it, with only a splinter of wood lodged in my calf from a bullet strike on the step above my feet.

I hit the ground, rolled behind a cabbage palm and belly-crawled toward a hedge that ran the length of the property. I peeked through the branches and saw the go-fast headed out to sea, the rifleman stowing his weapon and waving at me.

I stood and gave him the finger. I didn't know if he could see it, but I felt better for it. I assessed my wounded calf, and pulled out a half-inch splinter. Nothing to it.

I called 911 on my cell phone, identified myself and explained what had happened. I didn't expect anybody to catch the boat, but I thought a good citizen should report a shooting.

In a few minutes, a police cruiser came into the parking lot, its siren blaring. The officer parked and got out of the car, as I waved to get his attention. He trotted over, his equipment belt rattling.

"You okay, Matt?" he asked.

I recognized the young cop, but couldn't recall his name. "I'm fine, thanks." I told him what had happened.

He grimaced. "I'm afraid there's not much we can do," he said, "but I'll file a report. That go-fast is long-gone."

I agreed, and he drove me back to my condo.

* * * * *

I called David Parrish at home. "I think somebody's still after me," I said. I told him about the man in Mar Vista and the go-fast incident. "I want to talk to Conrad Foster."

"What good will that do?"

"I don't know, but I don't think it can do any harm. Unless your people are closing in on him."

"We've gotten nowhere with that. We can't find anything on

him at all."

"Maybe if I talk to him, he'll think you guys are close, and he'll slip up somewhere."

"Let me check around, and I'll get back to you. Keep your powder dry."

Whatever that meant. Parrish was from Georgia, and he didn't always make sense to sane people. I laughed and hung up.

Parrish called back at mid-afternoon. "Go for it," he said. "But be careful, and let me know what happens."

THIRTY-SIX

Monday morning. I called the senator's office and told the receptionist who I was and that I needed to see the senator as soon as possible. She put me on hold, and then to my surprise, told me he could see me at eleven o'clock that morning. I had two hours to get downtown.

Foster's office was in a tall glass enclosed building on the corner of Tamiami Trail and John Ringling Boulevard on the Sarasota bayfront. The glass was tinted, and the clouds hanging over the bay reflected off the face of the structure. There always seemed to be a piece of plywood covering a spot where a window should have been. Sea Gulls would fly directly into the building, not realizing it was mirrored glass, and in the process of killing themselves, would break one more window. I was sure this was not a hazard contemplated by the architect when he designed the place.

I took an elevator to the top floor and entered the double mahogany doors that had "Foster Enterprises, Inc." in polished brass letters attached to them. I was welcomed by a brunette who could have graced the pages of Playboy Magazine. She wore a short skirt and a body hugging cotton blouse that didn't quite hide her nipples. High heel sandals completed her wardrobe. She wasn't tall, about five-feet-four, and her hair flowed to a point below the shoulders. I guessed her age at twenty-five, no more.

Lisa, as she introduced herself to me, was a study in efficiency as she scurried about the office, getting me coffee and apologizing for the fact that the senator was running a bit late. I sipped my coffee and assured her that I was in no hurry.

After about fifteen minutes, I heard a discreet buzz from the phone console in front of the salubrious Lisa. She answered crisply, listened for a moment, and said, "Right away, Sir."

She rose and came out from behind her desk, smiled, and said, "The senator will see you now, Mr. Royal."

Who could ignore that invitation. I was on my feet and following right behind her, like a loyal dog. I was not unaware that the wasted fifteen minutes was deliberate on the senator's part, but I had enjoyed the view of Lisa so much, I decided not to mention it.

The senator was a tall distinguished looking man wearing a fifteen-hundred-dollar suit. He was about six-feet-two and trim as an athlete, with a long patrician face topped by a full head of white hair. He was in his late seventies, but could have passed for twenty years younger.

He had grown up in eastern Sarasota County on a large truck farm owned by his father. Once he inherited, the senator expanded the holdings, with a little help from his political cronies, until he was one of the largest land owners in the state of Florida. His holdings included cattle ranches, citrus groves and truck farms.

He employed many people, most of them Mexicans, and most of them illegal. He'd never been charged with any labor law violations himself, but once in a while the U.S. Border Patrol would sweep down on his properties and arrest some of the illegals. It didn't happen often, and the number of arrestees was small enough not to make a dent in the senator's operations.

There had been rumors for years that the senator paid off the politicians to keep his operations solvent and keep the flow of cheap labor unimpeded. No one knew anything for sure, and there had never been an investigation.

Lisa opened the door and stood aside as I walked in. "Senator Foster, Mr. Matt Royal," she said, softly closed the door, and retreated to her own desk. I was quite impressed. The office was plush, and the large windows overlooked Sarasota Bay and Big Pass out to the Gulf of Mexico.

"Mr. Royal," the Senator said, coming around his desk, hand outstretched. "I'm Conrad Foster."

"I appreciate your seeing me, Senator."

"Glad to do it. Have a seat. Would you like some coffee?"

"No, thank you. Lisa took good care of me," I said. I sat in one of the high back chairs facing his desk.

The senator took a seat beside me, abandoning the large executive chair behind the desk. "Sorry about the wait," he said. "There's always something unexpected coming up that I have to deal with it." He smiled. "I understand that you're working for one of my Mexicans."

"Excuse me?"

"Aren't you representing Pepe Zaragoza?"

"No, why would you think that?"

"I'm mistaken. I know you're a lawyer, and I just assumed you were working for Pepe."

That was an impossible leap of logic, unless he knew I was involved some way in the mess of the last few weeks. Even if he thought I was coming to see him on a legal matter, it didn't follow that it had anything to do with "his" Mexican.

"No," I said. "Somebody's trying to kill me, and I'm trying to figure out who and why. Your Mexican, as you call him, and I have the same interest. We want to stay alive."

"What can I do for you?"

"Call off your goons."

"My goons? What in the world are you talking about Mr. Royal?"

"Senator, I know you're behind this. I just don't know why you want me dead."

"Are you out of your mind, Sir? I'm a responsible businessman and member of this community. Why on earth would I want to kill you?"

"Maybe because you think I know something about your drug running and immigrant smuggling operations."

"Mr. Royal," he said, his voice steely, "I'm appalled that you'd think I'd be involved in anything like that. I hire my Mexican workers through brokers, just like every other farmer. I pay a fair wage, and I don't look into their legal status. That's not my job. I sure as hell don't know anything about drugs."

"Do you know Byron Hewett?" I asked.

"Yes. He's one of the labor brokers I use. He leases land from me down in Merrit County to house his employees."

"Ever heard of Jimmy Wilkerson?"

"Can't say that I have." He smiled.

He was lying, but I had no way of proving it.

"Senator," I said, "you're a liar."

He blanched, the color draining out of his face. "You bastard," he said, "I'll squash you like a bug."

"I might be a harder to squash than you think. Why don't we just call a truce? You leave me alone and I'll leave you alone."

He had raised his voice, anger flooding his face. "Get out!" he shouted.

His finger stabbed a button on the phone, and he said, "Marie, come show Mr. Royal out."

I can take a hint. I turned to leave and found Marie Phillips standing at the door, a look of trepidation on her face. I was as shocked to see her as she was apparently to see me. I was surprised to find that her "corporate world" was the senator. She smiled tightly, more in dismay, I thought, than surprise. I didn't think this was the kind of day she had in mind when she got out of bed that morning. I was quite certain she hadn't planned on seeing me in Conrad Foster's office.

"Thank you, Marie," I said, as I brushed past.

THIRTY-SEVEN

Large clouds painted in shades of gunmetal gray hung low on the horizon, their faces lightly daubed with the burnt orange glow of the setting sun. Lightning flashed at their edges, signaling the coming of the small storm that would sweep in from the Gulf during the night. An eddy of cool air teased my face, reminding me that it would rain soon. The sand beneath my bare feet was still warm, holding the last vestige of heat from the daytime sun.

I missed Anne. This was our time of day, walking the beach, holding hands, sipping from flutes of white wine. She would giggle at the antics of the sandpipers running from the small surf that passed for waves on our shores and rail at the raucous gulls, scavengers who chased the smaller birds and stole their food.

I hadn't heard from her since that day at the Sports Page. I hadn't called her, either. It's a fine idea for lovers to remain friends after the fires of passion have died, or been transferred to someone else, but the reality is altogether different. For me, there was pain, and regret, and pride, and loneliness, all wrapped together to create a bundle of irresolution. I was in that state where I didn't want to think about her, but couldn't get her out of my mind. Every mundane little thing reminded me of her.

I'd walk into a restaurant, or a bar, and remember the times

219

we'd been there together. A song, or a scent, or the sight of a long-legged brunette would send daggers to skewer my heart.

Waning love is like a balloon that deflates over time, growing ever less robust, until finally it's only a wrinkled mess; a mess that was once a beautiful emotion floating above an uncertain world. And when the air goes out of only one of the lovers, the other is left with jealously, a monster with a voracious appetite that sucks the logic from an otherwise engaged brain, leaving only memories that were once lovely, but at the end are bitter shadows that haunt the daylight.

So I walked the beach in the late afternoon, two days before Thanksgiving, feeling sorry for myself. People were trying to kill me for reasons I didn't understand, and my love had dumped me like so much outdated food.

I knew the senator was the bad guy, but I couldn't figure out a way to prove it. If the whole weight of the local, state and federal governments couldn't get him, I didn't think I would.

If we could get a line on Byron Hewett or the blonde woman who drove the van, we might be able to get somewhere. The crew of the *Princess Sarah* had been no help. They just knew that they delivered their cargo to the go-fast boats, and they were paid when they returned to Veracruz.

The go-fast boaters were low-level people who were paid in cash by their leader, who in turn was paid by the blonde woman at the house on Longboat Key when he delivered the drugs and immigrants. They seemed to be otherwise uninvolved.

Yet, someone in a go-fast was stalking me, and somebody else was asking my friends about my routines. They had to be the senator's men.

I'd asked Rufus Harris about Merc Maitland and Jeep in Orlando and was told that they had been left in place in hopes that when the drug connection came back up, Merc and Jeep would be part of it.

Interestingly, there was no thought among the various government agencies that they had stopped, or even hindered, the flow of drugs. When they rolled up one group, another took its place within a matter of days. Rufus said it was like King Canute trying to roll back the ocean waves.

I'd cut a man's throat, and the fact that he deserved it didn't make me feel any better. This wasn't the first time I'd killed somebody, and it wasn't even the first time I'd cut a throat. I remembered them all. I had committed that most intimate act, homicide, and I didn't even know the names of the men I'd killed. They'd died knowing I was their executioner, and they had no idea who I was. Most of them had been soldiers, good men probably, who were just doing their duty. And I knew for a certainty that they would have killed me had I given them the chance. Still... .

Recently, I'd killed two bad guys on Egmont Key and felt no remorse. Yet, now, knowing that the man I'd killed in that shed at the labor camp was looking forward to throwing me out of a helicopter, I was feeling - what? Regret? I didn't think so, but I'd have to chew on it a little; maybe talk to Jock who had more experience with this sort of thing.

Perhaps we hadn't solved anything. The drugs were still coming in, and the government seemed incapable of even slowing the tidal wave of illegals slipping across the border. We were no closer to finding out who killed the Mexicans or Dwight Conley. Pepe Zaragoza was in jail, charged with the murders of the migrants I'd found on the beach, and I thought he was innocent.

At least Buddy Gilchrist and the Mexican Consulate in Orlando had gotten Pepe a good lawyer. Richard Wright was as good as they came in a courtroom, but the clerk's computer had randomly assigned Pepe's case to Judge P. R. Linder. I'd heard that he and Wright, were old friends, and that might help. Linder was known in the circuit for his conservatism and was widely thought of as a hanging judge.

I briefly considered offering my legal service to the defense team, but then came back to reality. I was retired from the practice of law. Wright was one of the new generation of trial lawyers, feisty, brilliant and tenacious. But then, so was Judge Linder. Pepe was in good hands under the circumstances.

My thoughts circled back to my predicament. I could only guess at who was after me. I could prove nothing. I hoped that my conversation with the senator that morning had backed him off.

Marie Phillips was another matter. I'd been surprised to see her in the senator's office, and I was unsure of what her place was in the scheme of things. The coincidence of the blonde Marie Phillips in the senator's office and the blonde van driver was too exquisite to dismiss.

On leaving the building, I stopped to speak to the security guard in the lobby. They usually knew everything going on in their bailiwick. I asked if he knew Marie.

The man grinned lasciviously and winked at me. "Oh, yeah," he said, "she's Senator Foster's administrative assistant." He winked again as I thanked him.

What about the deputy we'd seen her with at the Bridge Tender Inn? Was he the source of the leaks? Was she using the poor guy, or was he part of the drug ring?

I'd called bill Lester as soon as I'd left the building, and he was looking into both Marie and the deputy.

Every time I thought I knew what was going on, something cropped up to change my outlook. I did know that I was dog-tired of people trying to kill me. I wanted my old life back, the one where my biggest worry was what kind bait to use for the fish.

It was nearing five o'clock; time to give up on the self-pity and head for Tiny's. A beer and conversation with friends never failed to cheer me up. I'd call Logan and meet him there. He'd recovered from his ordeal at the labor camp, and was talking about renewing his helicopter license.

* * * * *

I left the beach and crossed Gulf of Mexico Drive, walking at a fast clip. I didn't want to become road kill for some snowbird on his way to the Publix. The island was filling up with our winter visitors. They always brought an energy with them that was lacking during the summer, and I looked forward to their return. I also watched the traffic a little more closely.

I crossed the parking lot of my complex and took the elevator to the second floor. As I entered my condo, I noticed that the drapes covering the sliding glass doors out to my balcony had been drawn, casting gloom into an area usually awash with sunlight and a view of the bay. I assumed the maids had been in and for some reason decided to darken the place.

I was walking toward the drapes when I became aware of another presence in the room. My eyes had adjusted, and I could see a man sitting on my sofa.

"Good afternoon, Mr. Royal." It was the Cracker accent of Byron Hewett.

He reached up and turned on the lamp that sat on the table at the end of the sofa. He had a twenty-two-caliber pistol in his right hand, a long silencer affixed to the barrel. It was pointing right at me.

"If you'd have let me know you were coming, Byron, I'd have put some coffee on."

He laughed. "I won't be here long enough to drink it," he said.

"What do you want, Byron?"

"Ah, Mr. Royal, I brought you a message. 'Some bugs aren't

223

so hard to squash after all.'" He laughed again, a low rumbling from deep in his throat, ending in a snort. He stood up and took a step toward me, raising the pistol.

I'd moved a step or two closer to Byron while he still sat on the couch. "So, you work for the senator," I said. "If that's all you wanted to say, you can leave now."

"Can't do that, Mr. Royal. Me and this little old twenty-two are about to squash you, just like the man said."

I was only an arm's length from him now. His eyes tightened, his mouth twisting into a rictus of malevolence. "You pretty much ruined a good deal for a lot of people," he said.

"It wasn't much of a deal for the Mexicans, or the kids you infected with your damn drugs."

"Screw 'em, is what I say. Who gives a shit about a bunch of Mexicans? And those kids are gonna get their drugs somewhere."

"But not from you. And not from the senator. At least not for a while."

"You sure got a way about you, Mr. Royal. You just flat-out piss me off."

He raised the pistol higher, pointing at my face. I had to take the chance. I'd probably be dead before I touched him, but I wasn't just going to stand there and take a bullet.

In the split second that I was willing my arm to move toward the pistol, I heard a key slide into the lock of my front door. It turned loudly, back and forth. Out of habit, I had engaged the dead bolt when I came in. A key wouldn't open the door from the outside.

It was probably Larry, the condo maintenance supervisor, trying to get in for some reason, not realizing that I was home.

No more than a second had elapsed, though it seemed longer. My arm was coming up, when the noise from the lock distracted Byron. His eyes went to the door in a reflexive movement, and I grabbed his wrist with my left hand, twisting it up as I brought it over my head. I clasped the fist holding the gun with my right hand and twisted it down behind his back. That action put me behind him. I still gripped his wrist, and I brought it up forcefully behind toward his shoulder blades.

The pistol fired as I brought the arm around. *Pfft*. Almost no sound. The bullet hit the ceiling, and plaster fell around us. Byron screamed in agony as the head of his humerus was jerked out of the shoulder socket. The gun dropped on the carpet.

We went to the floor, my knee in his back. I was still exerting upward pressure on his wrist, twisting his arm up toward his shoulder.

Larry yelled through the door. "Matt, are you in there?"

"Call 911, Larry. Get the police here. Now!"

"Okay, Matt."

I could hear him talking on his cell phone, summoning help. I leaned down close to Byron, talking quietly, directly into his ear. "Listen, you scumbag. You've got one chance to get out of here alive. Tell me who runs this thing." I put more upward pressure on his arm.

"The senator," Byron said, between gasps of pain.

"How does he distribute the drugs?"

"I don't know."

I pushed his wrist higher on his back, my right hand grabbing a handful of greasy hair, pulling his head backward.

He groaned. "Honest. I don't have anything to do with the drugs." he said, "I don't think the senator does either. We just handle the Mexicans."

I pulled harder on his head. "Who's in charge of the drugs?"

"Don't know. The blonde woman handles all that."

"What's her name?"

"I've never heard it. Honest."

I put more upward pressure on his arm, eliciting another scream of pain. "You can do better than that, Byron," I said.

"No. We've been doing the Mexicans for about five years now, and last year the senator told me we were going to be bringing in drugs with the illegals."

I could hear sirens in the distance. "Tell me the rest of it, Byron. You've got about one minute."

"That's all I know. The senator didn't want to get involved with the drugs, but he said somebody was putting pressure on him."

"Who?"

"I don't know. He did say something about his daughter once, and I thought she might be involved, but I never met her."

There was a pounding on the door. "The police are here, Matt," Larry shouted.

"I'm coming," I said.

Then to Byron, "I've got your gun. If you move, I'll kill you."

I got up, backed to the door and opened it for Larry. He stood aside as two policemen came in, guns drawn.

"You okay, Matt?" said one of them.

"Yeah," I said. "That's Byron Hewett. He keeps trying to kill me."

Byron lay on the floor, groaning, his right arm resting at an unhealthy angle.

* * * * *

As soon as the cops left with Byron, I called Bill Lester and told him what had happened. "I think we've got enough now to arrest the good senator," I said.

"I'll have Sarasota PD pick him up. You okay?"

"Yeah. I guess I'm getting used to this crap."

Bill laughed. "Come on down to the station and give us a

statement while it's fresh," he said.

"Can I take a shower first?"

"Probably a good idea. Don't want you stinking up the place."
He hung up.

* * * * *

Thirty minutes later, I walked into the Longboat Key Police
station. The receptionist looked up and smiled. "Glad you're okay,
Matt. Go on back. The chief's waiting for you."

Bill Lester was at his desk in the small room that served as his
office. Stacks of documents and loose leaf binders full to overflo-
wing covered every surface. He always complained about the
futility of trying to keep up with the paper work. He'd rather be
on the street chasing criminals, even though there weren't that
many bad guys on Longboat Key.

He looked up as I knocked on his open door. "Bad news,
buddy," he said. "The senator's disappeared."

"Any idea where he's gone?"

"No, but his private jet left Sarasota-Bradenton about an hour
ago. His pilot filed a flight plan for Key West, but they're not
there. We don't know where he's headed."

I sat in the chair across from Bill. "He must have been feeling
the heat," I said.

"Guess so."

"At least we've got Byron."

Bill grinned. "There's that," he said. "Let me get a stenographer
in here and get your statement."

"Bill, we're back to square one, you know."

"What do you mean?"

"I was thinking this afternoon that the senator might have
backed off, but he obviously hasn't. The fact that we've got Byron

isn't going to stop others from coming after me. And I don't think Pepe Zaragoza killed those Mexicans."

"I agree with you about Pepe, but the forensic evidence is probably enough to convict him. I told the State Attorney I didn't think Zaragoza was guilty, but he's looking for a conviction."

"Maybe we'll find the senator, or maybe Byron knows something. Maybe pigs will fly."

Bill sighed. "Don't give up on the system, Matt," he said. "Byron's in the hospital pretty well sedated right now, but I'll make a run at him tomorrow. You put a hurtin' on the bastard."

Darkness had descended while we talked, and a light rain had begun to fall. Through the window of the chief's office, I could see that the asphalt parking lot that served both the police station and the firehouse next door, had acquired a wet sheen, causing the lights on the buildings to reflect into the night sky.

"You hungry?" I said.

"Yeah. Give the girl your statement and let's go to the Haye Loft. I get an erection every time I think about their coconut cream pie."

"You're getting old, Chief," I said.

THIRTY-EIGHT

On the day before Thanksgiving, the sun rose over the bay in burnt orange and yellow splendor. As dawn crept over the island, I sat on my balcony drinking coffee and reading the morning paper. Cold air was sweeping out of the north, and I was wearing a sweatshirt and long pants for the first time that year. The breeze kicked up small whitecaps on the gray surface of the bay. The tide was out, and the sour smell of the mud flats tickled my nose. Sea birds were wading in the shallows, picking at their breakfast. Gulls, the eternal scavengers, hovered nearby, squawking their displeasure at each other, waiting for a morsel of food to fall their way. Occasionally, a small boat with rods poking out of their holders would move up the Intracoastal channel, bound for the fishing grounds.

My phone rang. Bill Lester asked if I wanted to join him while he interviewed Byron Hewett. He would be by to pick me up at nine o'clock.

We drove across Anna Maria Island, turning east on Cortez Rd. At 59th Street we turned north and pulled into the parking lot of Blake Hospital. Bill parked in a spot marked for police vehicles only. I suggested that his unmarked might get towed. He shrugged, and we went inside.

We took the elevator up two floors, and the chief stopped at the nurse's station, his identification in his hand. He had a whispered conversation with a middle-aged nurse dressed in scrubs. He motioned to me and I followed him down to hall to where a Manatee County Deputy Sheriff sat in the hall outside a room. He recognized the chief and opened the door for us.

Byron was shackled to the bed by his left wrist. His right arm was in a sling, resting on a pillow placed across his chest.

"Byron," said the chief in a conversational tone, "you're in a heap of shit."

Hewett gave Bill a sullen look. "Who the hell are you?" he asked.

"I'm Bill Lester, Longboat Key Chief of Police. I want to ask you a few questions."

Byron moved in the bed, and grimaced in pain. "I got nothing to say to you," he said.

Bill pulled up a chair and sat. "I think you do," he said, "and the sooner we get finished the sooner you'll get some meds for that pain."

"You can't do that," said Hewitt.

"Do what?" said Bill.

"Withhold my medication."

The chief gave Byron his most innocent look. "I'm not withholding anything," he said. "The nurse just told me she can't give you any meds until we're through here. Afraid they might make you incoherent. We might have to stay a while, just to keep you company."

Byron shifted in the bed, trying to find a comfortable spot. "I'm expecting to hear from my lawyer any time now," he said. "He'll straighten you out."

Bill chuckled. "Ah, Byron," he said, "didn't you know that the senator took off in his jet yesterday about the same time you were getting the hell beat out of you by my buddy Matt? I'm betting he didn't call a lawyer for you, and besides you're not under arrest, yet."

"If I'm not under arrest, why am I handcuffed to the bed?"

"Just looking out for your welfare, Byron," the chief said. "If we arrest you before you finish your stay in the hospital, the town will be liable for your bill. We can't have that, now, can we?"

"You're lying about the senator," Hewett said.

Lester picked up the bedside phone. "Here," he said, handing it to Byron, "call him. I know you've got an emergency number. Let's see if he answers."

Byron looked at the phone. "How the hell do you expect me to hold that thing with no hands?"

The chief looked perplexed. "Tell you what, Byron," he said, "give me the number, and I'll dial it and hold it up to your ear."

The dumb Cracker recited a number from memory. I knew that within minutes of leaving this room, the chief would know where that number was located.

Bill dialed the number and held the receiver to Hewett's ear. I could hear the sound of the rings coming out of the ear piece. The longer it rang, the more Byron's face drooped, the look of hope draining slowly away. He was beginning to realize that he alone would take the full weight of retribution demanded by society and the State Attorney.

The room was still, the quiet broken only by the forlorn sound of a telephone not answered. I heard something metal drop on the floor outside the room, making a small noise, probably a spoon or a fork. The food service people were picking up the breakfast trays. A siren wailed in the distance, becoming louder and more urgent as it approached the hospital. I wondered what tragedy was propelling the ambulance toward the emergency room.

"Son of a bitch," said Byron. "Hang up the phone, Chief. What do you want to know?"

Lester smiled. "Tell me about the operation," he said.

"Ain't much to tell. The senator had a connection with some guy in Mexico who'd ship the illegals to us. We been working that deal for about five years. I told Mr. Royal all this."

"I need to hear it from you," said the chief. "I'm more interested in the drugs than the Mexicans."

"Don't really know nothing about the drugs. I just handled the Mexicans."

Bill leaned over in his chair, putting his face right next to Hewett's. "You told Mr. Royal that the senator's daughter was involved in the drugs," he said. "He doesn't have a daughter. I checked."

"I can't swear to it. I just heard something about his daughter, but I never saw her. The only person I ever saw was the blonde woman, and I don't think she even knew the senator."

"Why do you say that?" said Bill.

"I called him by name one time. Said something to her about 'Mr. Foster.' She didn't know who I was talking about. When I told her that was the senator's name, she just shrugged and walked off."

"How long has she been involved?" said Lester.

"About a year. The senator called me one day and said the next shipment of Mexicans would include drugs and the blonde woman would take care of it. He didn't like it, but he said she had him over a barrel. That's when he said something about it being his daughter, but I must have misunderstood."

"Did you or he ever bring up the daughter again?"

"No. It never came up."

I stood and walked across to the door and back. My legs were going to sleep sitting on the hard chair. "Tell me about Jimmy Wilkerson," I said.

Hewett laughed. "Boy, I sure got you and your buddy on that one, didn't I?" he said.

"You did. Tell me about the name."

"I just picked it out," said Byron. "I needed a name, and I didn't want to use my own."

"How did Jimmy Wilkerson get involved in the drug trade?" I asked.

"He wasn't," said Hewett. "I never got close to that end of the business."

I was quiet for a moment. "Do you know Merc Maitland in Orlando?" I said.

"Never heard of him."

"How about a guy named Jeep?"

"Nope."

"He knows you," I said.

"Mr. Royal, I swear to you, I ain't never heard of the man."

"He's a black guy running drugs in Orlando. Don't lie to me, Byron."

"Wait a minute. One time the senator had me call a guy in Orlando to tell him to go to a bar in Tampa to meet somebody named Tank. He sounded like a black guy on the phone. That might be the one you're talking about."

I leaned over close, lowered my voice. "Why are your people trying to kill me?" I said.

"I don't know," said Byron. "The senator just told me some Mexican had tried to kill you because you was messing in the drug business. Then when you showed up out in the mines, I figured you was after me."

"How did you know that was me in the Vagabond that day?"

"I'd told people out there that Jimmy Wilkerson was a friend of mine, and that some bad people were looking for him, and they might be posing as cops. They were supposed to let me know if somebody showed up. When you and your buddy started asking about me, I got a call.

"I called the senator and he described you, and he said I should take you out. Said that you were a danger to us all."

"What about yesterday?" I asked.

"The senator called and told me to go take care of you. He told me to tell you that thing about squashing bugs," Byron said. "That's all I know. You oughta find a better hiding place for your spare key." He laughed, or grunted. I couldn't tell which.

Byron was squirming on the bed now, the pain showing in his face. "Can I have some pain killer, now?" he said.

Bill looked at me. "I think we're done here," he said.

I nodded in agreement. "I'll send the nurse in," I said as we left.

We were in the hall when Bill used his cell phone to call his office and ask them to check out the phone number Byron had given us to call the senator. By the time we got to the car, the dispatcher called back with the answer.

Bill looked exasperated. "No joy in Mudville," he said. "We struck out. The number belongs to one of those pre-paid cell phones. No idea who bought it."

We drove back to the key, and Bill dropped me off at my condo. I called Jock in Houston to tell him what had happened.

"Maybe," he said, "you're off the hook. With Byron locked up and the senator gone, I'd think you're safe."

"Except that we still don't know who was running the drug operation. I think Byron was telling the truth about that. And Bill Lester tells me that the senator never had any kids. His wife died about ten years ago, and he lives alone on his spread out in eastern Sarasota County."

I also told him about the puzzling development with Marie Phillips. "I don't know how she fits in," I said, "and Lester hasn't come up with anything on her, yet. The deputy is some kind of hotshot with the sheriff's office, and they don't think he'd be involved in anything dirty."

"Hang in there, Podner," Jock said. "If you need me, I'll fly back over."

"No. You enjoy your Thanksgiving. I'll keep you posted."

The next day I had my holiday dinner at Logan's, along with fifteen other people who were made a little less lonely by our friend's generosity.

THIRTY-NINE

On the last Monday in November, I went jogging on the beach. It had been a quiet weekend and I'd used the beach each morning for my workout. I kept a sharp eye out for go-fast boats, but none came in close to shore.

I returned to my condo, showered and met Logan for breakfast at Izzy's. He was on his way to the airport for a trip to Atlanta to begin his work-week traveling the state of Georgia.

He took a sip of his tomato juice. "Think you'll be safe without me around this week?" he said, grinning.

"It looks like things are settling down. Maybe we took the wind out of their sails. The senator's gone and Byron's in jail. All in all, a pretty good Thanksgiving."

We chatted and ate our breakfast. I ordered another cup of coffee. Logan didn't drink what he called "that noxious brew" and had once declared that coffee-drinking was about the only vice he'd never indulged in.

Logan stood to leave. "Take care of yourself. I'll be back on Friday, and we can go fishing. Maybe K-Dog can join us."

That seemed like a good idea. K-dog was our usual fishing buddy, and the only one who took it seriously. I finished my coffee and sat for a while reading the paper. As I was paying the check,

236

my cell phone rang, and I stepped outside to answer.

It was Rufus Harris. "I've had a forensic accountant spend the weekend going over the senator's books," he said. "He made an interesting find."

"He got a line on the drug money?"

"Not yet, but he found some strange payments going to a lady in your hometown."

"Orlando?"

"Nope. Sanford."

Sanford is a small town just north of Orlando, and it's the place where Jock and I grew up.

"What's that all about?" I said.

"Don't know yet. The lady's name is Janet Horvath. Know her?"

"Never heard of her. Was it a lot of money?"

"No. But it was steady. Every month the senator wrote a check to Janet for a thousand bucks out of his personal account. There's no notation as to what it was for, and the payments stopped about ten years ago."

"Why do you think that's significant?" I said.

"I'm not sure it is, but I thought the coincidence of the payments going to a woman in your hometown was too much. Could this be a reason they were trying to kill you?"

"That doesn't make sense to me. I never heard of the woman. Let me do some checking in Sanford and see what I can turn up. I'll let you know."

I went home, and did a computer search for Janet Horvath. Nothing. I accessed the Property Appraiser's web site in Seminole County where Sanford was located. If Janet had ever owned property in the county, she didn't now, and the historical record was devoid of any mention of her name as a deed holder. There was no phone listing for her, so I called the information operator.

Nothing.

Maybe I could find out something in Sanford. I grabbed a change of clothes and my shaving kit and pointed the Explorer toward I-75 and Sanford.

* * * * *

My timing was good. At Tampa, I turned onto I-4, and passed through Orlando shortly after mid-day. The traffic on the express-ways had not begun to build for the afternoon rush hour, and I cruised through the city heading east, which on that part of the Interstate is actually north. Go figure.

I took the Highway 46 exit and drove into my childhood. Many things about Sanford had changed over the years, but as I entered the restored downtown, I felt as if I'd stepped through a time warp.

The old buildings, some dating to the late nineteenth century, lined the brick-paved First Street. Where, in my childhood there had been department stores, drug stores and other commercial establishments, there were now mostly antique and other specialty shops.

The town sits on the southern bank of Lake Monroe, a 9,400 acre body of water through which flows the St. Johns River. For many years Sanford had served as a great inland port, and later a rail center. It'd always been home for me, and though I had no relatives left there, I felt a stab of nostalgia as I drove into downtown.

I called an old friend, Mick Columbus, who'd practiced law in Sanford for more than fifty years and knew most of the people who lived there. He invited me by his office for coffee, a ritual that is largely missing from the modern practice of law.

Mick's office was in an old two-story building that once housed a hotel. It sat across from a decaying structure that in Sanford's

Murder Key

heyday had been the railroad terminal, long since fallen into disrepair, the tracks ripped out of the ground and sold for scrap. The "new" terminal, older than I am, was out of Highway 46, between downtown and the Interstate.

Mick greeted me effusively, and we spent some time chatting about the old days and people long gone. Finally, I told him I was working on a legal matter, and I asked him if he had ever known Janet Horvath.

"Oh, sure," he said. "She used to waitress down at the Colonial Room. Quite a gal. Died a few years back."

The Colonial Room was a small restaurant on First Street that served breakfast and lunch and was a favorite of the locals. At noon on weekdays, most of the courthouse crowd was there, savoring the daily special.

I sipped my coffee. "What can you tell me about her?" I said.

"Not much. She came to town twenty-five or thirty years ago, pregnant. She didn't bring a husband with her. She'd been here about three months when she had a baby girl. Rented a house out by Pinecrest School and went to work at the restaurant. Nobody ever knew who the girl's father was. It was quite a topic of conversation when Janet first came to town, but like everything else, that died down, too."

"What happened to the daughter?" I asked.

"I don't think I ever heard. I seem to remember that for a while she was bartending down at Wolfy's, but I don't know what ever became of her. I can't remember what her name is, either. I haven't seen her since her mom died."

We chatted for a little longer, and I took my leave, promising to stop by the next time I was in Sanford.

I drove the three blocks to Wolfy's to see if anybody remembered a girl named Horvath. The bar and restaurant sits on a city-owned peninsula that had been dredged from the lake bottom

239

years before. It was a popular nightspot with an unbeatable view of the lake. The municipal marina and a small hotel share the spit of public land.

The bartender filled my beer order, putting a Miller Lite and a cold mug on the bar. I asked her if she knew a girl that used to work there named Horvath, and she said she didn't.

She took a swipe at the bar with her towel. "I've only been here a couple of years, though," she said. "The manager will be here in a few minutes. He's been running this place forever."

I sat quietly, taking the occasional sip of beer. The flat water of the lake reflected the late afternoon sun, causing a glare that turned everything to shades of gray. It looked as if all the color were being leached out of the earth. I saw the snout of an alligator poking out of the water near the marina docks. Further out, a bass boat skimmed the surface, its wake curving behind, as the fisherman brought it in toward the marina ramp. At the far western end of the lake, I could see the I-4 bridge, full of vehicles heading through the rush hour traffic toward Deltona and Orange City. Orlando workers going home.

"I'm Tommy Bradseth," said a man, as he slid in next to me. He had a head full of unruly gray hair that looked like a Brillo pad. It hadn't seen a comb that day, or maybe that week. He wore rimless glasses perched low on his nose. Gesturing toward the bartender, he continued, "Paula said you were looking for somebody who used to work here. I'm the manager."

I turned to him, introduced myself, and we shook hands. "I'm trying to locate a woman whose last name is Horvath. I don't know her first name, but I was told she used to work here."

"Yeah," Bradseth said, "that'd be Beth Horvath. Her mother used to work over at the Colonial Room. She died a few years back."

"Beth's dead?"

"Not that I know of. Her mom died of cancer about ten years ago."

"What can you tell me about Beth?"

"She was a good kid. Hard working. She was going to school at the community college and working here at night. When her mom got sick, Beth had to drop out of school to help out. She worked double shifts every chance she got."

"Do you know what happened to her after her mom died?"

"Not sure. Last I heard she had gotten a waitressing job over in Orlando and was back in school at UCF."

The University of Central Florida was located on the eastern edge of Orlando. It had grown over the years into one of the largest universities in the country. One could get pretty well lost in a school with over forty thousand students.

I'd finished my beer, and signaled Paula for another one. "Can I buy you a drink?" I asked the manager.

"I could handle a Coors. Thank you."

I poured beer into my new cold mug. "Do you know where she worked in Orlando?" I said.

"No idea. Some bar. That's all I know."

We finished our beer, talking about how Sanford had changed over the years. I left Wolfy's and drove to the Hilton in Lake Mary, just down the road from Sanford. I got a room and spent the evening with a mystery novel.

* * * * *

On Tuesday, after a breakfast of eggs, bacon and grits in the hotel coffee shop, I headed to Seminole High School. The campus was off 25th Street, its buildings no longer new. It was from Seminole High School that I had left for the Army and Jock for college. It seemed a long time ago.

The building where I had gone to school no longer existed. It was a gracious old Greek Revival structure built in the 1920's. After seventy years, the school board decided to get rid of it. A lot of memories died that day at the working end of a wrecking ball.

I checked in at the office and told the secretary that I was an old grad, and wondered if I could peruse some past yearbooks. She took me to the library and pointed to the shelves where row after row of the books called "Salmagundi" were stored.

I had come looking for Beth Horvath. I pulled down several years worth of books, extrapolating from what I knew about Beth's age to come up with the years when she was most likely to have been in high school.

I looked at the senior pictures, because they were bigger, and closer in time to the present. If I didn't find her there, I'd check out the club pictures or sports teams. It's almost impossible for someone to spend four years in a small high school and not be in at least one picture in the yearbook.

On the third volume, I found her. I looked at the face that went with the name, and felt something like an electric shock course through my body.

A large piece of the puzzle clunked into place, and the answers I'd been seeking were, like a developing Polaroid photograph, coming rapidly into focus.

I knew Beth Horvath.

FORTY

I drove out 25th Street, past the Mayfair Country Club, and took the State Road 46A ramp onto I-4 Westbound. I wasn't sure what to do with the information I'd stumbled upon in that old "Salmagundi." I'd have to think on it.

As I was passing through downtown Orlando, my phone rang. I checked the caller ID. It was Bill Lester.

"Hey, Chief," I said.

"Where are you?"

"I'm going through downtown Orlando, on my way home."

"We've found the senator," he said.

"Where?"

"In Mexico, dead. Somebody called the police about a small jet that seemed to be abandoned on an airstrip outside of Veracruz. When the cops got there, they found the senator's body in a passenger's seat; shot once behind the ear."

"The pilot?"

"No sign of him."

"How do we know it's the senator?"

"The Mexican police tracked the jet by its tail number, and Rufus Harris was notified. They faxed him a picture of the body. No doubt. It's the senator."

"Bill, what are they going to do with the body?"

"I don't know. I'm not really in the loop. Rufus called me as a courtesy."

"Get somebody over there to get a DNA sample from that body."

"Matt, calm down. It's the senator."

"I know, but that DNA may help us find the person behind the drug operation. Can you get it done without anybody on our side knowing what you're doing?"

"What's going on, Matt?"

"I'll explain later. Try to get the DNA."

Just as we hung up, my phone rang again. It was Rufus Harris. "Matt," he said, "We've found the senator."

"I heard. Bill Lester just called. What else do you know?"

"Nothing. Just that the Mexican police found the jet and the senator's body was in it. Looks like he was executed."

"Have you got somebody on the ground down there?" I asked.

"Better than that," he said. "Emilio Sanchez is on his way to Veracruz."

I called Jock in Houston. He confirmed that he could get in touch with Emilio on his satellite phone. I told him I'd get back in a few minutes, and I dialed Lester.

"Bill," I said, "Emilio is on his way to Veracruz. I think he can get the DNA sample without anybody here knowing about it."

"Good, because I sure as hell didn't know how I was going to do it."

"Keep this close, Bill. I'll be in your office in about two hours, and I'll fill you in on what I've found."

I called Jock again and explained the situation to him. He assured me he'd get in touch with Emilio. Jock was going to catch the next plane to Sarasota, and he'd be at my condo that evening.

"That's not necessary, Jock. We're okay here."

"We're closing in, Podner, and I want to be there for the kill."

I drove west on autopilot, thinking, trying to make the connect-
ions that were bouncing around in my head. It was like that game
children play where they try to connect the dots to draw the outline
of an animal. I had a lot of dots, and the picture was starting to
come into focus, but there were still a few dots missing.

A plan was forming at the edges of my mind, but I couldn't
quite put it all together. I still wasn't sure who I could or couldn't
trust. Bill Lester was solid, as was Jock, and by extension, Emilio.
I thought Kyle Merryman was safe, but I wasn't certain about the
feds.

Sure, we got the drug shipment, and we messed up the
immigrant smuggling ring. With the senator dead, we had at least
plugged that leak in our border security. But the drug honchos had
gotten away. Had they had some advance warning, even with the
tight lid we had put on the *Princess Sarah* operation?

Maybe. If the ones in charge of the drug operation knew what
was coming down on them, they'd have known that we wouldn't
stop them before they got to the labor camp. They had a helicopter
standing by to take the drugs, and probably the leaders, to safety.

When we stormed the chopper, we may have ruined their
escape plan. Maybe they hadn't left early, as McClintoc thought.
They might have been in that car I saw leaving the labor camp as
Logan was taking us out of range of the rifles firing at the aircraft.

The more I thought about that, the more I became convinced
that the leaders wouldn't have left without the drugs. They'd
probably stashed the coke in the helicopter to take with them when
they left. They weren't in a real big hurry, because they knew the
swat team would take time to get into place.

But if they'd known about the operation in advance, why not
just change the plan and bring the drugs in somewhere else?
Because, if they did that, some bright bulb in one of the agencies

might guess that there was a leak, and with only a few people in on the planning for the raid, it'd be easier to narrow the field of suspects. No, they would've had to let it go ahead. The trawler and its crew would be easy enough to replace, and the drugs would be ready to sell on the streets the next day.

I'd have to chat with Bill Lester about who was in on the plan before we executed it, and see if we could begin to see a person through the smoke and fog.

I stopped in Lakeland for a quick lunch at a restaurant near the Interstate ramp, and continued on to Longboat Key. I left the Interstate and drove through downtown Bradenton on Manatee Avenue to 75th Street. I cut across to Cortez Road and over the bridge to Anna Maria Island.

Even when I'm gone for only a short time, I love crossing that bridge. The waterway is always busy with boats, large and small, their occupants enjoying a day in the sun. I had the windows in the Explorer down to catch a whiff of the sea that rode the onshore breeze. Late luncheon diners were sitting at the patio tables at The Seafood Shack near the foot of the span. I was back in paradise.

I drove directly to the Longboat Key Police station and chatted for a while with Bill Lester, both of us drinking black coffee. Jock called while I was with the chief, and we agreed to meet at Mar Vista for dinner. Bill begged off, and I drove south to the Village in the waning daylight of a late fall evening.

* * * * *

We sat on the patio overlooking the water, watching the lights across the bay wink on as full darkness descended. Jock was in a good mood, anticipating the end of our adventure. Cracker Dix stopped by to say hello and to tell me he hadn't seen the Hispanic guy again. He also said that he was going to England or a month-long visit with his parents. People don't leave the island without letting someone know.

Jock looked closely at me, as we sipped our beer. "What's the problem, Matt? You look a little down."

"I'm tired, Jock. Tired of people trying to kill me. Tired of killing people. I thought all that was over when I left the war, but it's come back to get me. I cut a man's throat last week."

"He was going to drop you out of a helicopter, Podner."

"I know, and he needed killing. But I keep thinking about the fact that somewhere there's someone who loved him; a mom or dad or wife. Somebody's going to grieve over him."

"You never get used to this, Matt. I've killed a lot of men, and I remember every one of them. They all left somebody."

"The North Vietnamese soldiers come to me in the night sometimes," I said. "Men that I killed; boys, really, like I was. They tell me about their families, their children.

"Once, my A team caught a ride on a C-130 that was re-supplying some Marines at a base camp that had a little airstrip. We came in at a sharp angle, a combat landing the pilot said, and set down between piles of burning debris. The smell was terrible, the odor drifting into the plane. Then I realized they were burning bodies in those piles.

"Sometimes, in the night, that smell wakes me up. Only it's not North Vietnamese bodies in the piles. It's my men; the ones I lost."

"You've never talked to me about the war," said Jock. "Have you tried to get some help with this?"

"Yeah, when I first got back. But I think it's just something I have to live with.

"I ran into that C-130 pilot a few years back when I flew into Atlanta for a court appearance. He was a Delta Captain, and he'd come out of the cockpit to say goodbye to the passengers. He didn't recognize me, but after the plane emptied, I went back and told him who I was. He remembered me and the team, and that god-awful day with the burning bodies.

"He was through flying for the day, and we went out to a bar near the airport. He couldn't drink in the terminal in his uniform, and I had a free night. I didn't have to be in the Court of Appeals in downtown Atlanta until the next morning.

"We drank more than we should have, and talked more than either of us had in a long time, about things best forgotten. I think the fact that we were just strangers passing in the night opened each of us up in a way that might not have been possible between better friends.

"He said that he thinks often about that day with the burning bodies, and sometimes, when he's not expecting it, he'll be landing at some modern airport, and he'll smell that fleshy smoke and see, for an instant, the pyres on the side of the runway."

Jock leaned back in his chair. "Matt, this last few weeks has put a terrible strain on you. Are you sure you're okay?"

"I'm fine, Jock. The dreams haven't been this bad in years. It's just all this killing going on around me. And then, I slit a man's throat."

"Look at it this way," said Jock. "You both learned something in the service. The pilot learned to fly, and you learned to cut throats. That day in the shed at the labor camp, which of those learning experiences do you think was the most useful?"

He was grinning, trying to joke me out of a somber moodiness that I hadn't known I was still capable of.

During the first few years after I got out of the Army, I would go off into my little corner of mental hell, and end up drunk and passed out somewhere that I shouldn't have been. Those days were interspersed with weeks of activity, lawyering on a grand scale. But it was those bleak days that finally ended my marriage and my law career.

"You've got a point," I said. "What about you?"

"I'm done. I told the agency I'm giving it up. That guy Diaz in Veracruz keeps popping up in my mind. He's like one of those targets on the firing range. He jumps up out of nowhere, and I have to shoot him again. I'll get over it, but I've lasted longer with the agency than most, and it's time to retire. I guess a man's only got so much killing in him.

"I know about the dreams. I have them, too. I've tried to square my life with my own conscience, and sometimes I'm successful.

"On an intellectual level, I know that I've only killed bad people, but somewhere down deep I know that my dead mother wouldn't approve. That haunts me. She was the gold standard when it came to right and wrong."

I said, "We're a long way from Seminole High School, Jock. Can we ever get back that sense of equanimity we had then?"

Jock frowned, and was silent for a moment. "No," he said. "Not in this life. We've crawled too far through the human sewer. Some of that ugliness rubbed off on us, and when we die, we'll carry that stain to the grave."

I knew he was right.

Jock's phone rang. He pulled it out of his pocket, looked at the caller ID and said, "It's Emilio."

They talked for a minute or two, and Jock hung up. "He's in Veracruz," he said. "He's meeting with the local police in the morning. He'll call when he's through. You got another woman on the waiting list? Guy's gotta have a woman, you know."

We were through being serious. Jock wanted to move on to a more enjoyable subject, and what is more enjoyable than pretty women?

FORTY-ONE

On Wednesday morning, Chief Bill Lester called. "I think I'm starting to get the run-around from Rufus Harris," he said. "He's not telling me anything, and Paul Reich hasn't returned the calls I made to him yesterday and this morning."

"Did anybody tell you what was being done with the senator's body?"

"No. I asked Rufus what they were going to do about it, and he said he didn't know. Said he was waiting for word from Washington."

"Maybe that's true," I said.

"And maybe not." He hung up.

It was close to noon, and I was antsy again. I'd read the paper, drank my two cups of coffee, showered, shaved, and couldn't think of anything else to do.

Jock came in from his run on the beach, wiping his face with a towel. He collapsed into a chair on the balcony, still breathing hard.

I handed him a bottle of water from the refrigerator. "Want to go fishing?" I said.

"That's a fine idea."

I drove to The Market for some deli sandwiches while Jock

recovered from his run and showered. We took the boat around to Cannon's for bait and fuel, and then headed out Longboat Pass. We anchored over the Seven-Mile reef, and fished without purpose, eating our lunch. There were no other boats in sight. The water was flat and blue, turning to turquoise closer to shore. The beach shimmered in the distance, kissed lightly by the autumn sun. A small breeze kept us cool enough for light jackets. The only noise was the whirring of the spinning reels as we cast and reeled the line back in.

The time passed quietly, both of us caught up in our own thoughts. We'd unloaded on each other the night before, and that was perhaps cathartic for both of us. Macho men did not lightly discuss their feelings, and I think we were both a little embarrassed by the outpouring.

The jarring ring of Jock's cell phone startled me. "Emilio," he said. He listened for a minute, and then said, "I'll pick you up at the airport."

He closed his phone and looked at me. "Emilio's flying in tonight,"he said. "I'll pick him up in Tampa. We've got a meeting at the federal building tomorrow morning, so I'll grab a hotel room up there."

The sun was hanging low in the western sky when we headed in. I tied the boat to its dock and washed it down. Jock went up to get changed, and left for Tampa.

* * * * *

I later learned about Emilio's trip. When the dust had settled, he told me this:

On Tuesday, he flew into Mexico City on a flight from Houston. Emilio carried a passport identifying him as a Mexican national living in the capital. After he cleared customs, he went

251

to the rental car counters and used a Mexican driver's license identifying him as a resident of Veracruz, and rented a car for a one-way trip.

He arrived in Veracruz and turned in the rental. He then went to another rental car company, and this time using the identification of a Mexican National Police officer from the city of Ensenada on the Pacific coast of Baja California, rented another vehicle. He found a hotel and called it a night.

The next morning, Emilio presented himself to the desk officer in the reception area of the Veracruz main police station, showed his ID, and asked to speak to the officer in charge of the case involving the *gringo* jet with the dead man. He was told to take a seat, and in a few minutes a small man wearing a cheap suit and a clip-on tie came down the stairs.

The man approached Emilio, and said, "I am the detective in charge of the case you are asking about."

Emilio held out his identification to the detective, and said, "I am Juan Gomez, attached to the police in Ensenada. We have been working a case involving what we think is the same airplane. I was here in Veracruz on vacation, and my superior called and asked me to look into this thing for him."

There really was an officer named Juan Gomez stationed in Ensenada, and he really was on vacation near Veracruz, visiting relatives. If the detective checked out Emilio's story, he would find it to be the truth. The person answering the phone at the Ensenada police station would, because of the large amount of money transferred that day into his checking account in San Diego, California, confirm the story. If the detective checked further, he would find that there was a Juan Gomez staying at a small hotel on the edge of the city of Veracruz. The agency was nothing, if not resourceful.

Emilio was taken to the airfield to inspect the plane. It had been impounded by the police and would not be released until the investigation was completed.

The small aircraft's passenger cabin was configured with four plush seats, two on a side, facing each other and a sofa across the back. One of the chairs had blood smears on its seat and back rest.

The detective pointed to the facing seat, and said, "Mr. Foster was sitting in this chair when he was shot through the back of the head. Blood and brain material splattered the facing seat. You can see where the bullet lodged in the seat back. It was a large caliber pistol, a forty-four."

"Where's the pilot?" asked Emilio.

"We don't know. The aircraft had been parked here for a couple of days before we were notified."

"How did you identify Mr. Foster?"

"He had his passport and Florida driver's license in his pocket. I called the American embassy in Mexico City and notified them of the death. They ran the plane's registration through their Federal Aviation Administration, and told us it belonged to Mr. Foster."

"Can I see the body?" asked Emilio.

"Yes, but I'm not sure why you are so interested in this."

"We've had a problem with drug runners in northern Baja. A jet with these tail numbers has been seen twice in the area. When word got to Ensenada, through the National Police, that you'd found this plane, my boss asked me to take a look. That's all I know."

"Maybe your boss is part of the drug cartel."

"Maybe," said Emilio, "but he hasn't offered to cut me in."

At the morgue in Veracruz, Emilio was shown the body of the senator. Unless Foster had a twin, this was his body.

"Detective," Emilio said, "would it be possible to get a DNA sample to take back to our lab in Baja?"

"I guess," said the detective, "but why would you want that?"

"I don't know. The boss asked me to get it. I have a kit in my pocket. All I need is a swab of the inside of his cheek."

"Ah, go ahead. The National Police are nuts. Not you, of course, but the bosses."

"I agree," said Emilio, pulling the small kit from his coat pocket.

FORTY-TWO

In Longboat Key, Thursday dawned cold. The first front of the year was pushing down from Canada, bringing winter with it. I decided to put off my jog on the beach and stay in. I just don't like cold weather.

Jock called at mid-morning to tell me that Emilio had arrived in Tampa and brought the DNA sample with him. They had taken it first thing that morning to a private lab that the agency used on occasion, and he was hoping to have some results by the end of the day. I relayed that information to Bill Lester.

I spent the day on the sofa in my living room reading a new book by James Lee Burke, drinking coffee, and later hot chocolate. Winter in Southwest Florida is not truly winter, but we pretend it is. It was in the low 60s outside, and the sky was cloudless, as it always is once a front has moved through. There were few boats on the bay, and a large flock of white pelicans was floating at the edge of the channel, uninterrupted by the wakes usually left by passing vessels.

As dusk approached, I ordered a pizza from Oma's on Anna Maria. It was delivered by a long haired teenager driving a new Jaguar. Things really were different in Florida.

I caught the TV news, watched an old movie on AMC, and

crawled between the sheets. The weather forecast for Friday was sunny with temperatures in the high 70s. Winter was over for a while.

* * * * *

The phone rousted me out of bed at six on Friday morning. It was Jock.

"We got a match on the DNA. We checked the senator's against our national computer database, and we got a hit. Your hunch was on the money."

"I'll call Bill Lester. You'll be in touch?"

"Right. See you later."

I rolled out of bed and made myself a pot of coffee. No use in calling Bill at this hour. He'd be in his office by eight. I got the paper and spent the next couple of hours in quiet contemplation of the world's peccadillos.

FORTY-THREE

I was enjoying my late Friday evening, the last day of November, at the Monkey Bar in the Colony Beach & Tennis Resort. Debbie Keeton was at the piano, her voice smooth as she sang "Longboat Blues," her own composition. Her husband Gary Deary played a softly muted trumpet in accompaniment. His range was extraordinary.

Sitting at a table in the corner, I was sipping bourbon. Debbie is too classy an entertainer for a beer drinker, so on my Friday forays into the Monkey Bar, I always ordered sipping whiskey. Jack Black on the rocks, or if I was feeling particularly expansive, Wild Turkey on the rocks.

My mind was restless, wanting the whole fiasco to come to an end. I wanted the killing and the fear to go away. I still didn't know why anybody would want to kill me, but I now had a good idea of who.

I felt a presence beside me. A soft voice said, "Buy a girl a drink, Soldier?

I looked up into the thousand watt smile of Liz Birmingham. I stood, fumbling my chair like some adolescent jerk. Her attire was perfectly appropriate for the Monkey Bar, a pink golf shirt with the logo of the Colony embroidered on the breast pocket, white shorts, white ankle socks and tennis shoes.

"Please, sit down," I said, pulling out a chair. "What in the world brings you to the Monkey Bar?"

She settled in, favored me with a smile that made me want to cry out with joy, and said, "Some of my sorority sisters and I get together here once a year for a little tennis and a lot of gab. I got tired of the gab and came looking for a drink."

I signaled to the cocktail waitress, and Liz ordered bourbon straight up. Some women just know how to drink.

"I saw you sitting here," she continued, "looking like you were about a thousand miles away."

"I was. It's been a long few weeks."

"I've heard about most of it, but I've been out of the loop. I don't know why. Do you?"

"No," I said. "I didn't know you weren't part of the whole thing. I just assumed you were."

"I didn't know anything about the bust here on Longboat until after the fact. I find that curious, since I've been the undercover guy on this thing from the beginning."

"Look, Liz, I don't know how your department works, but maybe somebody at the top thought there was a leak."

"Matt, you were there. You're a civilian, and yet you were part of the bust. You know more than you're telling me. Did someone think I was the leak?"

"I don't think so. I never heard that from anybody. As far as I know, your bosses think you walk on water. I think they were just playing it close, so that if there was a leak, they'd have narrowed down the list of suspects. The bosses were probably trying to protect you."

"That sucks. I don't need protection." A hint of toughness was slipping out. It didn't go well with her cool good looks.

"We got the bastards," I said. "Isn't that what counts?"

Murder Key

"Yeah, some. But we didn't get the drug guys, and that's what really counts."

"I guess you knew the senator is dead."

"Yes. Rufus passed that on to me yesterday, after he told me about the senator's involvement. He brought me up to date on the whole exercise. I think Foster was probably the drug guy, too, regardless of what Byron told you."

"What makes you think that?"

"It stands to reason," she said. "He'd been bringing in aliens for a long time, he had contacts in Mexico, and he was found dead there after he escaped arrest here."

"You could be right. But I think there's more to it than that. I'd like to find the blonde woman. She might be more than just a driver."

We sat quietly for a moment. Liz took a small drink of her bourbon, started to say something, thought better of it and took another sip. "What makes you think that?" she asked. "She's probably just some bimbo making a few bucks driving the illegals."

"I don't think so. She seems to show up a lot, and the agent we had with this last batch of illegals said the men showed her a lot of deference. She was also the paymaster. She paid off the go-fast captain in cash and was giving orders to the guys moving the coke."

"I didn't know you had infiltrated an agent among the immigrants."

I wrinkled my brow in surprise. "You mean nobody ever told you about that?"

"No," she said. "Rufus must have left that part out. Who was he?"

"A guy who works for another government agency. A one-shot deal. The Border Patrol or DEA or somebody recruited him for this exercise."

"Did you get a description of the blonde woman?" Liz said.

"No. I'm the only one who thinks she might be involved more deeply than it appears. Nobody's interested in my theories. I'm just a beach bum lawyer. And glad of it."

I grinned. I actually liked being a beach bum, and I didn't want Liz to think I was feeling sorry for myself. That's not very macho.

She changed the subject then, telling me stories of her years in college with her sorority sisters. We talked for an hour, drinking another shot or two, enjoying the music.

Late in the evening, she placed her hand lightly on my thigh, down near the knee. "There's a half moon out tonight. Interested in a walk on the beach?"

"As long as you don't have any ulterior motives," I said.

She winked. "Don't bet on it, Soldier."

I paid the check, waived at Debbie and Gary, who gave me the thumbs-up sign, and we left. We started toward the beach in front of the restaurant, walking arm-in-arm. She stopped suddenly.

"Matt, do you know Beer Can Island?"

"Sure, at the north end of the key."

"Why don't we go down there? It'll be deserted this time of night."

I drove the Explorer north, almost to the end of Longboat Key, a distance of about eight miles. Liz sat quietly in the passenger seat, deciding, I guessed, how the evening was going to end. Traffic was light on Gulf of Mexico drive, the island settling down for the weekend. I pulled into North Shore Road and parked at the end, near the wooden walkway across the dunes.

Beer Can Island is a misnomer in a couple of ways. Its actual name is Greer Island, but almost nobody calls it that. It's also not an island any more, but rather a spit of land where the key tapers to an end at Longboat Pass. The ever-encroaching sea had filled in the narrow slough that once ran between the end of Longboat Key and the little island.

The beach is wide as it wraps around the end of the island, and it's bordered by a stand of Australian Pines. These trees have shallow root systems and thrive in the salty environment. A good wind can blow them over, and the beach at Beer Can is full of fallen trees, their roots sticking up like Medusa's hair-do.

We walked north on the beach, barefoot now, wading in the shallow surf. The water had cooled the last few days, another sign that winter was approaching. A bright half-moon hung high above the horizon, painting the sea with a soft shaft of light. A cloud floated lazily across its face, its shadow reflected briefly on the swath of sea lit by the moonbeam.

Liz had her purse with her, a precaution that any sane Longboater takes when leaving his car at a beach access. About the only crime that regularly visits our island is the thieves who break into the cars parked there. I had mentioned this to Liz on the drive north and suggested she conceal her purse. Instead, she brought it with her.

She leaned into my arm, holding it with both hands, her purse hanging from a shoulder strap. She looked at me and smiled. We stopped, and she reached up to kiss me. I was tasting that smile, and like in that old Beatles song, it tasted of honey.

She broke away, stepped back and smiled at me. "That was nice," she said.

"Yes, it was."

"Matt," she said, "you know who the blonde woman is, don't you?"

"Yes, I do, Beth."

I heard a sharp intake of breath. "Beth?"

"Little Beth Horvath from Sanford, Florida."

She let out a long sigh. "How did you know?" she said, sadness tinging her voice.

"I saw your picture in the 'Salmagundi.'"

"God, Matt. I don't look anything like that now."

"That's for sure. But that smile hasn't changed, and like you said, a blonde wig just makes a girl."

"What else do you know?"

"I know that you're the senator's daughter."

"How?" she asked, surprised.

"DNA. We got a sample from Foster's body, and it matched yours from the DEA database."

"What put you onto me?"

"The senator sent your mother money for a long time. The forensic accountant found it, and I went to Sanford to find your mom. That led me to you."

"Foster was a son-of-a-bitch. I didn't know he was my father until just before my mother died."

"That must have been tough, growing up without knowing who your dad was."

"Tough doesn't get it, Matt. Mom would never talk about him. Then she got stomach cancer, and was dying a pretty rotten death. On the day before she died she told me that she'd called him when she got the diagnosis. She asked him for help so that his daughter, me, could finish college without having to pay for her treatment. He told her to go to hell.

"All those years busting her butt in the Colonial Room to keep us fed, and Foster wouldn't help when we really needed it. He deserved to die."

"What about your grandparents?" I asked. "Couldn't they help?"

"Her parents kicked her out when she was seventeen and pregnant. They were rock-ribbed Baptists who hated the sin, and the sinner, too. They told her never to come back. They said she would burn in hell, and they didn't want to get singed by the flames. How the hell do you do that to your only child? They died in a car wreck when I was four."

"But Foster was sending your mother a check every month."

"When she was in the hospital, Mom told me she called him when her parents threw her out and asked for help. The great senator told her she couldn't prove I was his, so he wouldn't help, except to send a little money every year. She was only thirty-six when she died." Her voice broke.

We were standing, facing each other, the small waves lapping at our feet. Tears were rolling down her cheeks.

"I'm sorry," I said.

"Mom asked me to bring her an envelope from her underwear drawer in the chest in her bedroom. It had my birth certificate and some other papers in it. It listed my birth name as Elizabeth Birmingham. She named me for her home town, since she couldn't give me my father's name."

I said, "We got your school records, and saw where you had given the school administration people your birth certificate and asked that all your records be changed to Birmingham from Horvath. The DEA didn't pick that up when they did the background on you. Somebody would have to be specifically looking for the change to find it."

"I did that after my mom died. Just as well. When I started to school at UCF I had to work in a bar out in East Orange County, and I wouldn't have wanted my mom's friends in Sanford to know what I was doing. The pay was good, but I had to screw the owner twice a week to keep the job."

I said, "I know from your personnel file that you went to work for the DEA when you graduated. How did that happen?"

"I met an agent during a drug bust at the hole I worked in during college, and he suggested I apply. My degree was in

Criminal Justice, so it was a good fit. I went through training and them spent five years on the Mexican border tracking drug runners. Do you have any idea how much money is in that?"

"A lot."

"More than you can imagine. Here I was, working my ass off for the pittance the government pays, and these third grade dropouts were taking home millions of dollars a year.

"I made a couple of contacts on the Mexican end of things, and when I got transferred to Orlando I saw a chance to open a new pipeline. I'd begun to look into my father, hoping to find some dirt on him. I wanted to ruin the bastard. I stumbled onto his immigrant smuggling operation, and I knew I had a hook."

I said, "How did you find out about Foster's smuggling gig?"

"Both Immigration and Customs were onto him. They couldn't prove anything, and they thought there might be a drug connection. That brought DEA into the picture, and I heard about it.

"I went to see the good senator, told him who I was and that I could protect him. The quid pro quo would be that he would use his immigrant pipeline to bring in drugs. My Mexican connection would take over the Veracruz end of Foster's operation."

"So you set up the distribution end of things."

"Yes, that was easy. I was working undercover at Les Girls, and I found a guy who was mean as a snake and offered to set him up in business. He never knew who I was. We only dealt with each other on the phone. He recruited the sales force."

"But you gave us Merc and Jeep in Orlando."

"Those idiots. I knew they couldn't tell you anything, and my snake had already scared the hell out of them with the head of the guy in Melbourne he had to take out. The only name they knew was Jimmy Wilkerson, and he doesn't exist."

"Do you know who killed Senator Foster?"

"I did, or at least I ordered it done. The bastard was trying to run. I knew he'd make a deal and give me up. He was the only one in the world who could positively identify me."

"How did you know he was running?"

"That's the icing on the cake. His pilot is a Customs Service agent named Graham Rutan. He moonlighted as a drug courier for me sometimes. Foster didn't know about that. He thought Graham was a free-lance pilot who worked for several jet owners.

"The senator thought he was going to Cancun to hole up while he made a deal with the feds. Graham took the stupid bastard to Veracruz and shot him. Good riddance."

"Sounds like a good operation. What happened?"

"That lawyer, Conley was getting close. He was using Pepe Zaragoza as a mole in the senator's organization, and Pepe stumbled onto me. I had to take him out, but I wanted it to look like a drug deal gone bad. Some of my Mexicans flew in and killed the other two, and thought they'd killed Pepe. Stupid bastards left them on the beach for you to find.

"It's interesting, isn't it?" she said. "If we hadn't tried to kill you, we might have gone right on with our business."

"Why did you try to kill me?"

"It wasn't my idea. Mendez, my guy in Mexico, had one of his killers watching the beach that day to see what would happen when the bodies were found. He saw you bend down to Zaragoza and then call the police. He thought Pepe had said something to you, and he called Mendez. That idiot over-reacted and ordered you killed in Tiny's. Stupid, stupid."

"We have to talk to Chief Lester," I said.

"I don't think so, Matt," she said, moving back a couple of steps and putting her hand in her purse. It came out holding a nickel-plated thirty-eight caliber revolver. She held it in front of her, pointed at the ground.

"I'm sorry," she said. "I'm sorry you got mixed up in this, and

I'm sorry for all those dead people."

"Liz," I said, "you know that other people have the same information I do."

"Probably. But I came here looking for you. I had to know what you knew."

"So, there's no sorority reunion?" I said.

She laughed bitterly. "Those sorority snobs wouldn't let somebody like me into their houses. I was like a ghost on the UCF campus. I went to class, got my degree, and didn't even go to graduation. They mailed me my diploma."

"The others will come for you, Liz. Let's go see Bill Lester."

"I've got a head start on the others. I'll be out of the country within an hour, and I've got enough money stashed away to live large for the rest of my life. Rufus can look for me forever, and he probably will, but he won't find me."

"So, Rufus wasn't part of your operation?"

She laughed. "Good God, no. Old Rufus is Mr. Upstanding Citizen. He'll come looking for me, that's for sure. I've ruined his view of what a good little agent should be."

"There's still time to make some amends," I said.

"No. Sorry, Matt, I've got to do what I've got to do."

She raised the pistol, pointing at my chest.

An amplified voice boomed from the stand of pines. "Agent Birmingham, drop your weapon. Longboat Key Police."

A look of surprise and then resignation crossed her face. She hesitated for a moment, then said, "Good-bye, Matt. I wish we'd met in another time and place."

She raised the pistol, and was pointing it at my face when her head exploded. I was looking into her eyes when death shut them down. In the split second before, I saw the red dot of the laser scope painting the left side of her head. I tried to react, but only an instant had passed since she raised her weapon. Blood and brain matter and bits of skull exploded out of the right side of her head. She crumpled to the beach like a bag of rags.

Men were pouring out of the trees. Bill Lester and Jock Algren were in the lead. Five Longboat cops in battle fatigues followed, all armed with M-16s.

"You okay, Matt?" asked Jock as he ran up to me, a sniper rifle cradled in his arms.

"Yeah," I said, and sat down on the sand.

"We got it all, Matt," said Bill Lester. "That little device was broadcasting like a good stereo system."

I pulled my knees up, put my arms across them and rested my head on my arms. "Let's get her out of here, Bill. She needs to rest."

Jock helped me to my feet, and we walked off the beach.

* * * * *

Jock drove the Explorer the mile or so to my condo. I felt like a zombie, empty inside, but yet an indescribable sadness was settling over me. I kept thinking about the moment life deserted Liz. I couldn't get that image out of my mind.

We took the elevator to the second floor and sat on the balcony drinking bourbon. Beer did not seem somber enough to match our moods.

Jock lifted his glass. "To the end of death," he said. "I've killed my last person."

"You okay, buddy?"

"I guess. I liked her, but she wasn't what we thought. She was going to kill you tonight."

"I know. You saved my bacon again, Jock. Thanks."

"You took the risks, Podner. All I did was stand back in the woods with a rifle. Sometimes, it seems as if that's all I've done my whole life."

"She had a tough life, growing up as a bastard in a small town. She worked hard to overcome all that, got her degree, went to work for a good agency. What made her take that wrong turn?"

"Money, probably. We'll never know for sure."

"She said it was the money, but I think it was more than that. She'd built up a lot of anger at the world. Life had dealt her a bad hand, but she was doing so well for so long. What in the world turns a decent kid into a killer?"

My cell phone rang. Bill Lester.

"I called Rufus Harris," he said. "He's not happy about Liz's death, but he's coming here in the morning. Can you and Jock be at the station at ten?"

"Can I bring Logan?" I said. "He needs to be brought up to date."

"No problem."

"We'll be there. Bill, you covered my ass tonight, and I'm grateful. Tell your guys that for me. I wasn't tracking too well when I left the beach."

"Will do," he said and hung up. Bill Lester was a tough guy.

Jock and I sat and talked and sipped good whiskey. I knew I was going to regret it the next morning, but I also knew I needed a little anesthesia for the night. I hoped Liz wouldn't join those North Vietnamese soldiers in my nightmares.

FORTY-FOUR

Hammers were pounding my head when I awoke on Saturday morning. I hadn't pulled the drapes shut when I went to bed, and light was streaming into the room, adding to the pain brought on by too much bourbon.

I crawled out from under the sheets, stood for a moment to make sure that I could, and then padded to the bathroom. I took four aspirins and stepped into the shower. I stood quietly, letting the hot water and the analgesic work their magic.

I dressed in a T-shirt, cargo shorts and boat shoes, and made my way to the living room. Jock was sitting on the sofa, a look of pain on his face.

"We gotta stop this crap," he said. "I'm getting too old for it."

I laughed. "I know what you mean. Let's go get some pancakes."

I called Logan to meet us for breakfast. We drove to the Blue Dolphin Café and Jock and I ate a stack of pancakes, a side of bacon and about a gallon of coffee each. Logan sipped his tomato juice. I drank enough ice water to fill a swimming pool, and suddenly, I was feeling better. I suspected I was going to survive the hangover, and that is the first hope that slips into the psyche of the man who drinks too much bourbon.

Hope brings with it a resolution to never do it again. But that resolve will fade, along with the memory of how bad one can feel on a sunny fall morning in Southwest Florida. And in a few days, the bourbon will inevitably flow again.

Logan found our predicament humorous. He'd spent the night watching a full evening of "Cops," his favorite TV program. He was feeling a little superior.

I groaned as I finished my stack of batter. "Have you seen the morning paper?" I asked, looking at Logan.

"No. Anything interesting?"

"Yeah," I said. "While you were goofing off in Atlanta yesterday, we were busy. There was a shoot-out at Beer Can, and Liz Birmingham is dead."

"The DEA agent?" Logan asked, his face reflecting his alarm.

I said, "She was dirty, Logan, and she was going to kill me, when Jock got her with a rifle."

"I don't believe this. What happened?"

"We're going to the police station. Bill Lester will fill you in while he brings Rufus Harris up to speed. It was a bad night."

Logan said, "What about Reich at Border Patrol."

"He's out of it," I said. "Once the illegal ring was busted, he moved on to other things. DEA is in charge of the drugs."

We left the restaurant feeling better and drove the half-mile to the police station. The receptionist waived us through the gate leading back to the offices. Lester and Harris were waiting for us. Rufus didn't look too happy.

Bill told us to take a seat and said, "I've been telling Rufus about what went down last night. I'll finish up and you two can add anything you want to."

He told the agent that I had come up with the possibility that Liz was in fact Beth Horvath and Foster's daughter. He explained how we came to get the DNA sample, and how we matched it to

Liz.

Bill apologized for not bringing Rufus into the action. "We weren't sure who we could trust at DEA," he said. "Yesterday, we were trying to decide how to approach you when Liz showed up at the Colony."

Rufus interrupted. "How did you know she was on Longboat?" he said.

Bill smiled. "I called McClintoc down in Miami on Thursday and told him what we suspected," he said. "He had one of his guys in Orlando put a satellite tracking beacon on Liz's car. BLOC new where she was from the time she started her car. Customs was going to get involved, because they didn't know who to trust in DEA either.

"She left Orlando at mid-morning yesterday and drove straight to Longboat. That surprised us, but it gave us all afternoon to set up."

I turned to Rufus. "We didn't think you were on the wrong side," I said, "but things were moving fast, and we didn't have time to sort it out."

Bill nodded his head. "After BLOC let me know that Liz had stopped at the Colony," he said, "I called the front desk, and sure enough, she'd checked in. I called Matt to bring him up to date, and he told me that he always went to the Colony on Friday nights. If Liz's people had been tracking him, they'd know that."

The chief continued with the story, telling Rufus the whole thing, step by step. We'd decided that I would follow my usual routine and see if Liz tried to contact me. We put another tracking beacon on my Explorer and wired me for sound. I had a small device stuck to my chest that would broadcast everything said to a receiver Bill and Jock were monitoring.

The Longboat Key Police Department doesn't have anybody qualified as a sniper, and Lester was going to ask to borrow someone from Sarasota County. Jock volunteered instead, and Bill only had to borrow the sniper rifle from the county. Jock went to the sheriff's firing range to zero in the weapon.

There were four crews of Longboat Key Police officers stationed at intervals along Gulf of Mexico Drive, ready to go where the chief directed them. Bill and Jock were in an unmarked car parked in the Colony lot while Liz and I were in the Monkey Bar. They saw us come out and walk toward the beach. Bill was about to move his men into place when he heard Liz suggest that we go to Beer Can Island.

The chief radioed the crew near the north end of the key to take up position in the pine trees along the beach at Beer Can. He and Jock headed north, running at high speed. A police crew stationed near the New Pass Bridge got in position to follow my car as I left the Colony property.

Bill and Jock arrived at North Shore Road minutes before I did. They parked the unmarked in a parking lot at the Whitney Beach Condominium complex, next to the personal car driven by the team from New Pass Bridge. They were tracking my Explorer on a hand-held receiver and knew when I pulled into North Shore Road. They were able to pick up my and Liz's conversation from the transmitter taped to my chest.

The team following me arrived and took up position with the rest of the officers. The moon provided some light, and Jock's rifle was equipped with a night vision scope that had the laser finder built in. Bill was wearing military issue night vision goggles that painted Liz and me with an eerie green hue.

When Liz pulled the pistol from her purse, Jock raised the rifle to his shoulder.

Bill whispered, "Not yet."

Jock held his position, watching us through the scope. When Liz pointed the pistol at my chest, Bill put the bullhorn to his mouth and ordered Liz to drop her weapon.

She didn't. When she raised it to point at my head, Jock flipped on the laser sight and pulled the trigger. Liz was dead.

* * * * *

Bill was quiet then, letting the story sink in. Nobody spoke for a moment. Then Rufus turned to Jock, "You had no choice, Jock," he said. "You did what you had to do."

Jock made a face of resignation. "Yes, I did, Rufus," he said, "and I'll live with that for the rest of my life."

The chief said, "There's something else. One of Customs' pilots killed the senator. A guy named Graham Rutan."

"Did you notify McClintoc?"

"Yes," said Bill. "He was going to personally arrest the bastard."

Logan spoke up. "What about Marie Phillips and the deputy we saw her with?"

Bill said, "Turns out Marie is what she said she was, an Administrative Assistant. She has an MBA from the University of Florida and has worked for Foster for about three years. Her job was on the legitimate side of his business, and she didn't know anything about the illegals or the drugs."

"Logan asked, "Was she his squeeze?"

"No," the chief said. "She inherited that condo on the south end when her husband was killed in a car wreck a few years back. She also got a bundle in a settlement with the owner of the truck that hit him. The deputy is her brother."

I shook my head. "Man, I sure jumped to the wrong conclusion about her," I said. "Have they released Pepe Zaragoza?"

"That's being handled as we speak," said Bill.

Rufus turned to the chief. "I'd like to hear that tape now."

I didn't want to re-live any of that night. I told them I'd wait outside, and Jock and I left the office. Logan stayed.

We were standing in the police parking lot talking quietly when my cell phone rang. It was Anne.

"Matt, I just read the morning paper, and there's a story about the death of that woman at Beer Can last night. It said you were there. Are you okay?"

"I'm fine, Anne. I think the troubles on the key are finished. I found out who was trying to kill me and why. Now, it's over. How're you?"

"I'm doing good. I miss you."

"How's the stock broker?"

"I don't know. Turns out he's kind of a jerk."

My heart beat a little faster, but I'm nothing, if not cool.

"Sorry to hear that," I said.

"If I come out tomorrow, will you take me to Egmont? It's supposed to be a nice day."

"Sure," I said. I wasn't exactly playing hard-to-get.

I closed the phone and related the conversation to Jock. He said one word. "Sucker."

I agreed, and smiled for the rest of the day.

FORTY-FIVE

On the first Sunday in December, the temperature slid into the high seventies. A slight breeze blew out of the south, bathing our paradise in currents of warm air. Light clouds moved slowly across a cerulean sky, and Anne wore her red bikini. Life was good.

I took the Grady-White out Longboat Pass, cutting in close to the jetty at the south end of Anna Maria Island. The sea had a light chop, but not enough to make the ride uncomfortable, as we headed north to the mouth of Tampa Bay.

Jock had left on an early-morning flight to Houston. He and Logan and I had spent the evening at Moore's, eating crabs and drinking beer. We finished up the night at the Haye Loft, drinking more beer and talking with Eric and Teresa, the bartenders. Several people stopped by to ask about the Beer Can Event, as it was becoming known on the key. I told them that the police had asked us not to talk about it. I just wasn't ready to discuss it.

Anne brought sandwiches and beer for lunch. We found a spot on the beach at Egmont, anchored and waded ashore. The sun was warm, and the company was magnificent. I didn't know if this meant that Anne and I were together again, or if this was just her way of letting me down easy. I decided I'd eat my lunch and wait for the other shoe to drop.

She put her hand on my arm and looked closely at me. "You look like hell," she said. "Friday night was awful, wasn't it?"

"Yeah. Liz was a girl with no hope who turned herself into a hell a woman. Something happened along the way, though, and she went bad. I think she had a lot of demons chasing around in her head, and she just couldn't control them."

"It wasn't your fault, you know."

"I know, but still... ."

"You couldn't have saved her, Matt. By the time you met her, she'd already turned the corner. The goodness in her was gone. She was a killer and a drug-runner. She was going to kill you, for heaven's sake."

She leaned into me, took my face in her hands, and kissed me long and hard. The other shoe had dropped, and we were going to be okay. At least for a while.

I didn't tell Anne that in the instant before Liz died, as she pointed her little pistol at my face, she removed her finger from the trigger. And smiled.